Humanity's Fight

Space Colony One
Part Two
Book 2

J.J. GREEN

Cover Design: <u>Erik J. Andersen</u>
Editing: <u>L.M. Lengel</u>

Sign up to my reader group for a free ecopy of *Night of Flames,* the prequel to Space Colony One, and for more free books, discounts on new releases, Review Crew invitations and other interesting stuff:

<u>https://jjgreenauthor.com/free-books/</u>

CONTENTS

You cannot love a thing without wanting to fight for it.

CHAPTER ONE

The escape capsule was falling. The interior was tiny, accommodating only one individual. Only one individual was required. Most of the bulk of the capsule was made up by the thickness of the hull. The capsule had no landing gear and the hull was designed to absorb the shock of impact on a planet surface. The thick shell was also designed to protect the occupant from the high temperatures generated by falling through a planet's atmosphere.

The capsule had drifted into Concordia's exosphere without incident. At this point, the small vessel was already trapped by Concordia's gravity and impact on the surface was inevitable. It was only a matter of time. The thing inside it remained motionless, waiting. Its artificial mind calculated the predicted velocity of the capsule's descent and estimated the peak temperature of the outer hull.

According to its calculations, the capsule would not heat up sufficiently to destroy the occupant, though burn damage would be inflicted. More importantly, the high temperature would not cause the capsule to disintegrate. If it did, the occupant probably would not survive the remaining fall to the surface.

The force of the impending impact was another consideration. The capsule had not been designed to land on a planet, and so its destruction was inevitable. Could the occupant survive the impact? There was a dissatisfying variance in the answer. The probability of unimpaired survival was only thirty-two point nine two eight four. However, the probability of functional survival was seventy-three point four zero eight three, rounded up. Nevertheless, that meant the probability of annihilation was twenty-six point five nine one seven.

The individual would have preferred better odds. If it was destroyed, its mission would fail. But there was nothing it could do to improve its chances. The intelligence thought it was odd that its creators had not designed a more robust craft but it was forced to accept it could not know their motivations and intentions.

Time passed, and the capsule entered Concordia's thermosphere. Its velocity increased as the tug of the planet's mass grew stronger. Where would it fall? Its trajectory was not yet entirely set. The capsule was light and would be subject to the forces of the jet stream when it dropped deep into the stratosphere. At that point it would also be on fire.

Given the predicted high temperature of its hull (what remained of it at that point), it would be preferable if it landed in the ocean, even considering the fact that the sudden drop in temperature might create a differential in thermal expansion that caused the hull to crack. If the capsule crashed into land, it would cool down much slower, reducing the heat differential and maintaining the structural integrity of the hull. However, the force of impact would be greater. Overall, the probability that the capsule would break open, reducing the likelihood of the individual's survival, was lower for an impact on water than on land.

When the capsule reached the mesosphere, its

exterior rapidly heated up. The metal alloy that formed the outer layer began to glow. At first, insulation protected the capsule's interior from the rising heat and the occupant registered no rise in temperature.

That state quickly changed. One-tenth of a second later the capsule's hull was melting and burning, sending out a long tail of flame. A human on the surface who was looking at the right part of the night sky at the right time would have seen a streak of light in the sky and thought they were looking at a meteor.

Another tenth of a second passed, and the individual inside the capsule registered the rapidly increasing temperature of its surroundings. Fortunately, it did not breathe air, or it would have discovered its throat and lungs scorching in the heat. Its skin was a manufactured substance designed to mimic human skin. If it had been organic, it would have been bubbling and peeling away.

By the third tenth of a second, the capsule was a fireball and its interior was a furnace. But it was maintaining structural integrity. The occupant sat and waited as its circuits heated. The artificial hair on its head dissolved and evaporated. The ends of its faux fingers crisped.

Estimated time to impact was point two nine—

The capsule hit. Against the probabilities, given the comparative volume of water compared to landmass on the surface of Concordia, the capsule had come down on land. The innermost wall of the capsule shattered but for the most part the vessel remained whole. One reason for this was the fact that what was left of the hull was molten at the time of impact, and the liquid, more flexible structure absorbed some of the shock.

The occupant completed a damage assessment. The results revealed a considerable number of breakages. Its inner frame had broken into many pieces and some of its wires had dissected. Self-repair was automatically activated. As the hull cooled, the individual healed itself. Not all parts were able to be saved, but it would be functional. When it had repaired to the greatest extent possible, it would find a way out of the wreck.

CHAPTER TWO

Cherry lifted a whistle to her lips and blew it so hard her ears rang.

"Exercise over. Get in line!"

The troops shuffled slowly to their positions in the training yard. Some didn't even seem sure of where the line was.

"MOVE IT!"

Cherry's missing arm was itching, which was doing nothing to improve her mood. She didn't think she'd ever seen such a bunch of useless recruits. If they weren't dropping their weapons they were bumping into each other, and if they weren't bumping into each other they were screwing around when they thought she wasn't watching.

Dammit! Where was Aubriot?

His subordinate officer's face had been a picture when Cherry had turned up unannounced that morning. Then the woman had tried to make up excuses for her CO, stuttering out some lame excuses for Aubriot's absence during the training exercise. That had only made Cherry madder. Loyalty was a virtue but not when it extended to covering up irresponsibility.

From the corner of her eye, Cherry saw a tall figure striding toward her. The sight of Aubriot finally arriving only made her more irritated. She glared at him as he approached.

"I'll take over, General," he said as soon as he was within hearing distance.

Cherry waited until he was close enough for her to speak to him without the recruits overhearing her. "Where the *hell* have you been?" she hissed. "You should have been here two hours ago. What kind of an example do you think you're setting?"

"Hey! I—"

"I don't want to hear it." Cherry pulled the whistle over her head and thrust it into Aubriot's chest. "These men and women are a disgrace, but now I see the attitude of the person responsible for training them I'm not surprised. You've got one week to whip them into shape. I'll be back to run them through a training exercise of my choosing, and if they don't behave like something resembling soldiers, you're discharged."

Aubriot's handsome features darkened. "You don't mean that. You wouldn't dare."

"I wouldn't dare?" Cherry struggled to keep control of herself. "Try me, Aubriot. Just try me. The Scythians could return any day, and when they do, we'll be relying on these idiots for our defense. Stars help us! If this is an example of the best you can do, our military is better off without you."

Cherry walked away before she had to take any more of Aubriot's attitude. The man was beyond exasperating. She knew why he'd been late. Antisocial as she was, even she had heard the rumors. Aubriot was late because he'd been with some young woman, one of the latest in a long line to fall victim to his charms. He was disgusting—working his way through the female half of the colony like a bad algae sandwich.

Cherry had heard he'd been fraternizing with

recruits too, though she had no evidence to prove it. His behavior in that regard was bizarre. Aubriot was the one who had written all the rules for Concordia's defense forces, basing them on his memory of armed service regulations back on Earth. Now he was the one flouting them.

She should have given him a dishonorable discharge a year ago, when his attitude started to slip. And she would have, except for the fact that when he concentrated on his job, he really knew what he was doing. Aubriot knew stuff about military training and tactics that wasn't in any of the colony's data banks. He also knew how to manipulate people into doing what he wanted. In the early days, he'd been too authoritarian and overbearing, pissing off the more independently minded Gens in the defense force. But Cherry had persuaded him to tone it down, and the nature of the people he was working with had altered too. These colonists were a later generation who had not revolted against Woken and Guardian control. They were softer, more malleable, and more tolerant of being bossed around.

When he put his mind to what he was doing in Concordia's military force, Aubriot produced excellent results. *When* he put his mind to it, and he wasn't giving priority to that other part of his anatomy.

Cherry swung herself into her autocar, started the engine, and told the car her next destination. The vehicle locked its doors and pulled out of the lot. The Concordian countryside rolled past Cherry's window as the car headed east in the direction of the site that was formerly Sidhe, the colony's underground settlement.

Was Aubriot's deteriorating attitude only due to the fact he was getting older, she wondered. She wasn't sure exactly how old he was. He didn't seem to show any signs of aging, but she guessed he had to be in his late forties or early fifties. He'd expanded his family's already huge business empire until it was vast before sinking all his assets into funding the *Nova Fortuna* Project. Then the project had taken many years to complete. Kes would probably know Aubriot's age when he left Earth. The xenobiologist was the only other living Woken who had embarked on the *Nova*. But since that moment, how much time had passed for the man?

Aubriot had spent a hundred and eighty-six years frozen aboard the colony ship—did people age while in cryo? Cherry had no idea. A little more than a year after Arrival, Aubriot embarked on the mission with her to the Galactic Assembly. Six more Concordian years or roughly three Earth years had gone by since their return.

But while they'd been away, time on Concordia had moved on another one hundred and six Concordian and fifty-three Earth years. How old did that make Aubriot now, or her for that matter? It was confusing.

Still, however old he was, aging didn't justify Aubriot's bad behavior. Whatever the reason was, it was up to him to fix it. He was a grown man. If he continued to be more of a liability than an asset to the colony, he had to go. Cherry wasn't going to place the safety of tens of thousands of men, women, and children in his hands.

Her car arrived at the destination and parked itself. She climbed out and walked to the stairs at the side of the parking lot, stepping over the crack that ran around the lot's outer edge. The line in the pavement was the only sign of the vast man-made cavern that lay under her feet.

She went down the long flights of stairs that led to the cavern's entrance and passed through the security at the door.

Cherry regularly inspected Concordia's armament depots. Everything always seemed in order when she carried out a visual inspections of each depot, but she liked to meet face-to-face with the officers in charge. People tended to be more open and honest when communicating verbally, often saying things they would not commit to writing. She perched on a camp stool and balanced an interface on her knees as she double-checked that month's report from the officer responsible for Cerberus.

Putting aside the interface, Cherry rose and walked to the nearest missile launcher. The points of four missiles protruded from the ground and rose to the ceiling. The frames that held them upright had been sunk into the ground far below.

"General," said a voice. "Welcome to Cerberus."

A fresh-faced young man in uniform was approaching. Cherry squinted, peering through the dim lighting and shadows. The man was a colonel and therefore the person in charge of the depot. She didn't recognize him. Aubriot must have reassigned the previous officer but hadn't informed her.

"Colonel," Cherry replied. "Please don't call me General. Ma'am is fine, or even sir if it's easier to remember. What's your name?"

The officer's stiff posture eased somewhat. "Fletcher, ma'am. I hope you'll find everything as it should be."

"I'm sure I will but it doesn't hurt to check, and also to meet new staff. You didn't write this month's report so you must have taken up your new post recently."

"Yes, ma'am. I've only been here two days. I received my promotion last week."

"Right. Well, how about you take me on a tour and show me what you know about the place?"

"It'll be a pleasure."

Fletcher took Cherry to the pulse emitter first and explained what it was and how it operated. An entirely different construction than the ground-to-space missiles, the emitter had been built according to plans Faina, captain of the Guardians' ship, *Mistral*, had dumped into the colony's data banks before crashing her vessel into the Scythian flagship.

The silo also contained a ground-to-air missile launcher to be deployed if the Scythians made it into Concordia's atmosphere. Stacks of missiles sat beside it.

As Fletcher led Cherry around the other armaments in the depot, her mind turned to her long day ahead on her bi-monthly visit to all the four military sites, code-named Cerberus, Minotaur, Medusa, and Hydra. Cerberus was the oldest, built in the earliest days of the colonization. Work had begun on the silo not long after Cherry had left to go to the Galactic Assembly.

Minotaur sat deep within the cliff face several kilometers from Oceanside, the second major settlement to be built and Concordia's capital. Medusa lurked beneath the mountain range that bisected the main continent, an offshoot of the extensive mines that riddled the mountains. Hydra held the title of the newest of the four. Built with the permission and help of the Fila, it lay in wait beneath the shallow waters of the continental shelf off the shores of the largest continent and original site of colonization, Lyonesse.

Hydra would eventually lose her status of most recently constructed depot. Work was underway on Chimera. The fifth silo was being constructed on Suddene, the second largest and recently colonized continent on Concordia.

At the end of his tour, Fletcher returned to the four ground-to-space missiles. Dust lay thick on their metal surfaces. Despite the dust, the silvery hue of the metal shone through. The missiles had been constructed from the search-and-destroy spiders the Scythians had sent down to kill the humans in their second attack. First to be built, they had sat there more than eighty Concordian years, awaiting the return of the Scythians.

Eighty years was a long time, and no missiles had

ever been launch tested. When the moment for their deployment came, would they work?

J.J GREEN

CHAPTER THREE

Wilder reached armpits deep into the guts of a pulse emitter and slipped a wrench over a nut. She'd lost count of the times she'd serviced the Cerberus emitter and those at the other depots, but Cherry had asked her to carry out yet more maintenance checks on top of those carried out by the regular crew.

Wilder understood Cherry's concern but the work bored her. It irked her too. Humans had lived on Concordia for a hundred and twelve Concordian years. They had spread across the planet's surface to both of its continents. They had built roads and railway lines, schools and hospitals, factories and offices. They had built a new civilization. If that didn't give them the right to call Concordia their home, she didn't know what did. It seemed unfair that they were forced to go to this effort to defend themselves.

There were so many more interesting things she could be doing than servicing pulse emitters, like—

"Hey, Wilder," said a voice behind her.

Startled, Wilder dropped her wrench. The tool clattered into the depths of the machine. "Damn!" Straightening up, she turned and saw Kes.

"Sorry," he said. "I thought you heard me come in."

"No, I didn't, but it's okay," said Wilder. "I was lost in thought." She squatted down next to her tool box and riffled through its contents, pulling out a magnetic gripper and placing it on the emitter's shell. "I didn't expect to see *you* in here. Things getting boring over at the Aliens Office?"

"You mean the Department for Extra-Planetary Affairs?"

"Exactly. The Aliens Office." Wilder ducked down again and picked up a rag to wipe her hands, hiding the smile that was creeping over her lips. She loved to tease Kes, whose love of his job bordered on obsession.

"Well, I guess you're half right," he replied. "I have been learning a lot about other members of the Galactic Assembly. But my job entails..." Kes paused. He laughed and punched Wilder on the shoulder.

She grinned. "Seriously, though. What brings you here? It isn't like you to venture out during daylight on a work day. Is a big disaster brewing? Have the Fila decided to emigrate?"

Kes' eyebrows rose in alarm. "The Fila leave us? Don't even talk about it. What a disaster that would be. No, it isn't anything as serious as that. It's probably nothing, in fact. I would have comm'd you about it, but you turned off your button. I thought I might find you here."

"Whoops." Wilder turned on her ear comm. "Sorry. I don't like to be disturbed when I'm working."

"No problem. I do that too sometimes. So, someone brought part of an object they found into the office today and I was wondering if you might be able to help us identify it. They found the thing way out beyond the mountains a couple of weeks ago."

"What does it look like? Did you bring it with you?"

"It's metallic, and it appears to have been burned, but that's as much as I can tell you. It doesn't resemble anything I've ever seen. I couldn't bring it with me unfortunately. I'm not allowed to take it out of the building. The director is worried it's something dangerous. Would you mind coming over to take a look at it?"

"Sure. Any excuse to get out of servicing these emitters. Give me a few minutes." Wilder reached into the emitter with the magnetic grip. The wrench hadn't fallen far. It was caught between two parts of machinery. But bumping the tool could send it clattering into the depths of the machine, which might entail days of taking the emitter apart in order to reach it. She opened the jaws of the gripper and delicately closed them around the wrench. She felt a satisfying clunk as the magnetism took hold.

As she pulled out the gripper, Wilder said, "Do you have any pictures of this thing you want me to look at?"

"I do. The person who brought it in also took pictures of the whole object they found. I've already sent them to you."

She found the files. "Got them. I'll take a look at them on the way over. I'm nearly done. I just need to close this thing up."

After Wilder had returned the emitter to a working state, they took the autocar Kes had arrived in to go to the government buildings where he worked. Concordia was governed from its capital, Annwn, which lay between Cerberus and the original farming district. Annwn was a small place. Mostly only government workers lived there. The Leader at the time had chosen it as an administrative center in order to discourage larger cities from vying for control of the planet later on in the colony's development.

Despite its small size, the capital was Wilder's source

of groceries and other supplies. Not long after returning from the Galactic Assembly, she had built herself another tree house in the small patch of forest that remained after the construction of Cerberus. Many of the trees had been cleared or had died due to the fitting of the military depot's underground dome. She loved the quiet and seclusion of her little forest home, though living there sometimes made her nostalgic about the days when Tycho, Stephie, and other friends had shared the dream of building an entire settlement beneath the canopy.

Now, Tycho and Stephie were married and had grandchildren. They lived out at Oceanside and Wilder rarely saw them. Their differences in age and experience had created a gulf their former friendship couldn't cross. And the tree settlement Wilder had dreamed of had been built and then later abandoned while she was flying at near light speed between the stars.

"Are you going to look at the pictures I sent?" Kes asked.

"Oh, yeah," Wilder replied, remembering what she was supposed to be doing. Wondering why she seemed to be becoming more absent-minded, she took out her interface and opened the files. The first pictures were of the large object that had been found beyond the mountains.

The thing was an irregular lump of buckled, twisted, scorched metal. The dimension measurements overlay the image and informed Wilder the object was two point eight-seven meters in width at its widest point, one point eight meters deep, and one point five meters tall. Lush vegetation surrounded it.

"The person who found it suspected it might be alien in origin," said Kes. "That was why she came to my department. What do you think?"

"I guess it's strange that something *we* made could

get burned up way over on the other side of the mountains," Wilder said. "Unless it's a crashed aircraft? But we would have heard about it on the news."

"That's what I thought too," said Kes.

Wilder's gaze shifted from the unidentified object to the greenery encircling it. She touched the image and widened it with her fingertips, revealing greater detail. "Look at that." She pointed at an area next to the mysterious artifact.

"What am I looking at?" asked Kes.

"The surrounding area was burned by the heat and flames from the object. You can see the scorched soil. But new shoots are growing. Judging by the dimensions of the object, they were about ten centimeters tall when the picture was taken. We're in the warm season now and everything's growing fast. I would guess the area was burned about three weeks ago, though it's hard to be exact without knowing the plant species."

Kes smiled. "I knew I'd come to the right person."

"You said the finder of this object waited two weeks before they brought it in to you?"

"That's right. She's a miner and she only recently had enough free time to bring it to Annwn."

"That makes it five weeks ago that thing was on fire. I'll check the news reports."

There was no mention of any aircraft crashes, fires, or any other unusual occurrences in the region of wilderness beyond the mountains around the time Wilder estimated, or within two weeks before or afterward.

They had arrived at Kes' place of work. After leaving the autocar in the lot they walked in through the wide doors of the government building. Kes took Wilder into his department on the first floor. It was an open plan office. Wilder drew some curious glances as Kes led her through the desks.

The object sat on an empty table. Wilder picked up

the piece of metal. It was clearly bent out of shape, but even mentally unbending it and imagining the original form gave her no clues as to what it had been. A sharp edge indicated it had been sheared off, probably prior to the major burning of the larger object it came from. The edge hadn't slightly melted and then cooled and solidified again, which is what appeared to have happened to the rest of the object. But even the edge was somewhat scorched like the rest of the thing. Wilder wasn't sure what to make of it.

Kes' colleagues had come over and gathered around her as she examined the object. Two were peering over her shoulders.

"I thought perhaps it was Scythian," said one of them, a young, balding man. "Remains of some of the spiders, melted together. We've certainly found plenty of those over the years."

"None of them were burned, though," said the other person next to Wilder, an older woman.

"Perhaps a container burst in the upper atmosphere and the spiders heated up as they came down," said the young man.

Wilder felt the object's weight. "It isn't part of a spider." She'd handled enough of the search-and-destroy devices to know how much the thing should weigh. It was too heavy. "I think it's a metal alloy, though."

"The chief engineer from Civil Works volunteered to test it and find out its exact composition," said the woman.

"That's great," Wilder said. "Knowing what it's made from will narrow down the field of possibilities." She turned over the object in her hands a few more times before returning it to the table top. "Are you busy with work at the moment?" she asked Kes.

"I'm always busy. There's always something to do, but why are you asking?"

"Do you fancy coming on a heli ride?"

"You want to go out there?"

"I do. This mystery is going to bug me until I've figured it out."

"Sure," said Kes. "I can make time for that. We can take a government heli."

"That's exactly what I was thinking."

Kes smiled. "Okay, let's go tomorrow."

Unable to glean any more information from the object that had been brought in, Wilder decided to call it a day and go home. Kes accompanied her to the outer door of the building. Before leaving, she halted and said, "What I don't understand is, how did it get there? It's in the middle of nowhere. It couldn't have been taken there by truck because there are no roads. We've ruled out the possibility of it being a downed aircraft. The only other vehicle capable of reaching that location is a flitter, but they're all locked away, even the ones with remaining power." A sudden thought struck her and she sucked in a breath.

"What?" asked Kes. "Have you figured out what it is?"

"Uh, no," Wilder replied. "I was thinking about something else."

Kes turned to look at her inquiringly. When Wilder ignored him, he said, "Something entirely unrelated to this object that made you gasp?"

"Look, it's personal, okay?" It wasn't personal, but Wilder couldn't think up a better excuse for not telling Kes the truth at short notice.

"Personal," Kes said. "Right." He folded his arms and leaned on the door, gazing at the view. Several awkward minutes passed in silence. Kes glanced behind them into the empty lobby before saying, "You know, if you're doing something *under the radar*, so to speak, you can tell me. Just because I work for the government it doesn't mean I would turn you in."

"Oh, I know you wouldn't," said Wilder, touching the older man's arm. "It isn't that. It's something I can't talk about yet, to anyone, that's all. And I don't think it's related to this burned up thing the miner found, okay?"

"Hmm, if you're sure. You know I'm only trying to look out for you."

"I'm sure, and I appreciate your concern." Wilder was moved. Kes had always been there for her, ever since that day he'd brought her sluglimpet repellent to spray on the trees in her settlement. He was the closest thing to family she had. She hugged him before leaving.

On her way home, she thought more about the connection she'd made between the mysterious burned object and her little project, until she was convinced there was none. Her initial thought had been that perhaps the object was a failed experiment along the lines of the ones she'd been attempting, but who else in Concordia would be trying to build an a-grav system?

CHAPTER FOUR

It was getting dark. The sunset colors that had brightened the office where Kes worked had disappeared and the encroaching gloom alerted him to the lateness of the hour. He turned off his interface and slipped the device into a bag, then rose from his desk and stretched.

The office was empty. All of his colleagues had already gone home. He was the last to leave, as usual. He walked to the exit, going over the day's events in his mind. He smiled and gave a slight shake of his head at the memory of his encounter with Wilder.

What secret lay behind that gasp she'd given? What was she up to? His young friend had clearly embarked on yet another project that skirted the border of legality.

Out in the hallway, Kes turned his steps toward the rear of the building. The front doors would already be locked and he would have to let himself out of the fire door. Not for the first time, his tired brain dwelt on how remarkably similar the shadowy, quiet building was to the kind of places he used to work at on Earth. If he didn't look too closely, he might have imagined he was back there and the intervening centuries and light years of space were nothing but a fiction of an over-excited imagination.

Kes pushed on the bar that opened the fire door and let himself out into the coolness of late dusk. He descended the steps and walked out into the office parking lot, which he wasn't surprised to see was empty of cars. They had all been taken by departing government workers.

Sighing, he sat on a low wall and ordered an autocar via his ear comm. As he did so, he saw three messages from his wife. A twinge of guilt hit him. He knew what the messages said and he didn't answer them, deciding to cross that bridge when he arrived home.

While he waited for the ordered car to arrive, Kes wondered to himself about his growing sense of deja vu about his workplace. He hadn't felt that way about any place on Concordia before. It had only been in what he saw as the second phase of his life there that his mental shift had appeared, after he'd returned from the trip to the Galactic Assembly.

Experiencing events that later turned out not to be real but a simulation artificially generated in his mind had had a profound effect on him. He'd felt psychologically destabilized and left with a distrust of what was real and what was not.

Then, when he'd returned to Concordia and discovered that the planet had moved on by more than fifty Earth years, he'd undergone another psychic shift. This second effect had occurred more slowly than the first. In the beginning, he'd been amazed and delighted. The colonists had worked wonders in just a few decades. And when he'd found out about the secret military depots they'd constructed in anticipation of the Scythians' return, he'd been even more impressed.

But within weeks a sense of displacement had set in. The new Concordia was nothing like he'd imagined it would be when he'd signed up to embark on the colony expedition. He'd imagined a lifetime of enormous challenges, hardship, and toil as the generational colonists and scientists fought to survive. Instead, after returning from the Assembly, he found he was living a reasonably comfortable existence with all his immediate needs catered for.

He had a comfortable home, a wife and child as well as another on the way, and an office job. If it weren't for the fact that he was studying alien sentient species, he could easily have thought he'd never left Earth.

The whirr of an autocar drew Kes from his musings. The vehicle pulled up in front of him and the doors unlocked. Kes shivered as he stood up. The evening was turning chilly. He looked up at the clear sky and overhanging starscape.

"You're different," he told the stars. "I can say that, but not much else."

He opened a door and climbed into the car, telling it his destination. The interior was warm. The car's heater had activated. It was yet another example of an Earth-like luxury, and it added to Kes' sense of alienation. He would almost have preferred the car was cold, the windows stuck open, and rain pouring inside.

The autocar purred as it pulled away and set off in the direction of Kes' home on the outskirts of Annwn.

Thinking about his life on the new Concordia and its similarity to his memories of Earth brought Kes to a sad recollection that often popped up unbidden when he sank into this mood.

When he'd returned from the Galactic Assembly, the first place he'd gone after emerging from the narrow Fila shuttle had been the Leader's Residence. He hadn't realized at first that the Leader was Meredith, Cariad and Ethan's child. Cherry had been the first to spot that.

At that time, Cariad was still alive and living with her daughter, but age-related dementia had taken over her mind. Meredith had warned him before he'd gone in to see her. However, the knowledge hadn't prepared him for what he encountered.

Against his expectation, she'd recognized him. Her eyes had screwed up to focus on him as soon as he'd gone into the room, and then her features relaxed in recognition.

"Kes, where have you been? Are you here to go into cryo too? I thought maybe you'd been taken to the OR already. Come and sit down."

Kes perched on the bed next to Cariad, a little shocked at the toll time had taken on her appearance. He'd known she would look older, of course, but to see it with his own eyes was another thing.

Cariad beckoned him closer. He leaned in toward her. She clutched his arm and whispered, "Kes, please help me. I changed my mind, but they won't let me leave. There's a nurse here who hates me and she won't let me go." Cariad's grip became tighter. "I changed my mind. I don't want to go on the *Nova Fortuna* any longer. I want to give up my place to someone else. I can do that, can't I? Someone can take my place. They can't force me, right?"

Kes had heard that the best way to deal with the delusions of the mentally ill was to go along with them. Telling them the truth would only make them agitated and unhappy and wouldn't help them at all.

He took her other hand in his. "No, they can't force you. You don't have to go if you don't want to."

"Good, good," said Cariad, her hold on Kes' arm softening. "I decided I can't leave my family. I can't do that to them, and I'll miss them too much."

Kes bowed his head. "I know how you feel. But don't worry about it. I'll speak to the doctors and tell them not to prep you for cryo."

"Thank you, Kes. Thank you. I knew I could rely on you."

Though Cariad appeared to have forgotten everything that had happened since she woke from cryo, her memory of the years leading up to the departure of the colonization expedition was vivid. As Kes sat and talked with her, she referred to many aspects of that time he'd entirely forgotten. The snatched moments of intimacy they'd shared, the utter exhaustion of the long days of work, office politics and gossip, and the escalating strength of the public protests.

By the time she'd become tired by their conversation and fallen asleep, Kes had been transported back into that time. He'd also felt anew the same doubt and indecision that now plagued Cariad's aged brain.

If he had his time again, would he decide to remain on Earth? If he'd known how much his expectations would be thwarted, it was possible he would.

The autocar drew to a stop outside a small house fronted by a yard covered in the rubbery, low-growing Concordia ground cover plant that grew naturally in that area. Kes exited the car and walked up the path. The front door opened before he reached it and yellow light silhouetted the pregnant figure of Isobel, his wife.

She waited until he was inside and the door was closed before she began her admonishments.

"You promised," she said. "You promised you'd be home early today."

"I know, I'm sorry. Someone brought something into the office, and I had to—"

"I don't want to hear it. Whatever it was, you could have at least comm'd me. You could have replied to my messages."

"You're right. That's what I should have done. I got carried away, I guess. Look, why don't we do something special this weekend? I want to make it up to you."

"It isn't only me, it's Miki too. She hasn't seen her Daddy in three days. You leave before she wakes up and come home after she's gone to bed. Three days is a long time to a two-year-old."

"I know." Kes hung his head. "I'm sorry." He reached out to hug Isobel, but she stepped backward, avoiding him.

"I've never said this before," she said. Her chin began to tremble. "If you continue like this, always working, never making time for me or our children, our marriage isn't going to survive. I know that sounds like an ultimatum, but it isn't. It's the truth." Isobel turned around and walked into the kitchen at the back of their house.

He knew she didn't want him to see her cry. Kes stood in the hall, his arms hanging loosely, feeling like an absolute asshole. What was going on with him? The amount of work he had to do was overwhelming. He was studying the available information on other members of the Galactic Assembly, learning as much as he could about the anatomy, behavior, environmental conditions essential for life, history, and culture of more than two dozen species. Realistically, it was several lifetimes' work for everyone in his department, let alone himself.

Yet none of it was as important to him as his family. Why was he neglecting them?

CHAPTER FIVE

Meredith had requested that Cherry pay her an informal visit at her private residence. The 'request' was not something Cherry, as the colony's general, could refuse her Leader, but she didn't mind going to see Ethan's daughter. Her grief at Ethan's passing and missing out on a lifetime of his friendship had, over the years, become something she could lock away. It was only during quiet moments she had to herself that she allowed the pain to surface. Also, as time had passed, remembering Ethan increasingly brought her many moments of sweet nostalgia.

As Cherry's autocar approached the Leader's Residence, she noticed that Oceanside had grown larger since the last time she was there. The streets of one-story houses spreading out from the central district at the clifftop had grown longer and more numerous. The views out to sea and inland over low hills made it easy to see why so many Concordians chose the place as their home.

Proximity to the Fila was another great selling point for the town. A large metropolis of the beings stood in the shallow waters offshore, where, decades previously, the *Nova Fortuna* had crashed into the planet. The flotsam of the ship's remains after the Scythians destroyed it had washed away long ago and now the waters had returned to their shades of azure and turquoise.

Relations between humans and their aquatic friends grew stronger every year. In the little spare time she had, Cherry would go to the beach at the foot of the cliff. Families also gathered there. Parents relaxed while their children played in the waves, entirely unafraid of accidental drownings. Cherry had even seen some of the youngsters speaking a rudimentary version of the threads' language, if 'speak' was the right word to describe their vigorous gesticulations.

Cherry's autocar halted at the entrance to the Leader's Residence. She climbed out and mounted the steps to the double doors. The assistant who let her in passed on Meredith's message that she was in the bunker. Cherry immediately knew what that meant: Meredith was talking to the threads. Probably Quinn, who had acted as the spokesperson for the aliens for as long as Cherry had known him.

Cherry took the elevator and descended through the vertical tunnel that had been dug through the cliff. She emerged into a circular room well below sea level. Half of the wall was transparent and looked out directly into water. The threads had also cut a passage through the rock at the base of the cliff so they could meet with the colony's Leader face to...tentacles. Cherry recognized Quinn's distinctive patterning immediately.

"Cherry," Quinn said via the room's speaker. He'd recognized her too, though she guessed her missing arm made her easily identifiable to the aliens. "It feels good to see you again."

"It's good to see you too, Quinn."

"Thanks for coming at short notice," said Meredith. "I didn't want to make a big fuss and order you here. I don't want to run the risk of this getting out before it's official."

"You have already arrived at a decision?" Quinn asked.

"Not yet," Meredith replied. "I want to hear what Cherry has to say."

"I understand," said Quinn.

Meredith said, "Cherry, the Fila comm'd me this morning. They received a transmission from outer space. A delegation of Galactic Assembly members is on its way to meet with us."

"A delegation?" Cherry asked. "Of what? I mean, who?" She was taken aback at the news and uncomfortable at the notion of unknown aliens turning up on Concordia's doorstep unannounced. The last time that happened things hadn't gone well.

"From what Quinn tells me," Meredith replied, "I believe you encountered this species when you visited the Assembly's space station."

"Do you mean the organizers of the station?" asked Cherry. She imagined the gigantic creatures striding through Oceanside, spreading terror and panic.

"No," Quinn replied, "they told us you met them during your simulation."

"Oh." Cherry recalled she had seen one other alien species at close quarters. "But I thought they were holos." The simulation had included a fake attack on the station. She and her companions had each been given the choice of sacrificing their own lives to help others, or saving themselves and letting hundreds of other beings die. Cherry, Wilder, and Kes had made the choice to sacrifice themselves, unaware the situation was not real. Aubriot had decided to save himself, to no one's great surprise when they found out later.

"The beings in the simulation were a fabrication," said Quinn, "but the species is real. They heard they were chosen to play the victims in the test scenario, and they are grateful that most of you chose to save one of them."

"Okay," said Cherry. "I see. But that was years ago. Why are they coming now, and why are they coming here?"

"I'm surprised you are not more aware of how the rate of the passage of time is affected by the observer's perspective," Quinn replied.

"Ugh, all right. I get it." The passing of over one hundred Concordian years while she went on her mission to the Galactic Assembly remained a sore point. Even more importantly, it was a factor that limited the Assembly's ability to help Concordia when the Scythians finally returned. Cherry had gone to the Galactic Assembly's space station in the hope that humanity would be accepted into their alliance. Her mission had been successful, but her expectation that other Assembly members would turn up to help defend her home in the event of an attack had proven wishful thinking.

The Galactic Assembly had warned the Scythians that the human colony had its support and it would not countenance any acts of aggression, but starships took weeks, months, and years to travel interstellar distances. If the Scythians wanted to annihilate the humans they could do it and face the consequences later. Whatever reprisal the Assembly chose to inflict wouldn't matter to the dead.

"This delegation has been traveling to Concordia since they received the pertinent information," said Quinn. "We passed on their message as soon as we received it, and the delegation lags their communication by only a short while. Of course they must come here if they want to meet you."

Cherry frowned at the swirling, tentacled alien. She focused on the center of the creature, where she guessed Quinn's brain was. He had no eyes and it was the best she could come up with for a focal point. The threads were notorious for their inability to exactly convert their measurement of time into the human scale. Though, to be fair, no Concordian colonist had managed to make the conversion going the other way either. The threads' method of measuring the passing hours, days, and months was an utter mystery to human perception.

"What do you mean by 'a short while'?" Cherry asked.

Quinn didn't answer. He seemed to be thinking.

"Ah, tomorrow, I think," he said eventually.

"After the sun rises and it's light here again?"

"Yes, that's right."

Was that so hard? Cherry silently asked.

"I guess we should welcome them," Meredith said.

"I guess so," said Cherry, "but it won't hurt to play this safe. The last time a new species arrived from outer space, it tried to destroy us."

"You don't really think these creatures you saved during your test would mean us any harm?" asked Meredith. "Do you think they're interested in Concordia too? Like the Scythians?"

"Who knows?" Cherry replied. "If they're members of the Assembly it's unlikely. But we only saw them during a simulation. We didn't meet them. I have no idea what they're really like and I'm worried about security issues. We can't afford the slightest suspicion of the existence of our armaments depots coming to the attention of the Scythians. Our secret weapons are the only defense we have, but visitors from offplanet wouldn't need to do much digging to find out about Cerberus, for example. That place is no secret to anyone here because nearly everyone has a grandparent who was living in Sidhe when construction began. And it's been hard to keep the locations and contents of the other depots under wraps too. If that information falls into Scythian hands

—or whatever it is they have—we might as well forget any element of surprise if they attack."

"What do you suggest?" Meredith asked.

"Well, we also can't afford to turn this delegation away either," Cherry replied. "They're fellow members of the Assembly. We have no valid excuse not to meet with them."

Meredith said, "And we would be foolish to refuse an opportunity to secure the close friendship of another galactic force."

"The *Opportunity* is available if you would prefer the visitors don't come down to the planet surface," said Quinn.

The starship the threads had built for the humans to travel to the Assembly's space station had remained in orbit ever since its return. It was impossible to hide the starship but Meredith had decided not to allow any more interstellar missions aboard it out of fear of triggering a visit from the Scythians.

"Yes," said Meredith to Cherry. "That's another option, if you're really worried about the visitors coming here."

"The *Opportunity* is tiny," said Cherry. "It was barely large enough for four passengers. I can't imagine hosting an official meeting of two galactic powers aboard it. No. They'll have to come here, providing they can survive in Concordia's environment."

"If not, they may invite you to come aboard their ship," said Quinn. "The *Opportunity's* EVA suits are still available."

"Yes," said Cherry. "They might. I hadn't thought of that." She might almost prefer the effort and potential danger of going aboard the aliens' ship to having them visit Concordia. "I think we should accept their meeting proposal and wait to see what they suggest."

"I was coming to the same decision myself," said Meredith. "But if they do want to come down to the surface, I'll need you to arrange the security operation."

"Of course," Cherry said. "That shouldn't be a problem. As I recall, these aliens are quite small and probably weak too. It won't be hard to keep them exactly where we want them. Time is short, so I'll begin the preparations now in case they want to come here. We can hold the meeting at the government offices in Annwn."

"I agree that's the best place," said Meredith. "Use whatever resources you need, with my full permission."

"Thanks. Let me know as soon as you hear anything," Cherry said. She was about to say goodbye when she remembered a pertinent question. "What are the visitors called, Quinn? I never knew the name of their species."

"As with many advanced galactic life forms, their name only translates into your language as 'people', but..." Quinn was silent for a couple of beats. "Yes, Kes has given them a name. It's *Parvus wilderensia*."

"*Wilder*ensia?" Cherry echoed. "Wilder. He's named them after Wilder. I don't believe it. He's done it again."

Meredith's smile told Cherry she knew exactly what she was talking about.

"We'll just call them Parvus," Meredith said.

Cherry sighed. "Thanks, Quinn. I'll be sure to pass on the bad news to Wilder." Cherry said goodbye to Meredith and Quinn and took the elevator to the first floor.

She was almost certain the visiting aliens would want to come down to the surface if they could. Quinn had once mentioned that life-supporting planets were rare in the galaxy. The visitors would probably be curious about Concordia and want to see it with their own eyes...or experience it with whatever sense organs they had.

But on her way to Annwn to organize the security around the landmark meeting, Cherry wanted to make a small detour.

CHAPTER SIX

Three small, two-seater helis were secured to the roof of the government building by docking clamps to prevent strong winds from blowing them away. The helis were restricted to government use only, as Wilder had known perfectly well when she suggested that Kes accompany her to the site of the mysterious object beyond the mountain range. The trip would have taken her days by any other mode of transport, even if she'd managed to hitch a ride on one of the ultra-fast trucks that collected metal ingots from the refineries near the mines.

She and Kes walked to the nearest one and Kes released the locking mechanism with a code.

Wilder said, "Mind if I fly it?" Without waiting for an answer she climbed in the pilot's side.

"Have you flown one of these before?" asked Kes, opening the passenger door while Wilder settled herself at the controls.

"Oh yes, lots of times," Wilder replied. She started the engine and under the noise of its whirr she added, too quietly for Kes to hear, "In a sim."

"How come?" asked Kes. "I didn't think non-government personnel were allowed."

"You know Cherry," Wilder replied. "Always asking me to do one thing or another." She didn't mention this last fact, though true, had nothing to do with her practicing flying helis.

"In that case," Kes said, "be my guest."

Wilder checked the surrounding airway was clear—it would have been a miracle if it wasn't, considering how few aircraft flew in Concordian skies. The danger of attracting unwanted attention from the Scythians was too great. But she checked nonetheless. Unsurprisingly, nothing was in the sky for cubic kilometers all around. Wilder disengaged the clamps that held the landing skids, engaged the heli's rotors, and lifted the machine up into the atmosphere. The rooftop retreated swiftly below them.

"You know," Kes said, "It's surprising what I miss about Earth. I always knew I would miss certain foods and things like going to the cinema or visiting theme parks, but I never thought I would miss birds."

"Those animals that fly?" Wilder said. "Yeah, I can see that. They must have been amazing."

"I took birds for granted," Kes mused. "They were always just *there*. Pigeons and sparrows in the streets, blue jays and robins in the countryside, geese migrating in the spring and fall. I never took the time to properly observe them. I was too busy thinking about life forms on other planets to pay any attention to the creatures on my own."

He sounded uncharacteristically pensive.

Wilder asked. "Are you feeling homesick?"

"I guess so, though I'm homesick for somewhere that no longer exists."

There was a tone in Kes' voice that caused Wilder to turn and look at him. "Are you okay, Kes?"

"I'm fine," he replied. "Don't worry." He gave her a

smile, but Wilder wasn't convinced that all was well with her friend. However, he didn't seem ready to talk about what was bothering him, so they chatted about other topics as they flew toward the mountains.

At one point, Kes put a hand to his ear and said, "Hi, Cherry...Uhuh...Really?" His eyes widened and he turned a shocked face toward Wilder. "When?... Sure. Of course. I wouldn't miss it for the world. It'll be good to meet the little guys in the flesh, so to speak."

"What is it?" asked Wilder after Kes finished speaking to Cherry.

When he related the news that Concordia was about to receive a visit from another member of the Galactic Assembly, Wilder was surprised but delighted. "That's fantastic. When do I get to meet them?"

Kes' features fell. "I don't know if you can. I don't know if the Leader will allow it. This is an official visit."

"Ugh, you're right," said Wilder. "Why would she arrange for them to meet up with me?" Maybe she should get a job after all, she pondered. A government job. It would be nice to have a heli at her disposal and she might get to do something interesting, like meet visiting aliens.

Mountain peaks were rising above the horizon. "Where are we going exactly?" she asked.

"I'll put in the coordinates," said Kes. He pressed the interface screen, transferring the numbers from his files.

Wilder relinquished the controls to the autopilot and folded her arms as she gazed out at the view. The landscape was passing swiftly beneath them, transforming from farmland to wilderness. To one side the road to the mountains cut through the vegetation. Autotrucks ran along the gray line.

To pass the time, Wilder asked Kes about his latest discoveries about the Fila. Though the research had been going on all the time they'd both been away, and

Kes had continued it during all the years that had passed since their return, there was always some new discovery to be made about the alien species.

Wilder listened with half an ear as they neared the mountain range and then rose to the height of the pass. She was interested to hear the latest finding about the Fila, but she was also puzzling over the strange object they were about to investigate beyond the mountains. The more she thought about it, the more intrigued she became about what it might be. She felt that familiar tug of desire to find out the truth about a mystery, no matter how long it took.

Her earlier fear returned. Had someone else managed to re-invent a-grav? Had their vehicle cruised to such a height that, when the machine failed, it had burned as it passed through Concordia's atmosphere? Wilder hoped she was wrong, for two reasons. Firstly, she would hate for another inventor like herself to have died horribly, and, secondly, *she* wanted to be the one to provide the colony with a-grav. Was that somewhat narcissistic of her? Perhaps. But there it was.

They crossed the mountain range through a cleft between two of the tallest peaks. Snowy slopes rose on each side of them and the air inside the heli grew chill, though the vehicle automatically supplied the cabin with additional oxygen. Finally, the heli began to descend. However, it wasn't until they were nearly at ground level that Wilder spotted the crumpled, twisted wreck. Tall vegetation had already begun to overhang it, obscuring the scorched, dull metal from view.

As the heli touched down in the closest patch of rough ground, several meters from the wreck, Kes lifted a hand to his ear comm.

"The results from the tests on the object's material came through," he said to Wilder. "Wait a minute, Aggy, let me patch Wilder in."

A moment later, he said, "Okay, go ahead."

"Right," came Aggy's voice through Wilder's comm. "I'm sending these over as I speak." She then proceeded to reel off a list of substances and proportion percentages to four decimal points.

"Thanks, Aggy," said Kes when she'd finished

Aggy closed her comm, and Kes turned to Wilder. "Well that was gobbledygook to me. Does it mean anything to you?"

"I think it does," Wilder said. The list had begun to sound familiar after Aggy had read out less than half of it. As the woman had continued, recognition hit Wilder like the flick of a wet towel from a bully. It was a sensation she knew too well. She'd waited to have her conclusion about the material confirmed, but she could have finished Aggy's list for her.

The heli rotors slowed to a stop, and Wilder stepped out onto the knee-high vegetation. She strode toward the mystery craft that perhaps was no longer such a mystery.

"Well, what is it?" Kes asked from behind her as he followed. "Don't leave me hanging."

But amazement and disbelief was keeping Wilder silent. She wanted to set eyes on the object, otherwise she might not believe it was real. She didn't want to give Kes an answer because it would sound ridiculous.

The outline of the wreck peeked tantalizing through gaps in the trees and tall plants that surrounded it. Wilder forced her way between overhanging tree fronds and pushed aside a vine that hung in her way. Then she was there.

The sight that greeted her gave no clue to the object's guessed origin whatsoever. The outer surface of the misshapen lump had burned at such a high temperature it had partially melted. Stumps of what must have been some kind of instruments stuck out, their edges dissolved into obscurity. It was no wonder the person who had stumbled across it had thought the find was remarkable enough to report.

"Wow," said Kes as he, too, arrived at the scene. He walked directly up to the object and ran a hand over the strange, destroyed surface, walking around it as he did so. "Hey, look here, you can see inside."

Wilder joined him. A dark hole gaped in the side of the object, but it revealed little of the interior. The remains that hung off the hole nearly made Wilder's heart stop.

"What's this, do you think?" she asked, touching the broken protrusion.

Kes frowned. "I'm not sure. It's odd that it wasn't burned away like the rest when it was sticking out like that."

"It *is* odd, isn't it?" said Wilder. "What would you say if I told you I think it's a door?"

Kes' eyebrows rose. He squatted down in order to peer through the hole. "A door? You mean it opened after the object landed and that's why it didn't burn off? But that would mean there was something inside here and it managed to open a door and come out."

Wilder took a breath. "Kes, the breakdown of the object's metallic compound—it exactly matches the material the Guardians' weapons are made from."

"No," Kes breathed, straightening up. He stared at her. "No way. It can't. They were here decades ago, and you said this thing had been here only a few weeks."

"A vessel without power might float around in space for centuries," said Wilder. "Thousands of years or even longer, before the gravity of an astronomical body finally snares them."

"But the *Mistral* was annihilated when Faina flew it into the Scythian flagship. How could a piece this size have survived intact?"

"I don't know," said Wilder, "but I don't think it's impossible. I only know that the material this is made from matches the Guardians' weapons. It seems too much of a coincidence for there to be no connection."

Kes squatted down again. "Could it have been an emergency escape capsule that was jettisoned just before impact?"

"Maybe it was caught up in the explosion and its engine was destroyed."

"So, was a Guardian inside, and it's managed to open the hatch and get out?"

"That isn't as crazy as it sounds," Wilder said. "But if this *is* the wreck of a Guardian escape vehicle, where's the Guardian?"

CHAPTER SEVEN

Cherry's autocar rolled to a stop outside an imposing dwelling. The three-story, double-fronted house sat alone on an offshoot of the highway that ran from Oceanside to Annwn, in a low spot between the surrounding hills. A garden of architectural native vegetation surrounded it, though the plants were unkempt and overgrown, as if no one had tended them in a long while.

The house was constructed from reclaimed building materials that originally came from the *Nova Fortuna*. The plastiwood created for the building of the colony's first settlement had proven extremely tough and durable, and it remained the favored material for creating new dwellings, providing the builder could get it.

The house's owner was exactly the person to find a way to acquire this scarce, valuable resource.

Cherry opened the door of her vehicle but she didn't get out. Was she doing the right thing? It had been years since she'd been here and her visit was unannounced. Seconds passed as she hesitated. Finally, she got out. Since she had taken the precious time out

of her busy day to go there, she might as well follow through with her visit.

As she walked to the residence, stepping over green tendrils that snaked over the path, the front door opened. Aubriot stood in the doorway. He raised an arm and leaned on the frame, his expression inscrutable.

Cherry climbed the house steps and halted in front of him. "Can I come in?"

Wordlessly, Aubriot walked away from her and down the hall, leaving the door open.

Cherry stepped inside and closed the door. She followed Aubriot into one of the two front rooms but paused on the threshold. The place was a mess. Dirty laundry was strewn about, used dishes and cutlery cluttered the coffee table, and dust lay thick over every surface.

Ever since Cherry had known Aubriot, he'd been generally neat and tidy in his habits. It was a fact that had surprised her, knowing his privileged upbringing, which had included servants to attend to all his needs.

Aubriot was already sitting on his sofa in his characteristic sprawl, legs splayed and arms resting along the sofa back. Defiance gleamed in his eyes as he took in Cherry's reaction to the state of his room, yet there was no hint of embarrassment in his face about his living conditions.

"Mind if I sit down?" she asked.

"Make yourself at home," he replied in a sarcastic tone.

Cherry picked up some clothes from an armchair and hesitated as she looked for somewhere to put them. No surface was empty. Finally, she placed the clothes carefully on the floor.

Aubriot watched her movements. When she sat down he said, "Want a drink?"

"I do, thanks."

Without asking what she wanted, Aubriot got up and

strode from the room.

Cherry was already regretting her decision to visit her former lover. It would be so much easier to simply discharge Aubriot from his duties and appoint someone else in his place. That was what he deserved after his behavior at the training exercise, and he'd deserved the same for similar behavior over the previous few months. She knew that retaining someone who had demonstrated he was unfit for service set a bad example.

But Aubriot was a good military strategist, or he was when he chose to be. He was probably better than her and so the best in the colony, considering no one living except he and she had taken part in any actual battles. If only Cherry could return him to his previous enthusiasm for his job. It could mean the difference between defeat or victory when the Scythians returned.

The problem was, she didn't know why he'd begun behaving so oddly. She didn't know what was wrong with him, and so she had no idea how to fix him.

Aubriot reappeared, holding a steaming mug. He hadn't poured anything for himself. Cherry took the drink and sipped the brown liquid. It was a beverage made from chicory root and her usual drink. "You remembered."

Aubriot shrugged and returned to his seat, but Cherry thought she detected embarrassment underlying his nonchalance. She took another sip of hot liquid and, failing to find anywhere to put the mug down, cupped it between her hands on her lap.

"You know why I'm here, right?" she asked.

Aubriot smirked. "Yeah. You can't keep away from me. Want to go upstairs?"

Cherry tilted her head. "Don't kid around, okay? This is serious." The kind of activity Aubriot alluded to had ceased to be a part of their tenuous relationship long ago, prior to the mission to the Assembly. Aubriot's narcissistic rage over the fact that she'd loved Ethan had killed any prospect of a return to their convenient arrangement.

"Look," said Cherry, "will you tell me what's going on? Your behavior the other day...it wasn't like you. And that wasn't the first time something like that has happened. What's gone wrong with you? You used to love what you do. You lived for it. Now, it's like you don't care anymore." She glanced around her. "You seem to have stopped caring about anything."

"I was only a bit late," Aubriot replied. "That's all. No need to get your knickers in a twist."

"Oh, for stars' sake, will you speak English for once?" Aubriot's habit of dropping archaic sayings into his speech had annoyed Cherry for years. He appeared to love confusing her and everyone else with his weird use of language.

"I mean..." Aubriot leaned forward, rested his elbows on his knees, and looked Cherry in the eye. "You're overreacting."

"I'm not, and you know it," Cherry replied. "If our roles were reversed you would have kicked me out long ago."

Aubriot broke eye contact, leaned back into the sofa again, and crossed his legs at the ankles. "If our roles were reversed, things would be different."

"What do you mean? Concordia's defense force? How would it be different?"

Aubriot remained maddeningly silent.

"I'm doing the best I can," said Cherry. "If you think I'm doing something wrong, making some mistakes, I want to hear about it. All I want to do is protect the colony. Aubriot, I value what you have to say. I *want* you to help me. But what you're doing now is no help at all."

Her ex-lover folded his arms and gazed into the middle distance.

Cherry was quickly losing patience. Aubriot was

being unbearable, as usual. He didn't give a shit about the colony and never had. He'd only ever cared about himself and now even that seemed beyond him.

"Okay," Cherry said. "I know there isn't a chance in hell you're going to tell me what's been going on with you recently, but I need to know something and I need to know it now. You have to give me a straight answer. Do you understand?"

Aubriot smirked again. "Sure, *General.*"

"Do you remember the aliens in the simulation at the space station? The ones you decided not to save when the station was attacked?"

"Yeah, I remember. I stand by my decision. What about them?"

"A delegation of them is on its way here right now. I think they want a closer relationship with us."

"Really?" Aubriot rubbed his lips with a finger.

Cherry was relieved to get a reaction out of him at last. "Yes, really. I don't need to spell out to you how important this could be to Concordia. Things are moving on and I have to keep on top of the situation security- and military-wise. Now, despite what you say, I am *not* overreacting about your behavior. Your attitude has been atrocious for weeks. You've been late for duty and from what I've heard I suspect you've been drunk while on duty too. And I'm pretty sure you've been fraternizing with your subordinates. Those are just a few misdemeanors, but, worst of all, you've been failing to train the soldiers adequately. That exercise the other morning was a shitshow. I can't afford to have someone with your attitude in such a high position of responsibility, especially at the moment. What I've come here to say is, if you give me your word all that is going to end today, I won't discharge you."

"Give you my word?" Aubriot's eyebrows lifted.

He was playing with her. Though clearly something was bothering him deeply, on another level he was enjoying himself. But Cherry had gotten bored of his egotistical games long ago.

"What's it to be?" she asked. "You're an asshole and you know it, but I've never known you to go back on a promise. If you assure me right now you're going to change your attitude, you can remain in your position."

Aubriot's features fell into a deadpan expression. He studied her. Just as much as she was watching him for a response, he was watching her. What it was he was looking for, she didn't know.

After a few long seconds, his eyes turned dull. "Ah well, looks like the military life isn't for me."

Cherry almost gasped. His response was not what she'd been expecting. She'd thought that, faced with the prospect of losing something he had lived for for years, ever since the defense force's inception, Aubriot would decide to make a change. The last thing she'd thought he would do was toss the entire enterprise aside, especially not after hearing the news of this interesting development. Her heart sank into her stomach.

Suddenly aware her mouth was hanging open, Cherry closed it with a snap. Aubriot wasn't looking at her, though. He was studying his toes.

Cherry was tempted to ask him to reconsider, but she'd already given him way too many chances.

"What will you do?" she asked. It was all she could think to say.

"Actually, I was thinking I might start up a brewery." Aubriot spread his fingers and inspected his fingernails.

"A brewery?"

"Yeah, the beer around here is shit. Always has been. It's about time someone showed the colony how it should be done."

"Right." Cherry stood up and put her full cup of chicory coffee on the floor. "Good luck with that."

"Thanks." Aubriot continued to avoid eye contact.

"I'd better go. The delegation arrives tomorrow."

"Fine. I'll show you out."

"No, it's okay."

When Aubriot accepted her response without an answer, Cherry walked out of his dirty, messy living room and left.

CHAPTER EIGHT

Wilder tapped her ear comm. Five meters above her, within the overhanging tree fronds, an electric motor started up. A moment later, a cradle made from plaited vines descended. Wilder climbed into it and tapped her comm again to signal the motor to wind in the opposite direction, lifting her upward to her tree home.

She gripped the twisted vines affectionately. Despite the six Concordian years that had passed the strands remained strong, though they had worn to a shine in the place she always held them.

Other materials had been available to her when she'd constructed her dwelling not long after returning from the mission to the Galactic Assembly—living in a regular house had gotten old fast, especially after her long confinement aboard the *Opportunity*. But she preferred using the same tree fronds and vines from which she'd built her original house. Repeating the same process pleased her sense of nostalgia and the natural materials were perfectly suited to the project: they were light and tough and they blended into the surrounding vegetation, giving the added benefit of camouflaging her home against unwanted visitors.

Not that she felt in danger from other Concordians. As far as she knew, no serious crimes were ever committed, perhaps due to the genetic selection of the generational colonists or the equality and stability of the civilization they were creating. Yet there was nothing Wilder liked better than peace, quiet, and the certainty that no one would disturb her while she was working.

She stepped off the cradle and onto the platform that supported her living quarters. Except for the rustling of leaves in the evening breeze, the silence of the forest now surrounded her. Looking forward to an evening working on her pet project, she pushed open her front door.

Two slim, gray, four-legged creatures about twenty centimeters long stood on the floor on the other side, waiting for her. They'd been alerted to her arrival by the sound of the electric winch. Before Wilder even had time to close the door, the two creatures ran up over her pants and shirt until they reached her shirt collar, which they clung to with small paws while they sniffed her face and hair.

"Hi guys," said Wilder, petting the creatures. "What's been happening?"

The little animals ignored her question and continued to snuffle her hair and neck. Finally, they stared at her face, their bright black eyes shiny on each side of their long snouts. Apparently satisfied that Wilder was who they thought she was, they both climbed into the open neck of her shirt. After burrowing down to the place where her shirt was tucked into her pants, they snuggled there, comfortable in her body heat.

"Not much, I guess," said Wilder.

She crossed the floor of her small, one-room home and took out a box of crackers and a tub of yeast spread from a cupboard. She also took a plate from another cupboard and a knife from a drawer. One of the animals in her shirt wriggled, slightly scratching her with its short claws.

"Hey, be careful."

Pulling out the only chair at her table, Wilder sat down and flicked open the interface embedded in the surface. She opened the tub and spread the yeast paste on a cracker with the knife. Meanwhile, both of the creatures nestling in her shirt ascended to the open collar and peeked out.

"Here you go, Puddle," Wilder said as she broke off a piece of cracker and lifted it to the right-hand animal, who took it from her fingers and inspected the morsel carefully before popping it into its mouth. A moment later a bulge appeared in the animal's cheek.

"And one for you, Piddle." Wilder handed a second crumb to the left-hand creature, who did the same as his—or her—counterpart, Piddle. Wilder hadn't yet figured out what sex the creatures were, assuming they reproduced sexually.

She'd had a couple of years to spend on the problem, since Piddle and Puddle had first emerged from the tree trunk at the center of her home. She'd named them after their poor toilet habits, but she hadn't learned much more about their behavior or anatomy.

She also hadn't told Kes of their existence, despite being fairly certain that neither he nor any of the other xenobiologists had discovered the species. She didn't like the idea of her little friends being prodded and poked by scientists.

Wilder scanned the latest news scrolling across her interface. The top headline jumped out at her.

DELEGATION OF PARVUS ARRIVES TOMORROW

Parvus? They had to be the creatures from the Galactic Assembly. Kes had received a message from Cherry about them but Wilder didn't know any more than what he'd told her.

She opened a comm and stated Cherry's official title.

Cherry answered immediately. "Hi Wilder, I can't speak right now. I have to get ready to meet the Parvus delegation."

"I guessed that," said Wilder. "What I want to know is, why has this only been announced the day before they're arriving? This is a huge step for the colony."

"Sorry," Cherry replied. "I'll explain later."

A tone from Wilder's comm told her Cherry had severed the connection.

Wilder tried to contact Kes, but her friend's comm was busy. She decided to wait awhile and try to find out more about the alien visitors. Were they members of the Galactic Assembly? She ate the cracker spread with yeast paste. Piddle and Puddle begged for more food, climbing up Wilder's neck and tugging on her earlobes and hair.

As she chewed her sparse meal and broke off two more pieces of cracker, Wilder wondered about the synchronicity of the day's events. It seemed an odd coincidence that the strange object she'd been investigating had arrived only a few weeks before the surprise visit of an alien delegation.

Then it occurred to her: Was Cherry even aware of the other arrival on the planet? There was no reason she should be, unless Kes had told her, and he probably hadn't said anything yet. They didn't know if their guess was correct. Yet the colony's military commander *should* know of the potential link.

Wilder requested contact with Cherry again, only to hear the 'no contact' tone. Dammit. Wilder guessed Cherry had set her comm to only receive from certain personnel. She considered contacting Meredith, who was probably one of the people who could speak to Cherry, but she didn't know Meredith well. Would it be too presumptuous of her to contact the Leader about her worries? After all, the object out in the wildlands beyond the mountains was just a lump of twisted metal. Everything else was guesswork.

She decided to think it over some more before making a decision. Perhaps she would talk to Kes and they could decide together.

Wilder ate a final cracker and read the rest of the day's news. A woman had given birth to quintuplets and all the babies were healthy and doing well. Multiple births were common on Concordia but from what Wilder understood they hadn't been common on Earth. Had that been something Cariad had factored into her selection when she'd picked the original generational colonists and the frozen gametes stored on the *Nova Fortuna*? Wilder didn't think the information was mentioned in the colony records and now no one would be able to find out. Cariad had died two and a half Concordian years previously. Her funeral hadn't been anywhere near as well attended as Ethan's, which Wilder thought was a shame. The woman's contribution to Concordia had been huge, but obviously not as well recognized.

After scanning the other headlines and not finding anything of particular interest, Wilder scooped the crumbs from her table, opened a window, and threw them outside. While she was doing this, Piddle and Puddle climbed out from her shirt, dropped onto the table, ran down one of its legs, and raced to a corner of the room where they had constructed a bed of dried plant material. Only the finest, softest strands of vegetation were deemed suitable for the bed. Wilder thought of the place as their 'grooming corner' because that was all the two seemed to do there. The two creatures set about licking and smoothing each other's short head fur.

Wilder turned off her comm and went to a covered mound in the center of the room. Lifting off the cloth, she revealed a circular machine roughly one and a half meters in diameter and half a meter tall. Half of the domed surface was covered by a shell. The other half was bare, the intricate, detailed circuitry and mechanisms displayed.

She had spent months working on the a-grav device after spending years, off and on, deciphering the explanation of the principles of a-grav outlined in the Guardians' data. Colony scientists had also stumbled across the information while she'd been away at the Galactic Assembly, and now only they had official permission to work on developing a-grav due to the—in Wilder's estimation, extremely small—chance of a serious accident. But others were working on re-inventing the process too. They had a little community where they discussed their work, and they had even managed to acquire a flitter engine to reverse engineer. But it all had to be kept secret.

Many times Wilder had given up on her work, throwing the cloth over the machine in disgust and turning her attention to a new puzzle. The problem was, the Guardians' data only recorded the theory, not the exact details on how to neutralize gravity. It was the application of the theory that was proving to be the stumbling block, and had done for years, even prior to her return from the Galactic Assembly.

Despite her lack of success, Wilder had never gathered the resolve to throw the prototype out. The machine remained in the center of her living space, taunting her. Over the previous few weeks, however, she'd felt she was making real progress.

The Guardians' data was complex, but Wilder felt the problem boiled down to balancing the proportions of the combined particles during each stage of the process. Others in the group working on the problem weren't convinced by her idea. They were sure the answer could not be so simple, but Wilder knew from her experience with the Scythian spiders that sometimes the solution really wasn't complicated.

She checked the previous balance she'd used, reached into the machine, and made a tiny adjustment. The effect would only increase the proportion of one type of particle by a few million, but the tiny increment could make all the difference.

Wilder activated the process. Instantly, she found herself pinned against the ceiling, a crushing pain emanating from her ribs. Her machine sat under her torso and was trying to force itself upward.

It had worked! She'd done it. She'd cracked the secret of a-grav.

But agony drained Wilder's elation. Red-hot knives were stabbing her chest. Her machine was driving into her with a dreadful force and she could barely breathe. She reached for the off switch but her hand only met smooth metal. The switch was too far away. She wriggled, trying to ease closer to it despite the pain, but she was pinned too firmly to move even a centimeter.

A creak came from above her. The ceiling was feeling the pressure pushing into it. If the material gave way, the a-grav machine would fly upward through Concordia's atmosphere and into space. It would move fast, probably too fast for her to climb off of it before it carried her so high she would fall to her death.

Ah! Her ear comm. All she needed to do was comm someone and they could come out and help her. Wilder touched her ear. The comm was gone! The impact of hitting the roof had popped it out of her ear.

She gasped in pain. Even if she could breathe enough to yell, no one would hear her. Her nearest neighbor lived kilometers away, near Cerberus. What could she do? Numbness was spreading from her arms and legs and she felt like she was going to pass out. How long could she last? How long would it take before someone realized she was missing and came looking for her? She frequently turned off her comm, so no one would think it strange if she was uncontactable, and she had no steady job, no boss to notice she hadn't turned up for work.

Potentially, days could pass before someone came to find her. Could she last that long?

CHAPTER NINE

An officer called Ellis was in charge of the security detail for the meeting with the Parvus. Cherry had chosen him because he was one of the few who seemed to take his position seriously. Major Ellis had posted guards along the route from the spaceport to the government office, but he had ordered them to wear dress uniforms, as if their position were ceremonial rather than military.

The idea behind the decision was to avoid offending the visitors if possible. Meredith had been adamant that she wanted the Parvus to receive a warm welcome and not be treated as a threat. Cherry understood the Leader's reasoning: Concordia could not afford to jeopardize the potential friendship of a galactic power. On the other hand, it was her responsibility to protect the colony.

Cherry was uncomfortable in her own dress uniform under the hot sun as she waited with Meredith, government department heads, and Kes for the Parvus to disembark their vessel. The Leader had wisely invited Kes as the colony's leading expert on intelligent alien life forms and veteran of the mission to the Galactic Assembly.

Their guests' ship was boxy and not at all aerodynamic, causing Cherry to wonder if the Parvus' home planet had a thin atmosphere. A portal had opened but, several minutes later, no one and nothing had emerged.

Cherry glanced at Meredith, who was sweating and looking stressed. From private conversations, Cherry knew Concordia's Leader was feeling the strain of her job. Everyone expected her to live up to her father's reputation and she had been re-elected year after year, following the pattern of Ethan's terms of office. The rule that a Leader could serve only one term had been dissolved expressly for Ethan's benefit, though, from what Cherry had heard, entirely against his wishes.

Meredith was a good Leader, but she lacked her father's calm pragmatism and levelheadedness, born of deep humility. The role had been thrust upon her the same as it had been thrust upon Ethan, but, unlike her father she wasn't rising to the challenge, she was sinking under it.

"At last," a voice breathed.

Figures were emerging from the shuttle.

The Parvus were as Cherry remembered them, EVA suits and all. Concordia's atmosphere was clearly not breathable for the visitors. Though on the space station she hadn't had much time to properly look at the creatures, she recalled their small bodies and six short limbs. They walked on all of them, their bodies parallel to the floor, like sluglimpets. As they walked down the ramp from their ship, Cherry noticed they also seemed to be struggling with the planet's gravity. The creatures walked slowly and heavily.

"Welcome to Concordia," Meredith said.

The Fila had put a translation system in place between the welcoming committee's comms and the

Parvus' EVA suits.

"We are glad to be here," came the reply. The Fila had used their usual artificially generated human voice to convey the Parvus' communication. Cherry wondered what the creatures really sounded like, or if they made noises at all. Maybe they had other methods of communication, like the Fila.

"Please allow us to escort you to our meeting room," Meredith said. She introduced herself, adding, "I am the Leader of this colony." She also introduced Cherry and the other dignitaries. Finally, she said, "Would you like to remain on Concordia after our meeting? I would be delighted to show you some of the most interesting and beautiful places on our planet. We have apartments where you can rest, but I'm afraid we would require more time to build a habitation where you could remove your suits."

"Your intention is noble," the Parvus' representative replied. "We observe that is the nature of your species."

Meredith looked understandably nonplussed by this reply. Cherry didn't know what it meant either. Did the Parvus want to stay a while and take a tour or not?

"Please come this way," Meredith said after a slight pause. "The place where we will hold the meeting is only a short journey from here."

The two parties proceeded to walk to the transportation that would take them to the government building designated for the meeting. Progress was slow. The Parvus moved with great effort, and it seemed to Cherry that sometimes their coordination of their legs got mixed up.

"Is your planet very different from Concordia?" Kes asked them.

"It is different in some ways. In some ways it is the same. It is smaller and there is much more water. It must be hard for you to live in a desert."

Cherry looked at the tree ferns that lined the route

and the vegetation in the distance. Were the Parvus mistaking the pavement and buildings for natural features?

Kes chose not to correct the speaker or to explain. It was clearly a topic for a much longer and more informal conversation than the occasion allowed.

The Parvus were transported separately from the rest of the delegation in a vehicle with a specially lowered floor. Cherry, Meredith, Kes, and the rest of the welcoming committee were driven in chauffeured government cars.

Eventually the delegates reached the room Cherry had chosen to host the meeting. She thanked the stars she'd picked one on the first floor. Forcing the Parvus to climb steps made for humans while also fighting Concordian gravity would have been embarrassing for all concerned.

Guards were already stationed within the room and Captain Ellis had fitted the place with recording devices too, according to the Leader's instruction.

When the members of the Parvus delegation reached the table they stood upright on their two hindmost legs and rested their upper pair of limbs on the tabletop. Their other two limbs hung in midair. Cherry noticed for the first time that tripod digits extended from the upper limbs. She couldn't see much of their faces through the dark visors of their helmets, but she thought she detected black, shiny eyes. More than two of them.

The human members of the party sat down.

Meredith opened the meeting by saying, "In our culture it is the custom to offer our guests refreshments as a gesture of welcome but unfortunately due to the fact you must wear environment suits we are unable to do so on this occasion. Please be assured we would like to extend our warmest appreciation of your visit."

This little speech excited the Parvus in what Cherry hoped was a good way. They wiggled their digits and turned to look at each other.

"Your refreshments are happily received."

What?

Meredith was similarly taken aback at the Parvus' response. Her eyes flicked to Kes, probably looking for some kind of explanation or reassurance. His shoulders moved in a slight shrug. Their resident alien expert had no idea what was going on either.

The obvious thing to move onto next was the reason for the Parvus' visit to Concordia, but it would have been rude to ask the question outright. Maybe the aliens were simply paying them a visit and traveling light years only for that simple purpose was normal in their culture.

The Parvus said, "We would also like to show appreciation. We are in your debt after you saved the life of one of our people while sacrificing your own."

"Thank you," Meredith replied. "But as I understand it, our members who went to the Assembly's space station didn't actually save anyone. They were experiencing a sim. So your thanks is welcome but not needed."

"No. Their intention was to save our people. That is not the same as saving them in reality. It is better."

"It's...Uh." Meredith paused again. Her gaze desperately sought Kes'.

"Um," he said, spreading his hands on the table top. "Am I right in thinking you see intention as more valuable than action?"

"Intention is more valuable. It is the accurate measure of a person's worth."

"I see," said Kes. "We think differently—"

"But we respect your position," said Meredith.

"We have come here to inform you in person, that if the Scythians attack you, it is our intention to aid in the defense of your planet."

"Right," said Meredith. "It's your *intention*."

The meaning of her emphasis was not lost on the humans present. The Parvus were either playing a weird game of pledging empty support or they genuinely believed they were offering something beneficial. Of course, their offer was actually worthless.

Cherry was annoyed. All the work everyone had done, all the stress and fuss over Concordia's first visit from a member of the Galactic Assembly, was all for nothing. The Parvus had nothing to give except words.

"I'm sorry," she said, "but your intentions are not going to help us. The Scythians aren't going to withdraw because we told them you *intend* to defend us."

"General," said Meredith, "I didn't invite you to speak. I apologize on behalf of my colleague."

Cherry leaned backward in her chair. Their visitors were a useless waste of time. She almost regretted saving one of them during the sim.

"May I ask a question?" said Kes.

"Go ahead," replied Meredith.

"If you do not act on an intention and someone dies as a result, isn't that a bad thing?"

"No," said the Parvus. "When a person dies they join the waters of the galaxy and nourish other life. That is a good thing."

Great.

Concordia's 'friends' harbored a death wish for humans and everyone else. At least the Scythians were upfront about wanting to kill them.

"As well as our intention of support," the Parvus went on, "we have another gift for you as a gesture of thanks."

You're going to do us a big favor and shoot us now? Cherry bit back her reply. She wondered if Aubriot would have managed to do the same if he'd been there. For once, she missed his sarcasm.

Meredith was looking like she felt seriously out of

her depth, but she managed to say, "It is very kind of you to offer us a second gift."

"This is less valuable than the first, and perhaps it is entirely worthless. It is information, but you may already be aware of it."

"Anything you would like to tell us, we're happy to hear," Meredith said.

"Humans are the most recent species to join the Galactic Assembly. We guess from this that your species is young in terms of galactic history. Our species is very old. We believe we are the oldest intelligent life form in the Assembly and, as far as we know, the galaxy as a whole."

Cherry wondered how the Parvus had managed to survive so long, given their desire to 'join the galactic waters'.

"Our knowledge of the development and spread of other species is vast. We have come here to bring you information about Scythian history."

Cherry sat up.

"This planet that you have settled, it is the Scythian origin planet."

The humans in the room became still. Looks passed between them.

"*What?*" Meredith whispered. She took a moment to compose herself. "The Scythians evolved on Concordia?"

"Yes," the Parvus replied. "Do you measure time according to the orbit of your planet around its star?"

"We do," Kes replied. "As well as the revolution of our planet."

"In your terms," said the Parvus, "the Scythians developed into intelligent life forms on this world approximately seven million orbits ago."

Seven million Concordian orbits was equivalent to nearly three and a half million Earth years.

Cherry was dumbstruck. Everything about Concordia

she'd thought she'd known to be true was being annihilated. The planet was not unclaimed. It was not a young world where higher life forms hadn't yet evolved. It wasn't *theirs*.

"It's clear you did not know this fact," said the Parvus. "We will tell you the rest of Scythian history as we know it. The details are sparse. Information from this sector takes many hundreds of orbits to reach us and we did not understand its significance at the time we began to notice it. Only a few records exist."

Tension was almost palpable in the room as every human present focused on what the small Parvus had to say. As always, the Fila's translator voice conveyed no emotion. It was impossible to tell how the creatures felt about the revelations they were providing.

"The Scythians developed space travel eight hundred thousand orbits ago. They began to travel to nearby stars. We saw they had begun to settle another star system two hundred and fifty thousand years later. The time interval was long, much longer than that of other species we were watching. It seemed the Scythians were not nomadic and preferred to remain on their home planet. Then suddenly we saw a huge increase in their expansion efforts. They were settling new worlds at a rate we had not observed before. Curious about the reason for the increase in migration, we looked closely at this world, hoping to discover the answer to the puzzle. What we saw was a slow catastrophe taking place. The atmosphere of the planet was undergoing a rapid change. The air was becoming poisoned by oxygen."

"Oxygen is poisonous?" Cherry blurted.

"To some life forms, yes," Kes replied.

The Parvus continued, "Something the Scythians had done during their millenia on their home world had created the perfect conditions for the proliferation of organisms that excreted a gas that the Scythians could not breathe. It appeared they were unable to reverse the process and so they were forced to abandon their planet in order to survive. They have not lived here for over one hundred and sixty thousand orbits."

"This is remarkable news," said Meredith. "I'm not sure what we can do with the information, or if there is anything we can do with it. But it certainly throws a whole new light on everything."

"No kidding," said Cherry.

CHAPTER TEN

As well as following the proceedings of the meeting and ruminating on the revelation about the Scythians, Kes was studying the Parvus. They were only the third intelligent alien life form he'd met in real life, after the Fila and the self-described 'organizers' of the space station—and he had yet to discover the latter's species.

The thrill of sitting in the same room and speaking with these creatures who had evolved to a state of high intellect on another planet was almost as great as it had been when he'd first come into contact with the Fila. Though they were wearing EVA suits, he knew what they looked like. The Fila had passed on a raft of information on other Assembly members, after translating it as well as they could into English. They had included images and vids too.

Kes' first impression of the Parvus was that they reminded him of grubs. It wasn't a pleasant connection to make, and he tried not to allow the mental association to color his opinion of the creatures, but their round, plump, elongated bodies were unmistakably similar to grubs he remembered finding under rotting bark on his parents' land when he was a kid.

The Parvus' three pairs of legs were grub-like too, only thicker where they connected to the body, but the digits at the ends of their upper pair of limbs were unlike anything he'd ever seen. They were as prehensile as the end of an elephant's trunk but the three 'fingers' were equidistant like the points of an equilateral triangle. Their head contained seven or eight eyes above a central mouth.

Concordia's visitors lived on a high-water-volume planet where the land masses only occupied one-sixteenth of the total surface and were mostly flat and swampy. If he remembered correctly, the planet's gravity was about sixty percent of Concordia's. The creatures seemed to be dealing with their additional weight for the moment, but Kes guessed they would probably leave soon. Their soft bodies contained no internal or external skeleton to protect them against the increased gravity.

Meredith had been asking the Parvus for more information about the Scythians' history on Concordia, but the creatures had little more to offer.

"We will give you our records of the changes in your planet's atmosphere, but we did not have any dealings with the Scythians until recent times, when their expansion brought them into conflict with other intelligent civilizations. It was only when we examined the information we had on planets in this sector that we understood what had happened. The current Scythian-occupied worlds all have atmospheres approximating that of Concordia's in its ancient past. When we examined our data more closely, and we heard of the Scythian attacks on this planet, we came to the conclusion we have related to you. The Scythians cannot live here. There is no other reason we can think of that explains why they want this world for their own."

"So, what you're telling us isn't an absolute fact?" Meredith asked.

"There are very few absolute facts, and this is not one of them. Yet we feel a strong certainty about its truth."

"Can I say something?" asked Cherry.

"Go ahead," said Meredith.

"I still don't get it. The Scythians ruined their home planet, right? That much I understand. Humans nearly did that to Earth, according to everything I was taught at school. So they left and found other planets to live on. They didn't die out, and from the sound of it they're continuing to try to expand. But why would they want to come back here? Especially if they can't live here because the atmosphere is poisonous to them."

"It isn't that hard to understand," said Kes. "This is their origin world. It's where they built their first civilization. Of course they want to keep Concordia for themselves. How would you feel about someone else taking over your home without your consent, even if you couldn't go back there?"

"I wouldn't care at all," Cherry replied. "That happened all the time on the *Nova*. I lived in three care centers while I was growing up. As soon as I reached a certain age I was moved on to the next one, until I finally left and was given a single cabin. If I'd gotten married I would have left there and moved into married quarters. It was no big deal."

"Hmm," Kes said. "That's probably your upbringing talking. In regular human societies people often formed emotional attachments to the places where they grew up. They would sell the houses or move away, but they still felt a connection to the place. I wouldn't be surprised if the Scythians view Concordia as belonging to them even though they could never live here again."

"Well, it doesn't belong to them," said Meredith. "It's plain stupid to refuse someone the right to use something when you can't use it yourself. By all accounts, habitable planets are scarce. It's wrong to hoard resources."

"We must return to our vessel now," the Parvus said. "Your planet's gravity is making us uncomfortable and we need a respite."

"Of course," Meredith said. "I apologize for wasting your time with our personal discussion. Please allow me to accompany you to your shuttle."

The Parvus moved away from the table, dropping down onto all six of their legs, and waddled slowly toward the door.

Meredith rose to her feet and followed the creatures, and the rest of the human contingent did the same.

"Will you be returning for further discussions?" Meredith asked. "I'm sure we have plenty to talk about."

"We would enjoy that," the Parvus replied. "We have many intentions we would like to agree upon with you."

Kes saw Cherry roll her eyes. He bit back a smile. Inter-cultural relations had never been easy even on Earth, where all parties were the same species. The Concordians could expect plenty of difficulties over the next few centuries as they entered into galactic society and formed relationships with other intelligent life forms.

Assuming they lived that long. The more Kes considered the fact that Concordia was the birthplace of the Scythians, the more apprehensive he felt. Colonization of new worlds was one thing—disputes over valuable new territory were to be expected—but fighting over a homeland was another thing entirely. If human history was anything to go by, the Scythians would never give up their right to Concordia nor ever see humans as anything other than invaders. Even the 'tribute' they claimed might not be enough to persuade them not to annihilate the colonists. As time passed their attitude might change, as it had during their second attack.

The procession to the transportation and then on to the Parvus' shuttle took longer on the way back. When they were halfway along the walk to the vessel, Meredith said, "Perhaps it would be more convenient if I and a few others came up to your starship for our next meeting?"

"That would not be practical," the Parvus replied, without any further explanation.

Off the top of his head, Kes couldn't remember their planet's atmosphere, but if humans couldn't breathe on the Parvus ship they could have worn EVA suits. The Parvus would know that, so Kes guessed the problem probably related to the size of the areas within the ship. Humans must be too big to move around in them. They must seem like giants to the small creatures. Kes wondered what the Parvus made of the Assembly station's organizers, who had been giants compared to humans.

Cherry had eased her way toward Kes until she was walking with him at the back of the group.

"How are you doing?" she asked quietly. "I haven't seen you for months."

"I've been busy, the same as you, I bet."

"Ugh, you're not wrong. Some days I almost wish I was back aboard the *Opportunity* with nothing to do except argue with Aubriot."

"You must be really suffering," said Kes. "It would take a lot more than a heavy workload to make me wish I had nothing to eat except Guardian ration bars for months. What do you think of this news about the Scythians?"

"Like I was saying before, I don't exactly get the significance. I thought that finding out that Scythians can't live here would be good news, not bad. But I take your word for it that it explains why Concordia is so important to them. The knowledge doesn't make a lot of difference to me. I have to continue to do my best to prepare to defend the place, regardless."

"How's that going?"

"The hardware is in place, it's the software I'm worried about." In response to Kes' inquiring look, Cherry went on, "The defense force. They're undisciplined and ineffective. I think the problem is they don't take the threat seriously. None of them has ever lived through an attack. All their lives Concordia has been safe and peaceful. They can't imagine anything different."

"Surely Aubriot can help you with that?" Kes asked.

"He resigned."

"He did *what*?"

"Honestly, I pushed him, and rather than pushing back, he jumped. He doesn't give a shit about the defense of Concordia anymore. Not that he ever really cared. He was only concerned about saving his own skin. Now it seems he doesn't even care about that anymore."

"That doesn't sound like Aubriot."

"It doesn't, does it? Something's up with him, but I don't have the time to figure out what, and I'm seriously done dealing with him."

They had nearly reached the Parvus' shuttle, only the creatures were moving slower with every step they took. Kes felt sorry for them. He would have loved to offer to pick one up and carry it, but of course that would have entirely deprived them of their dignity.

Meredith was saying something formal in farewell, thanking the creatures for their visit and expressing her hopes that they could visit for another meeting soon, when a realization popped into Kes' mind.

"Hey, Cherry," he said in a low tone. "I haven't told you about the Guardian yet."

She turned toward him. "What Guardian? I thought

they were all long dead. If machines *can* be dead."

"Not this one, maybe. Honestly, it's just a guess, and nothing's turned up yet so Wilder's probably wrong, but —"

"Wilder thinks there's a Guardian who wasn't destroyed in the second attack? How could that be possible?"

"If you'll stop interrupting me I'll explain."

"Okay. Wait a minute. Our visitors are leaving."

The Parvus had slowly mounted the ramp to their ship. The Concordians moved quickly away from the landing site, just in case the Parvus weren't aware of how easily they burned.

"Phew," said Meredith as she caught up to Kes and Cherry. "I'm glad that's over. I thought it went pretty well, didn't you?"

"Not bad," said Kes.

"I thought you did a great job," Cherry said. "That was quite a revelation about the Scythians originating on Concordia, but I think Kes might have a revelation of his own."

"Is this about Wilder's over-active imagination?" Meredith asked.

"Oh, you know about it?" said Cherry.

"If you mean her idea that a Guardian crash-landed on Concordia, yes, Kes already told me. I don't think there's anything in it. And, if you don't mind, I'd like you to both join me along with some of the department heads here to discuss what we just learned."

"You want to have a meeting about the meeting?" Cherry asked.

Meredith smiled. "Exactly. After we get back take ten minutes or so to refresh and then I'll see you in the meeting room, okay?"

"Sure," Cherry replied, then, as she and Kes walked the remaining distance to the government car, she said to him, "Tell me the rest about this Guardian. It seems

I'm the only person who hasn't heard about it."

"Don't give me a hard time," said Kes. "I only told Meredith. I was going to tell you as well, soon. It only happened yesterday." He then went on to quickly explain about the apparently crashed escape vessel the miner had found in the wildlands beyond the mountains, and how Wilder had said the analysis of the metal alloy it was made from was identical to the one used in the manufacture of the Guardians' weapons.

"And is it?" asked Cherry.

"Yes, it is. Checking that was the first thing I did when I got back to Annwn."

"I have to admit, that is an odd coincidence," Cherry said.

Kes also explained how the new growth in the vegetation surrounding the site of the crash indicated it wasn't old. "Wilder guessed the undergrowth had been burned there about four weeks ago."

"So if a Guardian did survive the destruction of the *Mistral* and its vessel finally fell to Concordia a few weeks ago, it's been wandering around the planet all this time?"

"That's kind of where Wilder's supposition falls down. If something was inside that thing, and it's a Guardian, it isn't behaving anything like we would expect it to, given what we know about them."

"That's right," said Cherry. "Still, it's an interesting problem. I wonder what that thing out there really is."

"Perhaps we'll never know," Kes said. "Anyway, I think we have more important issues to deal with right now."

"I don't agree. Any unexplained, potentially alien, object that arrives on Concordia must be thoroughly investigated. I'll send a team out there to assess it and bring it in. Honestly, Kes, it was dumb of you two to just go there and take a look at it without informing me. What if it was Scythian? What if it was booby-trapped?

It can't be helped now, but, please, if anything else like that turns up, I want to know about it immediately. Sometimes I feel like I'm the only person who's taking the threat to our colony seriously."

Cherry took a breath. Kes looked abashed. Had she gone overboard? Maybe a little, but everything she'd said was true. "We'd better not keep Meredith waiting." Cherry climbed the steps into the building, and Kes followed her. "By the way, how is Wilder? I keep asking her for favors. I hope I'm not wearing her out."

"She was fine when I saw her yesterday. She looked a bit overworked, but that's normal for her, right? I haven't spoken to her recently. I tried to comm here a couple of times this morning but she had her comm turned off. She'll get back to me when she has a bit of free time, I'm sure."

CHAPTER ELEVEN

"Come on, Wilder," said Ben, "it'll be fun."

He was standing in the open doorway of their care center. Neither of the carers were at their stations. Both of the men had girlfriends who were going planetside and they'd gone to say goodbye to them, probably along with some yucky smooching. The men weren't doing anything wrong. The care center was for children aged ten and over, who were judged to be old enough to be able to look after themselves for short periods of time. Sometimes that trust worked out, sometimes it didn't.

"I don't know," Wilder replied. "What if Ras or Harry come back and check the dorm? We'll get in heaps of trouble." She was no stranger to getting into trouble, but she knew the limits. Sneaking aboard a shuttle to go planetside would be crossing them. She was already only seven points away from a category four punishment, which could mean anything from weeding the planting beds to scrubbing the toilets. She had far more interesting ways to spend her time.

"They won't check the dorm," Ben replied. "They'll

be too heartbroken and sad." He pulled a face of exaggerated sorrow and clutched his hands to his chest.

Wilder laughed.

"I tell you what," Ben continued. "Let's take some spare pillows from the cupboard and put them under our covers to make it look like we're sleeping in our beds. Ras and Harry will fall for it. I'm sure they will."

"Oh, all right," said Wilder. Stowing away on a shuttle did sound like fun, and she was dying to go planetside. She seemed to be the only person she knew whose turn to take a trip to their new home hadn't come around yet. She'd had to get by with pics and vids of the surface taken by others. They were a poor substitute for actually being there. She was desperate to know what the air smelt like and how it felt to look up at a real sky, not the fake one in the Main Park.

Ben trotted across the entrance room to a set of doors fitted into the wall and opened them. Bed linen, pillows, towels, and other domestic stores were stacked inside. Wilder helped Ben pull out four pillows. They carried them into the six-bed dorm, where their center mates were already in bed. One of them, Marjory, remained awake. She was reading her interface.

"I wondered what had happened to you—hey, what are you doing?" Marjory's eyes were round as she watched Wilder and Ben pull back their covers and lay the pillows length ways on their beds. "You're gonna sneak out, aren't you? You guys are DEAD."

"Shhh!" said Ben. "You'll wake up the others."

"Promise you won't tell on us, Marjory?" Wilder asked. Marjory was okay, but she could be a tattle tale sometimes.

"Why shouldn't I? If I don't, and Ras or Harry find out I knew about it, I could get in trouble too."

"How would they ever know?" Wilder asked. "Why would Ben or I tell them?"

Marjory was unconvinced. She frowned and pouted.

"Why should I keep your secret for you? What's in it for me?"

"I'll do tomorrow's homework for you," said Wilder.

Marjory's expression brightened. "Make it all next week's homework."

"Okay, all next week's homework." Wilder had pulled the bed cover over the pillows and was patting them to make them look like a sleeping body.

"It's a deal."

"Are you ready?" asked Ben.

"Have fun," Marjory called softly as they left.

Two children taking a transit carriage alone wasn't particularly remarkable, despite the lateness of the hour. The *Nova Fortuna* was an enclosed environment where even petty crime was extremely rare. Even fairly young children couldn't come to much harm, and everyone was used to older children testing their boundaries. Many of the adults had done it themselves.

The situation at the shuttle bay was different. The protocols for allowing Gens down to the planet surface were strict. The Woken could come and go as they pleased, of course. There were far fewer of them and they had scientific studies to carry out. But if the Gens had been allowed the same privilege it would have been chaos.

Ben and Wilder hovered around the shuttle bay entrance, trying to look inconspicuous. In fact, it wasn't too hard to remain unnoticed. Tonight was to be the first night the colonists would sleep on the planet and the passengers were milling around in excitement.

The preparations for the momentous event had been going on for a while. First the engineers had installed an electric fence to protect the compound from the native wildlife, even though no one thought any dangerous animals lived there.

Then the builders had gone down to erect barns where the colonists would sleep. Later on, the builders would build houses and roads, and the barns would be used to store the equipment and produce from farms. More trips down to the surface had taken place to install electricity within the barns and build latrines. The intention was to create a self-contained encampment that could survive several days without additional supplies. That way, the necessity of constantly ferrying workers between the surface and the *Nova* could be avoided.

Ben was peering into the bay. The last shuttle would be leaving in ten minutes. The announcement to board would come soon.

"Got any ideas on how to get inside?" Ben asked Wilder.

"Of course not," Wilder replied. "I thought *you* had a plan. This was your idea, remember?" She was having second thoughts. She didn't mind being punished for stowing away on a shuttle, but to be punished for *trying* to stow away on a shuttle seemed a monumental waste of time and effort.

Ben's gaze alighted on cargo boxes being transported across the bay. He grabbed Wilder's arm and nodded at the line of transporters. "If we climb inside a storage box, they'll never know. The bots are only programmed to take the boxes to the ship, not check inside them."

"Maybe that's because no one thought anyone would be stupid enough to hide in one?" Wilder said. Misgivings about the entire situation were bothering her again. Would it really hurt to wait another few days to see the planet?

Ben seemed to take her comment as a challenge rather than a rebuke. He grinned and gripped Wilder's arm a little tighter. "We can do it. I know we can. Think how much fun it'll be to spend the night down there."

"That's another thing," said Wilder. "Will there even be a bunk for us to sleep on? What if they've only provided exactly enough for the people on the schedule?"

"Then we'll sleep on the ground." Ben scanned the bay. If they were going to make the attempt, they only had a few minutes. One pallet of containers remained to be loaded. "I know. Pretend to chase me."

"What?"

But Ben was already off, running across the bay. "No," he called over his shoulder. "You can't have it. You'll have to catch me first."

Wilder hesitated, but decided Ben would look like a dumb ass or crazy if he was seen running with no one running after him. "Give me my...my doll!" She cringed as she sped after her friend. She was way too old for dolls, even if she'd ever liked them, which she hadn't.

Ben had reached the pallet loaded with storage boxes and disappeared behind it. Wilder also ran behind the boxes and found her friend squatting down and panting. She peeked over the top of a box. Ben's ruse seemed to have worked. No one was looking in their direction. All the adults were too excited about going planetside.

Ben was already busy removing the seal on a box of supplies. He lifted the lid. Inside the box were bags of flour. He began lifting them out and dumping them on the pallet.

"I don't think you should do that," Wilder whispered. "They'll need flour to eat."

"C'mon. There's plenty here. They won't miss it, and if they do they'll just comm the ship to send down more. Give me a hand, huh?"

But Wilder felt too guilty at the thought of tampering with the colony's food. She began reading the labels on other boxes to try to find something less essential. The transporter bots were already removing the boxes from the far end of the pallet.

Meanwhile, Ben had removed enough bags of flour to make room for himself. He climbed into the box. "Put the lid on for me. I can't do it from in here."

"Ben, I changed my mind. Come out of there. We shouldn't be doing this. It's dumb and wrong. Let's go back to the dorm."

"We can't," Ben replied. "Harry and Ras will be back by now and they'll see us walk in. They'll know we broke curfew."

"Then we'll spend the night somewhere else. We could go to Main Park."

"Don't be a wimp," said Ben. Then his expression grew angry and he said, "Fine. Don't come if you don't want to, but at least put the lid on for me."

"Ben..."

"You won't even do that? I thought you were my friend."

"Ugh, all right!" Wilder snatched the lid from the floor and snapped it on the box. A moment later, a transporter bot fastened its arms around the box and carried it away.

The announcement to board sounded over the ship's comm, and while the passengers crossed the bay to the shuttle, Wilder took advantage of the bustle and walked casually in the opposite direction. When she reached the exit, she paused and looked back at the shuttle. Only a few stragglers remained, hurrying toward the hatch. The cargo door was closed. Only a small pile of bags of flour sat next to an empty pallet.

Wilder came to abrupt and painful consciousness. She drew in a breath and nearly screamed at the agony that pierced her sides. Where was she? It was dark, and she couldn't move, and her stomach and chest hurt badly.

She remembered. Her a-grav machine had finally worked, but she'd been leaning over it when it activated. Now she was pinned between it and the ceiling of her home.

How long had she been stuck? At least a day. She

recalled the first night, when she hadn't slept at all, and the despair she'd felt when the morning breeze arrived followed by the graying of the light. Then as the day passed she'd shouted herself hoarse, desperately hoping someone might happen to be wandering through the isolated place where she lived.

She must have passed out from exhaustion. The dream she'd had was an old one, though she hadn't dreamed it for several years. She'd thought her mind had ceased replaying that memory. Poor Ben. He hadn't survived the First Night Attack. How close had she come to losing her life too? Her waking and sleeping mind had replayed the events leading up to her friend's death over and over again as she tried to come to terms with her role in it. She blamed herself for not arguing harder. She had thought up several ways she could have prevented Ben from stowing away on the shuttle. She could have told someone what he was doing. She could have held onto him and stopped him from climbing into the box. But she'd done nothing and her friend had died.

Was she about to die too? Was that why her brain was returning to that event? Was her fate some kind of inevitable destiny, a punishment for her misdeeds?

Wilder shook her head slightly and grimaced at the pain this small movement caused her. Her desperate situation and physical and mental fatigue were making her think crazy thoughts.

A scrabbling sound from below caught her attention. Piddle and Puddle! She'd forgotten all about them. They must have scrambled into their hole in the tree trunk in fear when the accident happened, and they'd finally gotten the courage to venture out. They were probably hungry and confused about what was happening.

"Hey, Piddle," Wilder croaked. She coughed, just a little, winced, and said, "Puddle, where are you?"

It was too dark to see anything. Even starlight wasn't

penetrating the canopy or the small window above her table. The night was cloudy.

More sounds of scratching and scrabbling arose from the floor.

Like a lightning bolt, an idea struck Wilder. Her ear comm was somewhere below her. If she could persuade one of her pets to bring it to her, she would be able to comm for help. Both her little friends were excellent climbers. They could even climb over the ceiling, upside down. She'd seen them do it many times.

"Piddle, come here." Wilder listened. "Come here. Come and see me. I'm up here."

She listened again. Sounds of tiny claws climbing the wall came blissfully to her ears. She heard Piddle, and Puddle too, walking along the ceiling. The small creatures reached her feet. Their claws dug into her pants as they climbed along one of her legs.

"Hey guys," said Wilder as her pets clambered along her side and over her arm. They commenced their usual habit of checking her hair and smell. When they tried to enter the neck of her shirt, however, they found the way blocked by the a-grav machine pressing into her.

"Go back and pick up my comm," said Wilder. "It's down there. I need my comm."

It was hopeless. Wilder had never trained her pets to fetch and carry. Piddle and Puddle climbed over her neck and head, trying to find a place to settle or something to eat. When they didn't find either, they climbed back onto the ceiling. There was just enough light for Wilder to see the gleam of their little black eyes.

After a while, Piddle and Puddle grew tired of hanging upside down. They ran across the ceiling and down the wall. Wilder heard them moving around for a few minutes, then silence returned to her home. Piddle and Puddle must have returned to their hole.

Wilder suddenly felt very alone. Blackness

surrounded her. She had no hope of anyone noticing she was missing for days, by which time it would be too late.

CHAPTER TWELVE

Kes pushed back overhanging foliage and frowned at the undergrowth. He thought he could see a faint, narrow path but he wasn't sure.

"Does that look like a track to you?" he asked Cherry, pointing at the thin snake of what looked like trodden vegetation.

"I thought you knew the way?" Cherry replied. "You said you'd been to visit her."

"I have, but only once or twice, and that was longer than a year ago."

"You haven't been to see her in more than a year?" said Cherry. "She's only seventeen. She's much too young to be living out here all on her own. I thought you were looking after her."

"I do my best," said Kes. "I'm busy with work, and Isobel needs my help when I'm home. And, anyway, who said I was looking after her? Wilder's nearly an adult, and you know how independent she is. She wouldn't allow anyone to look after her if they tried."

"Fair point," said Cherry. "Sorry. I guess I feel guilty. I should have been making sure she's okay too. I've been asking her to help me with lots of things, but I don't think I ever once asked her how she was doing."

"Don't feel bad," said Kes. "I'm sure she's fine. I bet she's only turned off her comm because she's absorbed in something."

"For three days?" Cherry asked. "I know she doesn't like people bothering her when she's working, but three days of silence must be a record."

Kes had been trying to sound upbeat for Cherry's sake, but he was worried. With all the fuss surrounding the Parvus' revelation that the Scythians originated on Concordia, he hadn't contacted Wilder until the previous day. And it was only then he discovered that her comm had been off for over 72 hours.

Immediately, a blanket of concern had settled over him. He contacted Cherry on the off chance she knew what was happening with their young friend, but she hadn't heard from Wilder either. They'd elected to go and check on her straightaway, only the little tree home was proving hard to find.

"Let's try this way," said Kes. "This patch of woodland isn't big. Even if this isn't the route she usually uses, her house shouldn't be too hard to find."

They ducked under heavy tree fronds that reached almost to the ground and stepped through the undergrowth. The light under the canopy was dim, but as his eyes adjusted, Kes saw that his guess had been correct. The trail that Wilder used was now clear. The vegetation was sparser in the lower light levels, and Wilder's comings and goings had worn a track down to the dark brown leaf mold.

Cherry had seen it too. She was already striding along the path. Kes quickly caught up to her.

"I'm amazed any of this survived," she said. "Cerberus mustn't reach this far." The construction of the underground military silo had affected the tree roots or the soil in some way and all the trees directly above the silo had died. No one knew why. Cerberus was deeper than Sidhe had been and the building of the settlement hadn't affected the growth above ground at all. It was a shame, but the colonists would have been forced to kill the forest anyway. When the time came, the roof to the silo would lift and open. Thousands of trees would have made the process difficult if not impossible.

"That's right," said Kes. "I think we walked over the edge of Cerberus about fifty meters back." He stopped and, with his gaze, followed the direction the path was leading. He pointed to a spot where trees crowded together in a shallow hollow. "That's it. I remember now."

"Are you sure?" asked Cherry. "I can't see anything there that looks like a tree house."

"That's the point," said Kes. He trotted toward the clump of trees. "Wilder! Wilder! Are you home?" He halted to avoid the noise of his crashing through the shrubs and plants drowning out his friend's reply. But no reply came.

Cherry also called Wilder's name. When silence continued to reign over the forest, Kes and Cherry ran the final few meters to the tree house.

Kes called out again. He high-stepped over tall plants until he was closer to the tree and could look upward at the underside of the floor of Wilder's home.

"How do we get up there?" Cherry asked.

"I think only Wilder can activate the winch that sends the cradle down, or at least I don't know how to do it."

"We have to climb up there?"

"I don't see any other way. It's either that or request a heli from Annwn and that would take as long as half an hour."

"We can't wait that long," said Cherry. "Can you manage it? I can't get up there with only one arm."

Kes assessed the trunk. It was heavily ribbed, but no

branches protruded from it for the first two meters. "I can try. Maybe you can help me."

"Of course. What do you want me to do?"

"Stand with your back to the tree and squat down."

Cherry did as Kes had asked her. "I wish Aubriot was here. He'd be up there in no time."

"Did you comm him?" asked Kes.

"Yeah, but he only replied to say he hadn't heard from her. He isn't talking to me at the moment."

Kes left inquiring about the reason for Cherry and Aubriot's falling out to a more convenient moment. "Get ready," he said. "I'm going to step on your knees."

Cherry pushed her back into the trunk, and Kes put one foot on her knees to help him reach the lowest branch. He managed to grab it with both hands, but swinging the rest of his body up onto the branch was harder. With considerable effort, he finally managed it.

The next few minutes were a struggle. Wilder's home sat another three meters higher, and when Kes reached it he had to gradually work his way through the floor. There was no alternative than to rip out the tough, dried, compacted fronds bit by bit. Cherry waited below in anxious silence for a few moments, then she said, "I'm comming for a heli ambulance. I have a bad feeling about this."

Kes didn't answer. He didn't disagree and he was too intent on what he was doing to formulate a reply.

Finally, he punched through into air. "Wilder!" he shouted through the gap. He couldn't see anything in the narrow view except the ceiling of the room above.

Then a small head poked through the hole, almost causing Kes to fall off the branch he was standing on in surprise. A weasel-like creature was looking out at him. Then in another second it was gone.

"What's happening?" Cherry called up. "Can you see anything yet?"

"No, not yet." What was that thing? Had Wilder been

attacked by an unknown life form? Was the creature he'd seen venomous? Kes redoubled his efforts to break through into Wilder's home. He tore out a large piece of the flooring.

Then he saw her. Wilder was stuck against the ceiling, pinned there by a machine of some kind. He couldn't see her face. It was obscured by her hanging hair. But her body was entirely limp.

"Shit!"

Hardly conscious of what he was doing, Kes ripped away more of the flooring and forced his arms and shoulders through the hole.

"Christ! Wilder! Wilder!"

He was standing inside the home. The machine that was crushing his friend into the ceiling hummed softly. Kes reached up and touched Wilder's foot, but she didn't respond.

CHAPTER THIRTEEN

Cherry realized her fingernails were digging painfully into her palm. She released her fist and squinted up at Kes' figure disappearing into Wilder's home. She heard him shout the girl's name.

"Kes," Cherry called, "what's wrong? What's happened to her?"

A window shutter opened and Kes' head and shoulders appeared. His face was chalky. "Call a heli. I think she's..." He choked up and couldn't complete his sentence.

"I've already called one, remember. It's on its way. Lower the cradle so I can come up."

Kes withdrew into the room and a moment later a motor started up. The cradle dropped down through the tree fronds. When it reached Cherry she climbed inside, but the cradle didn't go up. "Kes! Make it pull me up."

The motor whirred again and the rope tugged upward. Cherry rose into the tree. The cradle reached the platform and she climbed out of it. The door to the dwelling was standing ajar. Kes was standing with his back to her and—

"Stars! What's happened?" Cherry exclaimed as she caught sight of Wilder's legs. The girl was dangling from the ceiling, held there by a machine that was floating in midair without support.

Kes held a hand to his forehead. "I knew she was working on something," said Kes. "Something not quite legal. I didn't guess it was a-grav."

"How long has she been hanging there?" Cherry asked. "You don't think she's been there the whole three days?" She touched Wilder's foot. "Wilder, sweetheart, can you hear me? We'll get you down."

"Do you think we should move her?" asked Kes. "What if her back's broken? We could make it worse."

"What if that thing's crushing her lungs and heart and she's about to die? We don't have a choice. We have to get her down."

"Okay. Let's do it."

Moving the machine so they could release Wilder was easier said than done. Kes pushed everything off the table and dragged it across the floor to position it beneath the trapped girl. Cherry dragged over the chair with one hand.

"You don't think she's already...Do you?" asked Kes quietly.

"I'm not entertaining that thought," Cherry replied firmly. She'd already lost Ethan and Cariad, she wasn't about to lose anyone else if she could help it. "I'll take the table, you take the chair." She climbed up onto the flat surface and then stood up. The buzz of an approaching heli came from somewhere in the distance.

Kes climbed onto the chair. Cherry's first impulse was to move Wilder's hair so she could get a look at the girl's face. Her eyes were closed and her lips were pale. Cherry gently pressed her fingertips into Wilder's neck. She thought she felt a pulse, but she wasn't sure.

"Anything?" Kes asked.

"I don't know. I think so."

"Let's move this thing and get her down."

"Yes, but we need to go carefully. As soon as she isn't being held up anymore, she'll fall. We'll have to be ready to catch her."

"You're right," said Kes. "Wait a moment. Jump down and I'll move the table underneath her."

In a few more seconds they were ready.

Cherry was standing on the table again, preparing to push the machine away from Wilder's chest and stomach. Kes stood close by, his arms stretched out to where Wilder would fall into them.

The noise from the heli was louder. The pilot's voice came over Cherry's comm. "Heli ambulance ETA thirty seconds. Please advise landing area."

"I can't speak right now," Cherry replied. "Please remain on standby. One injured to evacuate."

"Received."

"Ready?" Cherry asked Kes.

He nodded, his features tense.

She gently pushed against the humming machine, easing it sideways across Wilder's body. The machine resisted, catching on Wilder's shirt. Only half of it was covered. The other half was open, its innards complex and spiky. Cherry pushed harder.

Suddenly, Wilder groaned.

"She's alive," said Kes. His eyes grew shiny.

Cherry swallowed. "I'm going to give it one hard push. For stars' sake, don't drop her."

"Of course I won't."

"Okay. Here goes." Cherry shoved the humming device. The spikes that had embedded in Wilder's shirt tore free, the machine slipped out from underneath her, and Wilder fell.

Kes caught her and rolled her toward himself to avoid dropping her, turning her onto her side. Her shirt was a mess of dried blood. She cried out in pain. Her eyes opened.

"My a-grav!"

When Cherry had slid the machine away from Wilder, it had risen quickly and bumped into the ceiling.

"Don't worry about that now," said Kes. "The important thing is you're okay."

Wilder reached out weakly toward the humming device. It continued to press upward, working its way into the overlapping dried leaves that comprised the roof. "Turn it off."

"I don't know how," said Cherry. "Kes, I'll help you get her down. Then we'll carry her out to the heli."

"My a-grav," Wilder repeated.

A rustling sound came from above. As Cherry was stepping down from her chair she looked up. The ceiling was parting. The a-grav machine had forced a gap in the leaves.

"Noooo," said Wilder.

"It's okay," Kes said. "You can build another."

Cherry told the heli pilot where to land, on the open ground where she and Kes had entered the forest.

Kes squatted down, still holding Wilder. For the first time in a long while, Cherry wished she had two arms so she could take the girl from him. As it was, she could only move out of the way as he carefully climbed down from the table.

A crack came from above. Cherry looked up just in time to see the a-grav machine disappear. One moment it was there, the next moment it was gone and only a hole in the roof remained.

CHAPTER FOURTEEN

Wilder was furious. They had let her a-grav machine go. They'd let it go! And now she wasn't sure she could ever get the balance of particle inputs correct again.

She reached for the interface Cherry had placed next to her bed. Pain flared in her chest, and she gasped and paused. Her arm fell to her side. The pain was constant but it got worse whenever she moved.

Wrapping her other arm carefully around her ribs, she tried again. This time she managed to retrieve the interface. She'd been making records of all her experimentation with the a-grav machine up until the night of the accident, so she had the rough figures already. But she wasn't sure exactly what she'd done prior to the machine activating. That part was hazy in her memory, along with most of the time she'd been trapped on the ceiling.

When she thought about her stupidity in failing to secure the device to the floor, she felt like screaming in frustration. She'd been trying to neutralize gravity. What had she expected might happen if she succeeded? She couldn't remember considering the possibility.

Maybe she'd thought the machine would hover a convenient one meter above the floor?

If only she hadn't been leaning over it to adjust the particle flow. If she hadn't been in the way of the machine when it flew up, she might have been able to climb onto a chair and turn it off before it broke through the ceiling.

But she hadn't, and her carelessness hadn't only nearly cost her her life, now the machine was gone. It was probably still traveling through space unaffected by any object's gravity well and generating none itself, and it would continue until its power ran out.

Wilder swiped the interface screen open and began jabbing at the surface, finding her personal files.

The door opened. Cherry walked in, balancing a tray on one hand. Wilder had lifted her head just long enough to see who was interrupting her before scowling and returning her attention to her interface.

"I thought you might have woken up," said Cherry. "I brought you something to drink and a snack." She set down the tray on a table next to the bed.

Wilder continued to focus on the interface. She'd found her files and she was opening everything pertaining to the a-grav experiment, hoping that if she ignored Cherry long enough, she would leave her alone.

"How are you feeling?"

No such luck.

"What's your pain level like? The doctor prescribed some medication and you're due another dose about now. Should I get it for you?"

Stars, couldn't the woman take a hint?

"Wilder."

"What?!"

"Would you like me to bring you your medication?"

"If you want. I don't care. In case you hadn't noticed, I'm trying to work."

"Don't you think you should rest a bit and

concentrate on getting better? You know I had to persuade the hospital to discharge you, and the only reason they agreed was because I said you could come to my home to recuperate. It'll be a week at least before you'll be well enough to return to your daily routine, and longer than that until your ribs are fully healed."

"Look, why don't you get me my medication?" Anything to stop Cherry from talking. She was making it impossible to concentrate.

"Okay. I'll be back in a minute."

When Cherry had gone out, Wilder pushed down her covers and slid her legs over the side of the bed. Standing up was hard. Her chest felt like someone was slipping knives into it repeatedly. Nevertheless, she managed to hobble across the room to the door, which Cherry had left open. She closed it and looked for a lock. With dismay she discovered there was none. Not to be deterred, Wilder looked around the room for something she could push against the door to prevent it from being opened from the outside.

A chest of drawers stood in one corner, but Wilder wasn't sure it was heavy enough. Perhaps she could manage to push the bed over to the door? Footsteps sounded outside. Someone was coming up the stairs. *Dammit.* She was too late. This time when the door opened, she was right behind it.

"Hey, what are you doing?" Cherry asked.

Wilder could only glare at her sullenly. Why was the woman insisting on bothering her all the time? Didn't she understand the importance of the a-grav work?

"Come on," Cherry said. "Let me help you back to bed."

Wilder allowed Cherry to put her arm around her and accompany her across the room. When she reached the bed, she climbed into it, reckoning that protesting about Cherry's presence was only going to delay her leaving.

She took the tablet from the woman's hand and

dutifully swallowed it with a sip of water. She looked up expectantly. Now would Cherry finally go away?

"Do you want something to eat? I think it would do you good to eat a little."

That did it.

"I don't *want* to eat!" Wilder exclaimed. "I want to work! Now leave me a...*Ahhhh!*" She clutched her chest. Her outburst had caused it to explode in agony. She was in so much pain she couldn't speak. She could only hold herself and rock as tears collected in her closed eyes.

Cherry sat sideways on the bed and touched Wilder's shoulder. "Take it easy, okay?"

Wilder opened her eyes long enough to glower at her before closing them again and nursing her chest, wishing the waves of pain would recede.

"I have to work," she whispered. "You don't understand."

"You're right," said Cherry. "I don't. You're still sick, Wilder. The doctor said you were seriously dehydrated when you arrived at the hospital and you wouldn't have lasted more than another few hours. The prolonged dehydration and crushing from the a-grav machine has affected your internal organs and it's going to take a while for them to recover. Your ribs will heal, but you may never be entirely healthy again."

Her words were an almost meaningless buzz in Wilder's ears. If she never re-discovered the secret of the a-grav field, her health and well-being wouldn't matter.

"I tell you what," said Cherry. "Let's make a bargain. If you have something to eat—two spoonfuls of soup, say —then you can read your interface for half an hour."

Alarmed by this proposal, Wilder blindly reached for the interface that was lying face downward on the bed. She slid the device toward her protectively. The pain in her ribs was beginning to ease. The medication she'd swallowed had started to take effect. She took an experimental breath, breathing deeper than she had before. The pain was definitely reducing.

"What do you mean?" she asked. "I can read my interface for half an hour? What does that mean?"

"It means, you need to eat before you can work. That makes sense, doesn't it? You need calories, Wilder. You're stick thin. I wish I'd paid more attention to how you were getting on but I've been too busy."

"I've been busy too, working on the a-grav system. I worked on it for years, ever since we got back from the Assembly and I found out the scientists here had discovered the information in the Guardians' data and had started up a research group. Years, Cherry. Years." Wilder was barely managing to restrain her rage, especially now the agony of her cracked ribs was fading.

"I understand you must be disappointed, but—"

"Disappointed? You let it go! You allowed all that work I'd put in—decades of work from tens of people— just fly away into the sky. How could you? How could you do that to me? To the colony? Do you have any idea how valuable an invention like that is? How significant it is in terms of our status in the galaxy?"

Cherry said, "We had no choice. We had to save you. We couldn't save you *and* the machine. I didn't know how to turn it off even if I could reach it."

"You could have done *something*," said Wilder, "but you didn't. You let it go. And I'll never forgive you."

Cherry stood up. "We saved your *life*," she hissed, her hand clenched in a fist at her side. "And I've taken you into my home to look after you because I was worried you would discharge yourself and try to go back to that hovel you live in if I didn't. Don't you think I have enough to do without looking after you as well? I have the responsibility of protecting this entire colony on my shoulders. Do you think I want to care for an ungrateful brat too?"

"I didn't ask you to look after me! I don't want your stupid soup. I want to go home." Wilder moved to get up.

"Hey, no you don't," said Cherry. "Sit down. You have to stay in bed. The doctor said so."

"I don't care." Wilder moved away from Cherry and tried to get out of the other side of the bed.

"Wilder! Sit down." Cherry tried to grab her arm but Wilder was too fast. She was out of the bed in moments.

"Where are my clothes?"

"Get back into bed this instant," said Cherry. "You're not going anywhere until you're better."

"You are not my carer and I'm not a little kid. You can't tell me what to do." Wilder pulled open a drawer, looking for something to wear. She was still in the flimsy gown she'd been wearing when she woke up in the hospital.

"Dammit, I am not going to let you leave and hurt yourself," said Cherry. "You aren't in any condition to be going anywhere."

"Huh, I'd like to see you try to keep me here." Wilder gave up her search. "You might be the general but I bet I could beat you in a fight, even with cracked ribs." It was no good. The drawers were empty. She would just have to wear the gown and bear the stares of onlookers. It didn't matter as long as she could get back to her tree house. If she'd known Cherry was a maniacal control freak she would never have agreed to go to her home.

Wilder strode toward the door.

"That's it," said Cherry. "I'm calling the CED and asking them to send some officers over." She tapped her ear comm.

"You can't do that," said Wilder. "I haven't done anything wrong."

"Like you said, I'm the general. I can do whatever I like. I'll tell them you're a threat to national security and must be apprehended at all costs."

"You..." Wilder gave a gasp of frustration. "How dare you! You have no right." Hot, shameful tears of anger sprang to her eyes. She thrust the balls of her wrists into her eyes to wipe them away. "How could you do this to me?"

"Believe it or not, I'm trying to help you. You're behaving like a little kid. You have to rest. Come and lie down."

"No! Get out and leave me alone."

"Look, you either get back into bed and calm down or I'll comm the doctor and ask her to come over and give you a sedative to *make* you calm down. I've half a mind to ask her to reassess your mental state anyway. What's it to be?"

Wilder stomped over to the bed and sat down heavily. Immediately, she winced as the pain from her ribs broke through the effect of the painkiller she'd taken.

"Good," said Cherry. "Now, do you want to eat something? You must be hungry."

"You just threatened to have me arrested and forcibly sedated. No, I do not want your soup. What I want is for you to leave, you bitch!"

Cherry looked like she'd been slapped in the face. Her features froze and her skin paled. Her gaze searched Wilder's for a moment as if trying to see if she'd really meant what she'd said. Wilder glared back, hoping Cherry would read what she wanted her to see.

A troubled expression fell over Cherry's face and she seemed to regret what she'd said, but a line had been crossed. Wilder had been angry enough as it was about losing the a-grav machine. Cherry's threats had only made matters worse. All her life Wilder had been fighting against people who tried to control her. At one time she'd thought of Cherry as a friend. That was all over now. Wilder would never forget or forgive what she'd done.

106

CHAPTER FIFTEEN

Kes checked the time. It was nearly four o'clock and he'd promised Isobel he wouldn't be home late that evening. He was determined to keep that promise. Things had been tense between them since the last time she had confronted him about putting his work before his family.

Since then, he'd been better about making it home before Miki's bedtime, but not perfect. Working with Meredith on relations with the Parvus had eaten into his time, and he couldn't easily refuse a request from the Leader. The visitors hadn't returned for another meeting yet, and Meredith was keen to encourage them to enter into more discussions. The small aliens clearly possessed plenty of information that wasn't available in the files the Assembly had sent—potentially extremely useful information. So, as well as deepening his knowledge on them and their culture, Kes had been liaising with them.

In some ways it was hard going. The Fila's translation system delivered the Parvus' communication in English, but the meaning was sometimes unclear. Sometimes, Kes thought he understood exactly what they meant, only to discover he was entirely wrong. He didn't find these times frustrating, however. Interest and curiosity drove him on to find the heart of the misunderstanding.

Despite knowing he should spend more time with his family, Kes had worked several weekends and several times he'd arrived home too late to see his daughter before she went to bed. Isobel had been frosty with him on each occasion, saying once that she might as well be single. He knew he was skating on thin ice regarding his marriage. Isobel wasn't an unreasonable person and Kes didn't blame her for her attitude. She'd been pushed to the edge by his behavior and had nowhere left to go.

He turned his attention to the recordings of the Parvus. The vids covered every moment of the aliens' visit, from the arrival of their shuttle to its departure. He'd already watched them several times but he hoped he might see or hear something important that he'd missed.

Something he was particularly interested in was their statements around the idea of intention. Clearly, the fact that he, Cherry, and Wilder had acted with the intention of risking their own lives to save one of the Parvus held great importance for the species. It seemed as though the fact that no human had actually saved any Parvus wasn't important to them. It was what the humans had *intended* that mattered, perhaps even more than the actual action.

Did Parvus culture value inner, psychological reality higher than external reality? It certainly seemed so according to the evidence. But it was early days yet. Far too early to come to any conclusions or make any definitive statements. Kes considered how to state his tentative hypothesis.

"Can I watch those too?"

Kes looked up. Tricia, a colleague, was standing over him. He hadn't heard her walk over. He paused the vid.

"Sure," he replied. "Your clearance is high enough,

but be careful not to repeat anything you hear. I'll warn you, there's a doozy in there."

"Now I really have to hear it." Tricia pulled over a chair from the next desk, which was empty, and sat down. "You were so lucky to go to that meeting. I'm deeply jealous."

"I have to admit, it was fantastic." Kes told her the channel for the audio. "You'll be amazed at some of the things they said."

"Do they actually speak?" Tricia asked. "I haven't done much research on the Parvus."

"Yes, they do communicate verbally. I even have a recording of the sounds they make, somewhere in my files. I'll find it if you're interested. It sounds kind of burbly."

"Later. I want to hear this amazing piece of information I'm supposed to keep secret."

"You'll have to wait a while. The recording is at the moment we had our first sight of them." Kes unpaused the recording.

The Parvus came into view, wearing their EVA suits.

A comm arrived for Kes. He paused the recording again. "Cherry?"

"Are you alone?"

"No."

"Okay. Come to the Leader's Residence. Right away."

"Huh?"

"Just do it. See you when you get here." Cherry closed the connection.

"Uh..."

"Is everything okay?" asked Tricia.

"I don't know. I have to leave. Sorry." Kes closed the recording of the Parvus and returned it to the high security files.

"What, right now?"

"Yes." Kes stood up.

"But I want to know what happened during the

meeting!"

"You'll have to wait. Or submit a request to view the recordings." Kes checked if any autocars were already in the parking lot. Two were available.

"But that'll take forever. Can't you just tell me?"

"Not here and now. You know I can't." In the open plan office, the news that Concordia was the Scythians' origin planet could be overheard by someone who didn't possess the clearance to know the fact.

Kes left his disgruntled colleague and headed out of the office and the building. What could be so urgent that Cherry wanted to see him as soon as possible, and so sensitive or inflammatory she didn't want to discuss it with him in front of someone else?

The travel time from Annwn to Oceanside was a little over an hour. When the car was on its way, Kes comm'd Cherry.

"I'm alone now. Can you tell me what this is about?"

"I'm not sure myself yet, but I can tell you what I know. About half an hour ago, someone picked up a stranger wandering around the manufacturing zone near Cerberus. The woman was in such a state, he didn't bother calling an ambulance. He brought her to the hospital at Oceanside, telling them he was bringing in someone on the brink of death."

Kes tensed. He had an idea of what was coming.

"So this woman was brought into the emergency department," Cherry continued. "*Carried* in, I should say. And the doctors started to work, only to get what I imagine must have been the surprise of their lives."

"It was a Guardian?" asked Kes.

"Whatever it is, it looks human, but it certainly isn't."

"Stars," said Kes. "Wilder was right! What's happening now?"

"The android is still at the hospital, in a secured room with guards outside. As soon as the doctors realized they were dealing with something entirely out of their league, they contacted the CED, who then contacted me. I haven't seen this thing yet, and I want you to be with me when I do. You and I are two of the four people who actually remember the Guardians. But it's been a long time. I'm not sure if I trust my judgment."

"If it isn't a Guardian, what else could it be?" Kes noted that Cherry hadn't asked Aubriot to help her. He could understand why she hadn't asked Wilder. The girl would still be recovering from her accident, and she probably hadn't had close dealings with the androids. But Aubriot was probably closer to the hospital than Kes and he'd known the Guardians very well—too well.

"If it isn't a Guardian," Cherry said, "we're really in the shit."

***

Kes stood outside the hospital room door, hardly knowing what to expect. Cherry was with the staff nurse, getting the most up-to-date report on the strange 'patient'. Two guards stood on each side of the entrance. Guards were guarding the Guardian, if that was what it was.

Unlike many of the Woken, Kes had only known the Guardians as androids. After he'd been revived, he heard the tale of Anahi, the agri-scientist's, attempt to control the Gens by using the Guardians as a paramilitary force, but while the crisis was happening, he'd been frozen in cryo. The first time he'd seen a Guardian had been when Cariad had reactivated them and they'd come down to Concordia from their ship to help with rebuilding after the Scythian attack.

He recalled his first impressions and his realization that, if he hadn't known they were artificial, he would have been fooled into thinking they were human too. According to what Cherry had said, the thing's appearance retained its human-like quality, at least enough to mislead the person who found it and brought it to the hospital.

Cherry came striding down the corridor.

"What did the nurse say?" asked Kes as she drew closer.

"She said to be prepared for a shock when we see the state its in, but it doesn't appear to be suffering any pain, though its functions are impaired. That might be why it isn't speaking. It hasn't spoken a word since it was found."

"Because it can't."

"Exactly."

"Did they give it an interface?" asked Kes. "Maybe it can write."

"No, they didn't, and I'm glad," Cherry replied.

"Why? If its speaking capability is shot, how else is it going to communicate with us?"

"Do you think it's a good idea to give an unknown entity access to Concordia's data?"

"Fair point. Still, it would need superior technical skills to find out anything sensitive from a regular interface connection."

"The Guardians had superior technical skills. Very superior."

"But if it is a Guardian, its primary motivation is to support the colony, isn't it? Where's the danger?"

"*If* it's a Guardian, that might have been what its primary motivation *was*. Even after everything they did to help us in the end, I'm still not convinced that was the case. But anyway, if one of them really has been floating around in space for the last several decades before nearly being destroyed on entering the atmosphere, who knows how its circuits have been screwed up? What if that program that guided it to save us is now telling it to destroy us? Let's go in and see this thing."

Cherry stepped up to the door. A guard moved aside, and she breathed into the security panel. The door opened.

The figure in the room was clearly visible through the doorway. As he caught sight of it, Kes took an involuntary step back. One of the guards glanced surreptitiously over her shoulder and gasped.

Cherry rebuked her before walking into the room. "Eyes front!"

Kes joined Cherry, unable to remove his gaze from the thing sitting in the hospital bed.

It was humanoid, but that was about as much as could be said about it. Kes could see why the person who had first encountered the being had thought it was human. What else could it be? To nearly all Concordians the Guardians were historical figures, if they believed they had existed at all. But its appearance must have made the finder wonder how it still lived and moved.

Half the head was simply *gone*. If the thing had once had hair, it had all been burned away. The part of the face that remained was blackened and disfigured. The body areas that were visible—it was tucked under covers, bizarrely, considering the thing was a machine— were also badly damaged. The right shoulder and arm, the same side as the missing area of head, were bent backward as if from a heavy impact. The hand and lower half of the arm up to the elbow was gone. The figure was naked. It had once been crafted to resemble a human female, but its charred surface bore barely evident details of its femininity.

Cherry was motionless, gazing at the thing, seemingly also taking in its appearance. "Can you speak?"

The damaged android regarded Cherry with its single eye. Its mouth opened. It worked its jaw and tongue, as if trying to respond or simply re-familiarize itself with the act of speaking.

"I... know... you."

Cherry raised her eyebrows at Kes. "You do?"

"I..." The android's mouth was moving but no sound was coming out. Then speech returned to it. "My systems are damaged."

"You can say that again," said Kes. "Is there anything we can do to repair you? Any way we can help?"

Cherry raised a hand and frowned at him. "What are you?" she asked the android. "What are you doing on Concordia? How did you get here?"

"I was here before. I do not know when. My timekeeping function is impaired."

Stepping closer to the android, Cherry said, "Why didn't you speak before? Why are you only speaking now?"

"I did not recognize this place. It does not match with my records. I was trying to reconcile my memory with this new environment."

Kes knew that sense of confusion all too well. He'd felt it too, when he'd returned from the Assembly's space station and discovered that Concordia had moved on more than fifty Earth years.

"You haven't answered my question," said Cherry.

Kes thought she was being rather harsh and demanding. Though he knew it was wrong to anthropomorphize, he couldn't help but feel pity for the android. He'd heard they felt emotions. How would it feel to be alone in space for decades, and then nearly burned to annihilation?

"I recognize you," the machine replied to Cherry. "I now think I am in the correct place."

"So you know Cherry from before?" Kes asked. "What about me?"

The bleary eye turned to regard him. "Yes. Though I do not recall your name."

Kes was about to give it when Cherry interrupted him. "What about you? What's your name?"

"I do not know, but my data files contain the information that I captained a starship."

The *Mistral's* captain? What was she called? Kes couldn't remember.

"Can you type?" Cherry asked. "Do you remember how to write in English?"

"I think I can type. And I can read and write English."

"How convenient," said Cherry. "Tell me, how did you get here? You didn't answer my question earlier."

"I remember falling. And I remember my system rebooting. I walked for a long time, but I could only travel slowly because my legs are damaged. Eventually, I found a road and I followed it."

"Why?" Cherry asked. "What were you hoping to find?"

"I am compelled to find humans. I don't know why."

"Right," said Cherry. "Wait here. Kes, could you come with me?"

As they left the room, Kes asked, "Are you going to give it an interface now?"

"Yes," Cherry replied, closing the door. "One that's been wiped, disconnected from the comm system, and modified to only record written language."

"Isn't that overkill?" said Kes. They were walking away from the room. "It seems obvious that what's in there was once a Guardian, the captain of their ship. What was her name?"

"Faina. *Its* name was Faina. It isn't a 'her' and it never was. When it said it captained a ship, I had a good look at it, trying to see the resemblance. It does look like a burned up Faina. That doesn't mean it is, though. And you and everyone else would be wise to remember that."

"Why? What are you suspicious about?"

"For stars' sake, Kes, you sound like one of those damned recruits who doesn't know which is the dangerous end of a gun. You're a smart man. Think about it."

Kes was taken aback. Everything he'd seen and heard about the thing in the hospital room added up. Could there really be any other explanation for the thing in the bed?

He recalled Cariad telling him once that Cherry hated the Guardians. She'd hated them ever since they were used to control the Gens, and that hadn't changed, even when they did so much else to help with the colonization later. Was Cherry's prejudice coloring her opinion of the new arrival? But she seemed to be implying something else.

"You think that thing isn't a Guardian? That it's some kind of threat to our security? But everything it says adds up. It knew your name."

"No, it didn't. You told it my name."

"I did? Well, it recognized you."

"It *said* it recognized me. All we can say it knew for sure was that I had to be someone important, because I was the one who was asked to go and see it. Nothing that came out of that thing's mouth has convinced me it is what it says it is. And until I *am* convinced, I'm not taking any chances."

"I guess you are the general of the defense force," said Kes.

"Damned right. But I want your opinion too. What did you think of it? Did it look like a Guardian to you?"

"It did. Or rather, it looked pretty much as I would expect one to look after nearly burning to cinders traveling through a planet's atmosphere and then crash landing."

"Do you know of any way we can check?"

"We could examine it internally, but no one ever got a look at their insides as far as I know. Their specs might be in the data files from the *Mistral*. And we have their weapons. That was how Wilder knew the crashed object was related to the Guardians, because the metal alloy is the same."

"Yes. The capsule it arrived in checks out in that regard. I had it retested, but it's a melted mess. There's not much else to be learned from it. I'll ask someone to search for everything we have on them."

"How's Wilder doing, by the way?" Kes asked.

"Ugh." Cherry's expression turned sour. "She's getting better, but she wants to leave. It's ridiculous. She's nowhere near better yet. I think she hates me too."

"Hates you? Why?"

"I threatened to call the CED on her."

"You *what*?"

"I know. Sounds crazy, right? We were having a fight, and things got out of hand. I don't even know how it happened. I guess I didn't have the patience to deal with her. She's mad at me for not doing anything to catch the a-grav machine."

"She's mad at me too, then. I didn't do anything either. But, seriously? Does she even remember the state she was in? We saved her life."

"She doesn't seem to rate that as highly as the machine she was working on. But I wasn't exactly reasonable either, and she is still a kid, while I'm the adult. Patience was never one of my strengths."

Kes was interested to hear more, but he'd noticed something through a nearby window. It was getting dark outside. Apprehension struck him. "Do you know what time it is?"

Cherry said, "About seven thirty, I think."

"Shit! I have to go." Seven thirty! Kes began to run down the corridor. It was an hour to Annwn. He wouldn't make it in time to see Miki before she went to bed. Isobel would be furious. No, she wouldn't be furious. She would be hurt and bitter and disappointed, and that was even worse.

CHAPTER SIXTEEN

Wilder lay awake in bed, facing the wall. When Cherry had come in to check on her, she'd pretended to be asleep. She never wanted to speak to Cherry again.

She heard the sound of a tray being placed on the table next to her bed and then Cherry's footsteps as she crossed the room. When the door closed, Wilder exhaled and turned over. The room was empty and a tray holding a bowl of breakfast cereal and a glass of juice sat on the table. Next to the glass was a pill.

Wilder picked it up, placed it at the back of her tongue, and drank a mouthful of juice to wash it down. She would have to wait for the medication to take effect before she made her move. It would take a few minutes, and Cherry hadn't left the house yet anyway.

Wilder waited in anticipation for the analgesic effect to wash over her. Her ribs had been bothering her for a couple of hours, but she'd been awake since before that, planning her escape. She wasn't going to spend a minute longer in Cherry's house than she had to. The woman was actually keeping her there as a prisoner. It was outrageous, and a gross abuse of her powers.

She'd thought Cherry was a kind, nice person. How wrong she'd been.

Wilder climbed out of bed and padded over to the door. Pressing an ear against it, she listened for Cherry's movements. She could hear her downstairs, walking around. Wilder listened impatiently. What did Cherry have to do that took so much time? What was keeping her from going to work? All she had to do was eat and then leave.

"Come on," Wilder breathed. Then she froze. Footsteps were climbing the stairs. Wilder sped across her bedroom on tiptoes, leapt into bed, and pulled the covers over her. As the bedroom door opened, she froze again.

Cherry came into the room. "Wilder."

When Wilder didn't answer, Cherry repeated her name. After another pause, she said, "I know you're awake." Wilder continued her pretense. She wasn't going to give the bitch the satisfaction of replying to her.

Cherry sighed. "I have to go out to work, but I'll be back as soon as I can. In the meantime, there's plenty of food in the kitchen if you get hungry. Help yourself to whatever you want. I wanted to talk to you before I left, but seeing as you're not in the mood it'll have to wait until later. I hope you feel a bit better today. Take it easy, okay? Get plenty of rest. Then you'll be able to get back to working on a-grav. I'm sure everything will come back to you then and it won't be long until you re-invent your machine."

Yes, I am going to return to working on a-grav, and sooner than you think!

The door closed. Wilder relaxed. She lay motionless, waiting. After a few moments, she thought she heard the front door close. She sat up. Suddenly realizing how thirsty and hungry she was, she drank the orange juice in several gulps and then quickly slurped the cereal in spoonfuls from the bowl. Wiping her mouth with her hand, she slid her legs out from under the covers and got up.

The room held no clothes. She had discovered that the previous evening after Cherry had left. Was that by design? Had Cherry intended to deprive her of her liberty from the beginning? Whether it was a coincidence or not didn't matter. Wilder needed clothes. If she went walking around Annwn in a hospital gown she would draw attention to herself and she would wind up right back where she was.

Wilder held her ear against the door again. This time, she heard nothing. She waited five minutes, counting the seconds under her breath. No sounds came from the house. Cherry had left.

Wilder turned the door handle, her muscles tense. To her relief, the door opened. Cherry hadn't locked her in. She stepped out onto the quiet landing. Two more doors led off from it and both were closed. Wilder peered over the railing to the hall below. Nothing stirred except motes of dust in the sunbeams shining through a glass panel in the front door.

When she'd arrived at Cherry's house, she'd been dopey with medication and hadn't taken much in. Now, it struck her how small and simple the place was, considering Cherry's position.

She walked down the stairs quietly, listening hard. The two doors leading from the hall were open. A kitchen and a living room were visible through them, both empty. The rooms were sparse, almost clinically so. Wilder disliked clutter too, but the walls of her tree house were decorated with sketches she'd drawn— fantastical machines and devices she'd dreamt up over the years. She also had a few drawings Tycho and Stephie's grandchildren had given her on her rare visits to her old friends.

In Cherry's home there was nothing like that.

Nothing sentimental or nostalgic. Everything was practical. There was nothing to warm the heart.

Cold and mean, Wilder thought. *Just like her.*

Feeling happier now she knew she would not be disturbed while she enacted her escape, Wilder climbed the stairs again. Her ribs were twinging despite the medication, so she knew she had to not take things too fast. She would also have to find the rest of the painkillers and take them with her. They did belong to her, after all.

She felt bad about taking Cherry's clothes, however. As soon as she got back to her own place, she would return them to her. Wilder opened an upstairs door. Here was what she needed. It was Cherry's bedroom, and an open closet door revealed hanging clothes. Wilder quickly stripped and grabbed the nearest things to hand: casual pants and a round-necked, warm top, suitable for the cool weather outside. The clothes were baggy on her and the pants and sleeves ended inches above her ankles and wrists, but they would do.

As she closed the closet door, Wilder saw a figure in the mirror. She gasped, not recognizing herself, before she realized that the gaunt, wild-haired girl with shadows under her eyes was in fact her. Slowly, she took in her appearance. It had been years since she'd seen a full length view of herself. She'd grown taller in the intervening time, but no wider.

She lifted the top and inhaled sharply at what she saw. Her abdomen and ribs were a blue-purple mess. That was what the a-grav machine had done to her. But she was also astonished by the concave depression that was her belly, and the prominent bones of her ribs that overhung it.

She raised a hand to her hair. Matted and messy strands stuck out all over. Her nose was sharp and her cheekbones and chin were jutting. Her resolve to escape Cherry's home faltered. Maybe the woman had a point. Maybe it might be better to wait another day or two and rest.

Then she remembered Cherry's threat to call the CED and to have her sedated. Her jaw set firm. She refused to remain in the home of someone who had zero respect for her rights.

She had to get out. When she was somewhere safe, then she would rest.

But she didn't have to leave right away. Cherry had implied she would be gone for hours.

Wilder returned to her room, undressed, and took a shower. She washed her hair, marveling at the handfuls of strands that fell from it. She gently soaped her bruised skin. The a-grav machine had really done a good job at crushing her. It was a miracle she'd survived.

She wondered how much force it had exerted. Had it been moving at the same speed as Concordia's gravitational acceleration? She didn't think so. That would have killed her. So the neutralization effect had not been complete? Wilder pondered the question.

Before she knew it, the shower room was thick with steam and her skin was as wrinkled as an old person's. How long had she been there? Wilder hastily turned off the water and stepped out of the shower, a terrible guilt weighing on her at having wasted so much water.

Her feelings didn't make a lot of sense. On Concordia there was water aplenty and the energy to heat it was free—Cherry's home might even be hooked up to the old geothermally heated water the Fila had supplied in the early days of the colony. But the creed that it was morally despicable to waste water had been bred into her bones during her childhood on the *Nova*, and she didn't think she would ever be free of it.

Looking at herself in the bathroom mirror, she saw the long shower had made little difference to her emaciated, bruised appearance, but she felt a whole lot better. She dried her hair, put on Cherry's clothes again, and went downstairs to the kitchen. She opened a cupboard, looking for food she could eat before leaving. On her third try, she found what she was looking for: crackers, yeast pastes, and cookies. Her favorite meal.

As she was stuffing her pockets with packets of food —Cherry wouldn't mind, and if she did, Wilder didn't give a shit—she spotted the pack of painkilling medication on the windowsill. She slipped that into a pocket too.

Out in the hallway she opened an under stairs cupboard and found her boots. Her washed socks had been placed on top of them.

Wilder hesitated as she reached for them. A quiet note of guilt sounded inside her in reaction to the thoughtful care Cherry had taken over her stuff. She gritted her teeth. It was a shame Cherry hadn't taken the same care over her right to liberty.

After putting on the socks and slipping on her boots, Wilder strode to the front door. She peered through the transparent panel in it. Had Cherry put guards outside to prevent her from leaving? The exterior looked empty. Cherry's small home stood in a short, quiet, dead-end street, somewhere in Annwn. She'd told Wilder she'd lost her farm during the long decades of their trip to the Assembly. She'd looked incredibly sad when she said it. At the time, Wilder had felt sorry for her. Now, that was all gone.

Wilder went to the back door, which led off from the kitchen, and pressed the door release. The door remained shut. Cherry had locked her in. *Bitch!*

Who on Concordia thought it was necessary to have their house doors fitted with locks? What was Cherry afraid of?

Wilder didn't feel particularly fazed. It would take a lot more than a lock to prevent her from leaving. If it was the regular kind, she could deactivate it with her eyes closed. Wilder inspected the device closely. *Damn.* It looked like military grade. She could probably override it, but time was a concern. Security alarms were fixed so that an alarm was sent to the CED if someone tampered with them. That wasn't a problem if breaking the device only took seconds, but Wilder didn't know how long it would take her to deactivate the military systems. She could be caught while still trying to escape. There was no way she was going to spend another day in that place, held against her will.

She took a step backward, away from the door. She had to find another way out. The window? As Wilder walked toward it, she saw that her luck was in. No locks held the window closed.

She climbed onto the sanitizer, opened the window, and took a quick look outside. All was still in the small yard. She jumped out, a rush of adrenaline hitting her as she crossed the threshold. She was free again.

But where should she go? Her tree house would be the first place Cherry would look when she knew she had escaped. She had to go back there to check on Piddle and Puddle, but after that she needed to go somewhere else—somewhere Cherry wouldn't find her.

Wilder crossed the small yard and climbed the fence. She didn't know where she was going yet but it didn't matter. She'd survived worse situations in the past and come out fine. She would do so again. And, more importantly, she would be able to return to working on a-grav.

CHAPTER SEVENTEEN

After Kes disappeared in a hurry, Cherry returned to the nurses' station. The staff nurse was going over something with another nurse. When Cherry approached she wrapped up the discussion and sent the nurse away.

"Our visitor will be moving to Oceanside Jail," Cherry said. "Guards and an army vehicle will be arriving in about half an hour. I want you to prepare the prisoner for transportation by strapping it to a gurney. The guards will also secure it with handcuffs and shackles."

The staff nurse's eyebrows rose in surprise. It was understandable. She was used to treating people in order to make them better. But that thing that had arrived from space was not a person and it wasn't going to get any better, at least not if Cherry could help it.

The staff nurse huwas intelligent enough not to question the order, however. "Yes, ma'am. Is there anything else you would like me to do?"

"Yes. I want you to take a sample from it for analysis. Any part of the main structure will do, but not any remnant of clothing or hair. I'm not sure how you'll do it. Maybe an orthopedic surgeon might lend you a saw."

"I can ask, but they're precious about their tools."

"A maintenance person, then."

"I'm sure I can find something suitable."

"As soon as you have a sample—I think a piece about this big should be fine—" Cherry lifted her hand and held her thumb and forefinger about four centimeters apart. "Send it express to the Engineering Department at the university. They'll be expecting it."

"I'll do it now, before the guards arrive to take her."

Cherry stiffened. "It isn't a her. It isn't human and it never was. It's important that you understand that."

"Yes, you're right. I'm sorry. It was a slip of the tongue."

"Don't worry about it. It's an easy mistake to make. Thanks for your help. I have to go now, but please comm me immediately if any problems occur." Cherry left, worrying about what seemed to be turning into an ongoing problem. Even Kes, who had always known the Guardians were androids, had fallen into the trap of thinking of the surprise arrival as a person. That faulty perception and its attendant dangers would continue until Cherry did something about it.

Was the thing really Faina? Cherry could see the likeness in what remained of its face. But if it really was the former captain of the *Mistral*, so what? The colony no longer needed Guardians, if it ever had. Cherry had often thought their arrival had created more problems than it solved.

And if it wasn't Faina, it meant Concordia was in grave, immediate danger. The only other explanation for a fake Guardian dropping from the sky was that it had been sent as a spy. There was plenty of sensitive information that, if it got out, could mean the end of the colony. The secret nature of the military depots would be as much of an advantage in battle as their contents.

Cherry had already made up her mind before she left

the hospital. The thing in the bed had to be destroyed, and quickly, before rumors of its presence spread. She wasn't sure how the job could be done. Guardians were made from tough materials, assuming it was one. That the thing was still functioning despite its near-destruction was testament to the fact.

Cherry ran quickly down the hospital steps. Her autocar was waiting at the bottom. She had to report to Meredith and ask her permission to destroy the android. As her car carried her toward the Leader's Residence, she came up with the answer. Out at the mountains, smelting plants turned the ore into metals to send to the manufacturing district. The furnaces there had to be hot enough to entirely destroy the unwelcome guest.

If it was a Guardian, it would be the last one. Their stain would be removed from Concordia forever.

***

Meredith took Cherry out onto the wide balcony that led off from the functions room. No function was being held at the residence at that moment, but Cherry could imagine the music, dancing, free-flowing drinks and stacks of food. Meredith held regular formal parties, as a way of smoothing strained relationships between important figures in Concordian society.

Meredith had often invited Cherry, but even the idea of a social event like that set her on edge. It wasn't the kind of thing Ethan would have done. The colony had changed a lot.

"Take a seat," Meredith said, indicating a table next to the ornamental wall that ran around the balcony's edge.

The breeze from the ocean was stiff but Cherry enjoyed the feeling of cleanliness it gave her. Spending time with the Guardian-like being had made her feel dirty.

"Drink?" asked Meredith, also sitting down.

"No, thanks," Cherry replied.

"Come on," said Meredith. "You never sit and have a drink with me when you come. It wouldn't hurt you to relax a little."

Cherry regarded the older woman for a moment. Was she lonely? Cherry guessed she might be. She was single and just as busy as Cherry was with her job. "Okay, I'll have chicory coffee." She sat down.

"Chicory coffee? I don't think I've heard of that. I'll ask the cook if we have any."

When the answer came back that the Leader's Residence didn't stock Cherry's favorite drink, Meredith apologized. "We only have the regular stuff."

Had Aubriot cornered the chicory coffee supply? Cherry herself hadn't managed to find any for years. "Regular will be fine."

Meredith sent the order through and sipped from a cup that was already half empty. She had been sitting on the balcony for a while. "So, tell me all about it."

"Thank you for not going to see it before I had a chance to check it out," Cherry said.

"No problem. What you said makes sense. If our visitor does have nefarious plans, it wouldn't be wise for our colony's Leader to offer up herself to it at close quarters."

"Have you had a chance to look at the vids the doctors took?"

"I've been studying them for a while." Meredith swiped open an interface set into the table surface. "They're pretty gruesome."

"It doesn't look any better in real life. It smells too, of burned plastic."

Meredith wrinkled her nose. "And did you come to a conclusion about what it is?"

"Not yet. I've ordered for the material it's made from to be tested, but even when we get the results I'm not sure it'll tell us anything definitive. I'm also moving it to the jail for better security, but my advice is the safest option is to dispose of it as soon as possible."

"Isn't that a bit hasty? We don't even know what it is. What if it is one of these Guardians? Perhaps it could be useful to the colony."

"Huh, you wouldn't say that if you knew what life was like when those things were here."

Meredith put down her cup. "Am I missing something? All the history books say the reason the Scythians stopped attacking us was because the *Mistral* flew directly into one of their ships. The enemy mistook the act as a sacrifice."

Cherry's coffee arrived, carried by Meredith's maid. She took the offered cup. "It's more complicated than that. A lot more complicated. Believe me, if it is a Guardian, those things are not to be trusted. Nothing it has to offer us is worth the risk of exposing ourselves to the danger it could bring."

"You aren't sure it's a Guardian?"

"I'm sure that's what it wants us to think it is."

"What gives you that impression?"

"Things it said."

"Wait a minute. It spoke to you?"

"Yes. After not speaking to anyone else, I'm the one it chose to *reveal itself* to."

"What did it say?"

"That it remembers me, but this place has changed. Oh, and it remembers Kes too. Conveniently."

"It all fits. Well, that throws a whole new light on everything."

"Does it?" Cherry asked. "I don't see how."

"If it can talk... If it can communicate..."

"An interface can communicate. A Guardian only has more processing capability."

"A lot more processing ability, and other abilities besides," said Meredith.

"You've seen the pictures," Cherry said. "That thing isn't capable of much any more, believe me."

"Which of the Guardians is it?"

"It doesn't remember its name, but it said it remembers it was the captain of a starship."

"Faina!" Meredith exclaimed. "I read about her."

Cherry's jaw tightened. She was getting tired of explaining that the word 'her' was inappropriate in this case. "It's best not to think of the Guardians as people. They're nothing more than machines."

"I know. Very sophisticated machines, though."

"The distinction isn't important here. We need to destroy that thing as soon as possible. I was thinking about how to do it—"

"I know. You already said. But I'm not sure I agree."

Cherry tapped the tabletop. She hadn't touched her coffee. "Why's that?"

"We don't know yet what this android has to offer us. Who knows what useful data might be stored in it? And besides, word has already gotten out about its existence. The man who brought it in and medical staff at the hospital have spoken to media outlets. I couldn't do anything to stop them. It was too late. There might even be images circulating. I'm not sure. But the colony knows about this crash survivor."

"Crash survivor?"

"That's what they were calling it in one headline I saw."

"Shit."

"It's regrettable, I admit. This has never happened before. We don't have any systems or regulations to control that kind of information. But what's done is done. If we destroy that android, it's going to look very bad."

"Does that matter if the safety of the colony is at stake?"

"We don't know that, and the safety of the colony also depends on a populace that feels secure."

"Does it?" Cherry could barely contain her anger. "It

would seem to me that the opposite was true."

"If we go around arbitrarily ending the existence of something that looks human, and like a severely injured, helpless human to boot, it'll undermine public morale. People will wonder if the same thing could happen to them."

"That's ridiculous."

"People aren't always rational or logical, Cherry. In fact, I'd say most of the time they aren't."

Cherry didn't know what to say. Or, actually, she did, but she bit back the retort.

Ethan wouldn't have hesitated. Ethan would have known the right thing to do. He would have destroyed it.

Instead, she said, "I hope you agree that it needs to remain in a high-security environment?"

"I do, for the time being. Until we're certain what it is."

"I don't think we'll ever be certain," said Cherry.

"Certain enough to know it poses us no danger."

Cherry wanted to repeat herself, but what was the point? Meredith's judgment was clouded. Like the rest of the Concordians, she didn't fear the Scythians enough. Her sense of danger had no edge, if she had any sense of danger at all.

Cherry looked out over the dark ocean. The breeze had dropped, and phosphorescence was sparkling on the calm surface, signaling the movements below. Threads were probably doing something down there and disturbing the water. She recalled the time Ethan and she had taken a trip to the creatures' underground city for her Joining Ceremony. They had spoken of the glittering sparks that adorned the water on still nights.

She missed him, so badly. She almost yearned for the peril they had lived under in the first year or two after Arrival, when the colony's existence had sat on a knife edge. Things had been much harder then, but they had been clear, and simple, and real.

"I have something I want to tell you," Meredith said. "I've decided to reduce the budget on Concordia's military next year."

"You've *what*?"

Meredith held up her hands. "Calm down. It isn't by much. You have to admit we do spend an awful lot on defense."

"Yes, for a very good reason!"

"Cherry, we have four missile silos, pulse emitters, and all kinds of equipment, nearly every able-bodied person has received military training, and one quarter of the adult population is a member of a military force, either full or part time. We're also building Chimera. I believe the investment in our military has been money well spent, but there has to come a time when we say we've done plenty and we should scale back a little."

Suddenly, Cherry couldn't stand sitting there with Meredith any longer. She stood up. "I should go."

"So soon?" Meredith asked. "I thought we had a lot more to discuss."

"Not really."

"Okay," said Meredith, perhaps sensing Cherry's mood and not wanting to push her further. "Let's talk another time."

When Cherry returned to her car, she nearly input her home address but then changed her mind. The conversations she'd had with Meredith, Kes, and the staff nurse left her wanting to speak to someone who understood where she was coming from.

Twenty minutes later, her car pulled up near Aubriot's house. She'd instructed it to stop thirty meters away, at a bend in the driveway where she could see the building but Aubriot wouldn't hear her car.

A few windows were lit up. He was home. Probably brewing, if he'd gone ahead with the new career he'd mentioned.

Of all four Concordians who had been alive at the same time the Guardians were at the colony, Aubriot was the one who knew in his core how dangerous the androids were. At one point, they had forcibly sedated him after judging him to be a threat to social stability. The Guardians had set no date when they proposed allowing him to return to consciousness. If it hadn't been for the objection of all the colonists to this heinous act, they could have effectively killed him. They could have kept him comatose until the moment they determined that he was no longer a threat. And if that was never? Well, never mind.

Aubriot would agree they needed to destroy the 'Guardian' in a heartbeat. And when he was motivated to do something he damn well got it done. But all the spirit seemed to have gone out of him lately. He was probably in his house getting drunk. Or maybe he had a woman over. Maybe both.

Cherry remembered her former lover's dead eyes the last time she'd seen him. She gave a slight shudder. She didn't want to see those eyes again right then. She input her home address. The autocar turned and moved up the driveway.

Wilder would be there when she got home. Cherry had been surprised how easily she'd taken to having the girl around. She'd thought she would hate to share her personal space after living alone for so long, but she'd found she enjoyed having a little company.

Ever since their argument, Cherry had been regretting what she'd said. She'd overreacted. She made up her mind to apologize and have a respectful discussion about how long Wilder should stay with her.

As soon as she got home.

CHAPTER EIGHTEEN

Bunny Giesen lifted his hard hat and rubbed his close-cropped hair. The gesture did nothing to ease the ache that had begun behind his eyes and was gradually working its way through his head. It was the endless grinding of the excavator that caused it. The same headache every day, starting about two hours before the end of his shift. Ear protectors did nothing for it. It wasn't the sound, it was the vibration, and there wasn't anything could be done about that.

He should have been a pilot like Ma. It would have been hard to live up to her reputation, for sure. The other trainees would have been watching him, looking for signs that he had her skill and reaction times. He doubted he would have. He wasn't that good, but he probably would have been okay. Ma could have given him pointers while she was still alive.

But hardly anyone flew planes on Concordia. Little, light, personal aircraft was all that was ever built, those and the government helis. Everyone knew why. It was because *they* were watching. The beings in the sky, from another planet. The Scythians.

Only, were they really? Ever since he was a little kid

he'd been warned his home was under threat, that there were aliens in outer space who wanted Concordia for their own. He'd learned all about the First Attack and Second Attack in history classes, as well as the Journey of the *Nova Fortuna*, Leaving Earth, and the Arrival of the Guardians.

But when he'd asked about the Scythians, what they looked like, where they came from, and when they were coming back, his teachers couldn't answer him. When he'd tried to find out the answers for himself, he'd drawn endless blanks. He'd wondered if any of it were true.

He'd seen the recordings. Watched them over and over again, in fact. But they could easily have been faked. The entertainment channels produced similar stuff all the time. He often wondered if the entire story about the Scythians was a conspiracy, put together by the government to get everyone to do what they said. People living in fear were more likely to do whatever they were told.

"Bunny, watcha doing up there? Taking a nap?" It was his supervisor, Alun. The words came from Bunny's ear mufflers, which were linked up to the work radio.

"Got a headache coming," Bunny replied. "I was just taking a little break." He hated it when Alun called him by his pet name, not his real name, Bernard. Only friends could call him Bunny, and Alun was far from that.

"Did you see the nurse like I said? Didn't he give you something for those headaches?"

"Yeah, I saw him," Bunny replied. He hadn't seen the nurse, but he didn't want Alun on his back about it. Bunny knew that all the nurse had to offer was medication, but who knew what was in that stuff? Maybe that was another way the government controlled people. He wasn't about to become a slave to the people in power.

"You can take a break when your shift's over," Alun said when Bunny didn't elaborate on his answer. "Start up again. We're on a schedule."

Bunny angrily threw down his hat and thumbed the button to start his machine. He let the noise drown out the curses he directed at his supervisor.

He checked the screen on the dashboard. Another two meters to go before he reached the outer edge of the chamber that would hold Concordia's fifth military depot. He wasn't supposed to know that, of course. He was only a tunneler. What right did he have to know the secrets of those who held the power?

But he did know. He knew the locations of all the military depots, because he'd worked on all of them. Not that it took much intelligence to figure it out. What other reason could there be for government-funded projects to hollow out vast underground chambers? Everyone knew about Cerberus, and the chambers he'd worked on had been about the same size and depth below ground.

When he'd asked Alun once or twice what they were building, his supervisor had pretended not to know. Maybe he really didn't. Maybe he really was that dumb. But Bunny knew.

Holding the control stick, he eased the drill forward until it bit into the rock. Dust and shards flew out from the surface. The air turned opaque and pinging sounds came from the excavator's plating and reinforced transparent screen. Though Bunny sat five meters from the drill tip, the debris from the excavation zone reached all the way back to him.

He didn't mind it too much. He was safe inside his machine. The entire site could collapse on top of him and he wouldn't be hurt. As long as he didn't try to leave his cab he would be fine until someone finally dug him out.

He wasn't worried about the rock shards hitting him,

it was the vibration he couldn't stand. He was already juddering in his seat and his headache felt like a second drill boring into his brain. And he had another two hours to endure before his shift would finally be over.

Suddenly, the excavator flew forward. All resistance ahead of it had disappeared. Bunny hit the brake. His machine halted, but Bunny carried on traveling. His head hit the window. He heard the *thunk* of his skull against the reinforced glass.

***

When Bunny came around, his face was on his dashboard. He felt the familiar edges and smooth surfaces pressing into his nose, mouth, and forehead. His headache was bad. Real bad. What had happened?

He opened his eyes. He could see the side window of the cabin. Outside, the air was dusty from his last round of excavation. He hadn't been out long. His machine had cut out. He must have released his hold on the dead man's lever when he passed out.

Wait. That was wrong. He hadn't passed out. He'd been knocked out. He'd braked hard and been thrown forward. He hadn't fastened his safety harness, and he hadn't been wearing his hat. *Dammit.* Alun would be all over him like a sluglimpet after this. He might even be let go.

He'd braked because the excavator had flown forward all of a sudden. He'd braked instinctively. Who wouldn't have?

But why had the excavator behaved as it did?

Bunny put his hands on the dashboard and pushed himself upright. This action had a weird effect on his machine. It began to—ever so gently—rock. Bunny froze. He could think of several scenarios that might cause an excavator to rock, and all of them were bad.

"Geisen!" Alun's voice came through to Bunny, harsh and angry. "What the hell did I just tell you? No more breaks, okay? We don't have time for your—"

"Shuttup!" Bunny hissed. "Just shuttup. Something's gone wrong."

"Wrong? What's gone wrong? What the hell are you talking about? You better have a damned good explanation for this."

"I don't know yet. I'm waiting for the dust to settle." Bunny was waiting for his machine to settle too. The rocking had continued and he wasn't sure that it was easing. He had a feeling it was getting worse.

One of the scenarios that might have caused the effects he was experiencing was an earthquake, but the fact that Alun wasn't feeling any tremors meant Bunny could rule that possibility out. The fact brought him a little relief. Though his cabin could withstand a heavy rockfall, it was no match against the forces that moved Concordia's tectonic plates. Nor would it be impervious to lava erupting from a crack in the mantle below.

Yet though he wasn't in the middle of an earthquake, his situation remained dire.

"I think I broke through into...something," he said.

"You broke through?"

"I was working, drilling, pushing the machine forward, you know."

"I know how excavators work, Bunny."

"And suddenly there was nothing there. Nothing to push against. The rock was gone."

"Oh shit. Do you think you hit a natural cave? Let me check the survey report."

Bunny was aware of his own breathing. In, out. In, pause, out. The rocking of his machine did seem to be slowing, finally. Bunny peered into the dust. His machine's lights bounced brightly off the tiny specks. The ground in that part of Suddene contained a lot of quartz, which made for hard drilling, but it created a pretty, shimmering effect.

What he was seeing wasn't looking good. Ordinarily, as the dust settled, a solid rock face would emerge.

Now all he could see was darkness stretching out beyond the shiny motes.

Hitting an unknown natural cave when excavating wasn't common, but it wasn't unheard of either. Bunny knew of two instances, though it had never happened to him. By itself the cave posed no danger. The problems lay in what it contained and how deep it was. The first problem could be ruled out. If the cave was filled with poisonous gas Bunny probably wouldn't have woken up after being knocked unconscious.

But the second problem... The second problem could explain the rocking of his excavator. It had stopped, thank the stars. Bunny was loath to do anything that might start it up again, but he had to know. Very slowly and keeping his back pressed firmly into his seat, he leaned toward his right. The scene at the side of his cab inched into view. Blackness was taking the place of falling motes of dust.

There was nothing except empty space to the side of him. And... Bunny leaned farther.

He swallowed. There was nothing beneath him. He was balanced on the edge of a precipice. The heavy machinery that drove the drill of his excavator rested on solid ground behind him. The heavy drill at the front of his machine was supported by nothing at all.

He was in the middle. A slight shift in his comparatively small weight could be all it took to tip the excavator over the edge. Centimeter by breathless centimeter, Bunny returned to an upright position. His head facing forward and his body rigid, his hands groped sightlessly for his safety harness.

How far below did the bottom of the cave lie? It could be tens or hundreds of meters. Would he survive the impact?

His fingers brushed the straps of the harness. Remaining as still as he could, Bunny pulled it over his shoulders, found the central lock, and snapped it closed.

Where was his hat? He couldn't see it from where he sat, and looking for it elsewhere would entail far more moving than he was prepared to do.

"Back again," said Alun. "Are you sure you hit a cave? There's nothing on the survey."

"Yes, I'm sure," hissed Bunny. "I'm damned well looking at it. And if I'm not very lucky, I'm about to become more acquainted with it than I'd like."

"Huh?"

"I'm right on the edge, hanging over it. Get someone over here to get me out."

"Whoa," said Alun. "No kidding! Okay, don't worry. I'm on it. I'll sort something out as fast as I can. Whatever you do, don't move."

"Thanks for the tip," Bunny said between his teeth.

His radio went silent again as Alun left to 'sort something out', whatever the hell that meant. Bunny could do nothing except stare ahead at the darkness that was growing deeper every second as the dust fell away into the expanse of the cave.

The excavator's lights were brilliant, designed for the darkest underground spaces where no daylight ever reached. Now the dust had nearly all dissipated, they shone far ahead.

Bunny began to make out shapes and shadows in the distance. At first, he thought he was seeing the far side of the cave, but as the shapes took form in his view, he became puzzled as to what he was looking at. He hadn't been in many natural caves in his time, but the ones he'd seen first hand had been irregularly shaped. Rocks and tunnels hadn't been uniform in their appearance, they'd been haphazard.

So what was he looking at? He could see spires rising from wide bases and narrowing to slim spikes. He also saw arches and sweeping curves. How had these shapes formed? He'd never heard of any geological formations like these.

The lights from his excavator only gilded the edges of the structures. He couldn't see any detail, so it was hard to estimate their size, but he guessed they were huge—larger than anything he'd seen on Concordia, and he'd seen the Observation Tower, which was the tallest building in the world.

Was he hallucinating? He had hit his head after all, and it still hurt like crazy. Bunny closed his eyes. When he opened them again, the strange structures were still there. He was fairly certain they were real.

Somehow, tens of meters below the surface of Suddene sat a vast underground cavern that contained hundreds, perhaps thousands, of structures. No human had built them, so what had?

CHAPTER NINETEEN

It was with some trepidation Kes unlocked the door of his house. To his relief, Isobel didn't come into the hall, angry at him for arriving home late again. He could hear her in the kitchen. The rest of the house was dark and quiet. Miki was already asleep, of course. Kes felt bad for not having set eyes on his child for the entire day for the second time that week.

He would make it up to her on the weekend. They would all go somewhere together, somewhere remote and beautiful, where he could forget about work and concentrate fully on his family. He'd heard about cabins in the mountains that were available to rent. He would look into it tomorrow and book something.

Bracing himself for the onslaught of Isobel's reaction to his broken promise that he wouldn't be home late, Kes stepped into the kitchen. Isobel was lifting a casserole out of the cooker. She was facing slightly away from him. Her bump seemed to have grown larger overnight.

"Isobel, I'm so sorry. Something astounding happened today. I don't think I can talk to you about it yet, but it was shocking and amazing. I had to go to Oceanside, and I confess I lost track of time. Otherwise I would have comm'd you."

Isobel had turned toward Kes during this speech. "It's okay. You don't have to explain."

Her smile seemed too fixed, too bright.

"Are you sure?"

She nodded. "Come and give me a hug."

Kes wrapped her in his arms and held her tight, though taking care not to squash her bump. "I really am so sorry," he whispered into her ear.

"Please, don't talk about it."

"How are you feeling?" Kes asked as he released her.

"About as you would expect. Late pregnancy is no joke, but I knew what I was getting into after Miki."

"It's a shame we can't have a baby the way they did on the *Nova*, and on Earth too before I left. Pop an embryo in a bag, feed it nutrients for nine months, and then take it out again. Voila!"

Isobel gave him that look she reserved for the moments when he reminisced about things that happened long before she was born: a mixture of boredom and irritation. Kes didn't blame her. He knew he talked about those times more often than he should, given that his wife couldn't relate to anything he said.

"You go and sit down," he said. "I'll bring dinner out."

Isobel took two plates out of the cabinet and cutlery from a drawer before going into the dining room. Kes brought out the hot casserole dish and placed it in the center of the table.

"There's some bread, too," Isobel said. "And wine, if you want it."

"Wine? Are you sure?" Kes asked. "I don't want to make you feel bad that you can't have any."

"I don't mind. Have some, and relax a bit. It sounds like you had a stressful day."

"Not exactly stressful, but weird." Kes returned to the kitchen to fetch the bread and wine. "What can I get you to drink?" he called.

"Shhh! You'll wake Miki."

"Sorry," he whispered. He seemed to be saying sorry a lot. He stuck his head through the dining room doorway. "What would you like to drink?"

"Water is fine."

Kes brought everything through into the dining room. His guilt and anxiety about being late had dissipated and been replaced with elation that Isobel was taking it so well. He was almost jovial as he sat down and opened the wine bottle. Discovering that someone had planted vineyards in the mountain foothills and had been producing wine for decades had been one of the nicer surprises of returning to Concordia fifty years later than he'd expected.

He poured himself half a glass of the ruby liquid. Meanwhile, Isobel was spooning the bean casserole she'd cooked onto her plate.

"I had an idea about something we can do during the weekend," said Kes. "I thought it would be nice to go up into the mountains. Maybe stay there a couple of nights. What do you think?"

"I don't think it'll be safe. I'm too far along. I might go into labor early, and we would be hours from the hospital."

"Yeah, you're right. I was forgetting. But it's something to keep in mind for after the baby's born."

"Hmm, maybe."

Kes asked what Isobel and Miki had done that day, and the conversation moved on through their usual topics of discussion. As was usual, too, Kes found it hard to muster interest in the mundanity of everyday life on Concordia, especially in the light of what had happened that day. He itched to tell Isobel about it, but though Cherry hadn't explicitly told him the arrival of the

Guardian was a secret, he guessed she wanted to keep it under wraps for now.

He loved Isobel and Miki deeply, and he knew he would feel the same about the new baby when she arrived, but he felt trapped. This life wasn't what he'd signed up for. He'd been expecting an adventure, not a cozy existence in suburbia.

"Have some more wine," Isobel said. "Don't hold back just for me."

"If you say so." Kes poured himself another glass. The bottle was now half empty. He hadn't drunk alcohol in a while out of consideration for Isobel, who couldn't enjoy it with him. He felt a little tipsy already after only two glasses.

"Dinner was great," Kes said, and he meant it. He wasn't a natural vegetarian, but Isobel managed to turn plant food into delicious meals that took the edge off his craving for meat. "I'll clear up."

"It can wait," said Isobel. "Leave the dishes for the morning. You must be tired."

"Only a little, but I can do them before I leave for work tomorrow."

Isobel stood up. "I'm tired, even if you aren't. Do you want to go to bed?"

"What, now? It's a bit early, isn't it?"

Isobel shrugged. "It's up to you. I thought maybe we could snuggle, but we can watch a vid or a holo if you want."

"No, snuggling's good," said Kes. "Snuggling's always good." He didn't know how far the snuggling would go, but physical intimacy between them had been predictably diminished due to the pregnancy, and the fights his constant lateness had caused hadn't helped. He would appreciate just holding his wife close for a couple of hours, even if nothing else happened.

Isobel said she wanted to shower, so Kes waited for her in bed. He was very tempted to comm Cherry and ask her what was happening with the Guardian, but he knew that if Isobel heard him discussing work stuff when she came out of the shower her apparently forgiving attitude would be shattered.

Kes removed his ear comm and put it on the bedside table. He didn't know what he'd done to deserve Isobel. The truth was, he didn't deserve her. He entirely understood her viewpoint on his behavior, which made his inability to improve it all the more inexplicable.

The bathroom door opened and Isobel came out wearing a floor-length, dusky pink, satin nightgown with shoestring straps. She'd washed and dried her hair and it hung around her shoulders, thick and lustrous. Kes' mouth dropped open. His wife looked gorgeous bump and all. In fact, it was partly due to her pregnancy. Her abundant hormones had made her skin especially plump, soft, and glowing.

"Sweetheart, you look stunning," said Kes. He was so moved at the sight of his wife that his eyes became moist.

Isobel's eyes were glistening too. She pulled back the covers and climbed into bed. "Hold me, okay?" She turned her back to him and he lay down with her, pressing close to the back of her body, folding one arm over the top of her bump. Their baby stretched in response, pushing hard against Kes' forearm. Kes chuckled and Isobel laughed softly too.

Kes folded his other arm under his head and rested his face in Isobel's hair.

"I love you, you know," Isobel said.

"I know, and I love you too."

Isobel turned over and put her arms on each side of his neck before kissing him full on the lips. Kes pulled her close, and they kissed deeply. He pushed back her hair and kissed her neck. Isobel ran her hands over his back.

Kes stopped what he was doing and pulled back,

making eye contact with his wife. "Is this okay? I mean, you're pretty far along."

"The baby isn't due for another four weeks. I'm sure it's fine."

Kes' heart skipped. It felt too good to be true. Smiling, he moved in close to Isobel again and resumed kissing her neck. His fingers found the strap of her nightgown and slid beneath it, easing it off her shoulder.

Their lovemaking lasted an hour or longer. Certain accommodations had to be made on account of Isobel's bump, but that only made the experience more special and pleasurable. Kes lost track of time. Things hadn't been so good between them for months. He didn't think he'd ever felt so lucky, so blissful.

When it was over, Isobel rested her head on Kes' chest and he sank into a heavy sleep.

When he woke, it was full daylight. He sat up, panicking. What was the time? He'd forgotten to put his ear comm in before falling asleep. He'd missed his alarm. He was going to be late for work.

As he reached for his comm, Kes noticed something else was wrong. Isobel's side of the bed was cold. It wasn't unusual for her to rise before him. Miki often had a nightmare in the early morning and had to be comforted in order to go back to sleep for another couple of hours. But Isobel's side of the bed felt like no one had slept in it all night.

An icy hand clutched his heart.

His breathing sped up.

No!

Suddenly, his wife's behavior the previous evening took on a new meaning.

Like an automaton, Kes climbed out of bed. In four steps he crossed the bedroom to Isobel's closet. The door stood ajar. He pulled it wide. A room holding only a few clothes confronted him. Isobel's packing case was gone.

Clammy with cold sweat, Kes walked toward his daughter's room. Her door was open and her bed was empty.

He stood in the hallway, motionless.

Isobel was gone. She was gone. She'd taken Miki and left him.

Last night had been her goodbye.

He fell to his knees.

CHAPTER TWENTY

Night was falling. Wilder estimated she had another couple of kilometers to go. All the way from Annwn, she'd kept to the side of the road that ran along the floor of the valley to avoid detection. Now the hillside was evening out, which meant she was nearing her journey's end. She could already smell the ocean, though the raised land had prevented her from catching sight of it.

She was dizzy with fatigue. Her medication kept the pain of her injuries and sore muscles at bay but it did nothing for her energy levels, which felt like they were already at zero.

And she wasn't even sure where she was going. It had been a couple of years since she'd been at Tycho and Stephie's house. The last visit had been awkward, and she'd never gone back. They were different people from the adolescents she'd left behind when she'd gone on the mission to the Assembly. It was obvious when she thought about it. They had a lifetime of experience that had changed them, while she was essentially the same person who had invited them to help her build a tree village more than fifty years previously.

But they were the only people whose location she— vaguely—knew. She had other friends, who were mostly people who were also working on a-grav, but she only ever talked with them over comm or very occasionally met up with them at a public location. She had some idea where the a-grav people lived but not the house or even the street.

She also had no comm and so no way to contact any of them. Even if she had a comm the minute she contacted anyone her exact location would show up on the system. If Cherry had instructed the CED to search for her their officers would immediately swoop.

Luckily, she remembered the whereabouts of Tycho and Stephie's home. They lived on the outskirts of Oceanside in one of the newer developments. She wouldn't have to walk right to the top of the cliff and into the town center to reach them. The most recently built housing was closer to sea level and set back from the water.

Or, they *had* lived there. If they'd moved, she was sunk. They were the only people who could help her and who she trusted to not tell anyone where she was.

Cars zoomed past twenty meters to her right. Commuters from the manufacturing site near old Sidhe were returning home for the evening. Wilder had heard that the factories and munitions plants were being relocated to an area closer to Oceanside. The manufacturing site's proximity to Cerberus had made sense in the early days of the colony, when the weapon parts had been transported underground through a tunnel, but Cerberus had long been built. Now the spread of the colony across Lyonesse and then over the ocean to Suddene made the delivery of armaments easier to disguise.

Moving the manufacturing site nearer to Oceanside would cut many Concordians' commuting time while also making the military silo less vulnerable if Cerberus came under attack.

It was all unimportant to Wilder. She loved her forest home and she fully intended to continue living there with Piddle and Puddle, just as soon as she could get Cherry off her back. Her heartstrings tugged at the thought of her little pets. She hoped they were okay. She'd been forced to abandon the idea of quickly visiting her tree home to check on them. It was too far and too risky. Her capacity to walk was severely restricted and she'd realized she had to save her strength for her walk to Oceanside and her only hope of retaining her freedom.

The minute she could manage it, she would return to her home and find Piddle and Puddle.

As she crested the next low hill, several streets of houses were revealed over the rise. In the low light they were shadowy shapes on the gentle slopes. This was it. She'd reached the outskirts of Oceanside.

But the streets didn't look familiar. Perhaps they belonged to a development that had been built since she'd last been there. Tycho and Stephie's house had to be farther in. To reach it she would have to walk along the streets, exposed to other pedestrians and passersby. She probably looked awful and she would attract attention, but that couldn't be helped. She was exhausted and almost beyond caring.

Dragging one foot in front of the other, Wilder made her slow way closer and closer to the residencies. She stepped onto the nearest sidewalk. Kids were playing in the front yards, screaming and laughing, probably dreading the moment their parents would call them in for dinner.

Concordians had continued to reproduce at an incredible rate all the time she'd been gone, and children were everywhere. Wilder didn't dislike them, but she also relished the seclusion of her home, which allowed her to pick and choose when to be in the presence of the loud, chaotic, emotional creatures.

As she shuffled along the street, Wilder watched the kids playing with their brothers and sisters and neighborhood friends. She was a little envious. The children were clearly happy. They had the love and security that came with belonging to a family. That opportunity had arrived too late for her. She'd been born into a life of slavery, entirely absent of her volition, serving the dreams of individuals long dead. That was what it meant to be a Gen, but Wilder didn't think she'd ever really felt the injustice of it until then, when she saw the children who belonged to loving families playing, carefree, in their front yards.

Some of the kids had noticed her and stopped what they were doing in order to stare. Wilder bore their curious gazes stoically. It wasn't like there was anything she could do about it. She certainly couldn't go any faster or change her appearance.

A street corner was coming up. She turned it gratefully. The next road was a larger thoroughfare and a fair amount of traffic passed along it. Wilder guessed it was a branch of the highway from Annwn, which led toward Oceanside's center. She thought she recognized it.

Soon, she approached a familiar street name. This was where Tycho and Stephie hopefully still lived. Neither worked any longer. They'd retired, but they were busy looking after their grandchildren and carrying out volunteer work.

Wilder walked around the corner, wracking her brains for her friends' house number. She couldn't remember it, and all the houses looked the same. By now, she could barely stand, let alone walk. She didn't have the energy to walk up and down the street, trying to figure out which house was the right one. Her legs muscles were shaking and her whole body ached, the pain returning as her medication wore off.

Then she saw it: a small bush of yellow flowers. Wilder recalled Tycho telling her it was one of the few flowering plants on the planet, and quite expensive to buy because the scientists hadn't figured out how to preserve the seed. It was only viable for a few days, after which it wouldn't sprout, no matter what conditions the scientists provided.

Wilder forced her legs to take another few steps. She walked up the pathway to the front door. She couldn't comm Tycho or Stephie to tell them she was there. She raised her hand and knocked.

No one answered.

Wilder raised her hand again, but her arm muscles wouldn't obey her. She only managed to lift her hand halfway before her arm fell limp by her side. She toppled forward, hitting her head on the door, and crumpled to the ground.

Somewhere on the edge of her consciousness, she felt the door open. She was unable to stop herself from falling into the opening.

"What the...?"

"Dad, someone's at the door. She's collapsed."

"Someone's at the door? We aren't expecting anyone else."

"Didn't you hear me? She's collapsed. I think you should call an ambulance."

"Get out of the way so I can see who it is."

Hands grabbed her shoulders.

"Wilder? Honey, it's Wilder!"

This was a voice Wilder recognized. It was Tycho. She'd found the right house.

"No ambulance," Wilder said.

"What? Why?" Tycho asked.

His old face came into Wilder's view.

"You need help," he said. "You're sick."

"I'm not sick, only tired. Please, no ambulance. I'll

explain later."

"Wilder!" Stephie had arrived. "Stars, you look awful! What's wrong with you?"

"She says not to call her an ambulance," Tycho said.

"Oh, but we must," said Stephie. "She looks like she's at death's door."

"No ambulance," Wilder said. "I mean it. I'm in trouble. I need your help."

"You need our...?" Tycho said. Then after a slight pause, he added, to people Wilder couldn't see, "Perhaps you should go home."

"Yeah, perhaps we should. We were on our way out anyway. We'll talk later."

Shadows passed over Wilder. Tycho was already pulling her into the hall. Wilder saw Stephie close the door and turn and face her. "Wilder, whatever has happened to you?"

CHAPTER TWENTY-ONE

How strange it felt to be carried downstairs by two friends who had been teenagers a few years ago, and who were now old people.

"You don't need to do this," said Wilder. "I'm sure I can walk by myself now. I feel better."

"It's no trouble," Tycho replied. He was holding Wilder under her armpits.

"Yes, we don't want you to slip and hurt yourself," said Stephie, who was holding Wilder's knees.

"Besides," added Tycho, "you're as light as a cracker. You were always skinny, but you haven't been eating properly lately, have you? That old habit is going to catch up with you one day."

"Stop nagging," said Wilder. "Can't you see I have enough problems?"

Tycho chuckled. They'd reached the bottom of the stairs and the basement of Tycho and Stephie's home. The old couple had taken Wilder's fear of discovery seriously, and they'd said she could stay in a room they'd had built for their grandchildren. It wasn't particularly secret, but they would put a rug over the trapdoor that led down there, which might foil a cursory search.

Though her responses were flippant, Wilder was deeply grateful that these two old friends, who she hadn't spoken to for years, had immediately agreed to help her without knowing what kind of trouble she was in or who was looking for her.

"Please put me down now," said Wilder.

"If you're sure," said Stephie. She and Tycho placed Wilder on the basement floor. She stood up, though not without difficulty. She was standing in a circular room with a low ceiling. Toys were scattered over the floor.

"This is it," Tycho said. "Our underground shelter for when the Scythians return. It's basic, but it'll do for now. We'll make the sofa up as a bed. The bathroom's through there." He pointed at the only door in the room.

"Let me help you, dear," said Stephie, in that grandmotherly tone that Wilder had never gotten used to. The Stephie she remembered had been twelve years old and had begged to be allowed to join the older kids in the tree village, not a sweet old lady, gray-haired and slightly stooped.

Nevertheless, Wilder didn't refuse Stephie's guiding, supporting arm as she crossed the basement floor in a few steps. She sat on the sofa with relief. Waves of pain were erupting from her ribs and abdomen like lava from a slow eruption. Wilder reached for the medication in her pocket. "Could I have some water? I need to take a pill."

"Sure," said Tycho. "We'll get you some, and some food. Our family was visiting and we have plenty left over."

"I'd like that," said Wilder. She'd eaten all the food she'd taken from Cherry's house and she was ravenous as well as very thirsty. "I can't thank you enough."

"Stop right there," said Stephie. "You don't have to thank us for anything. You gave us a place to stay that allowed us to escape forced living with fake parents, and you traveled light years to the Assembly in order to save the colony. Nothing we can do can repay that. We'll always be in your debt."

"Oh, that's ridiculous..." Wilder began, but Tycho interrupted her.

"Don't argue. Just sit there quietly while we get you some dinner."

Wilder didn't have the strength to argue, so she didn't object. Tycho and Stephie returned to the stairs.

"We won't be long," said Stephie.

It was the last thing Wilder remembered until she felt a hand on her shoulder, gently shaking her. It was Stephie again. Wilder didn't know how much time had passed. She guessed she must have fallen asleep. She'd been sitting on the sofa, but now she found she was lying on her side.

"Please, let us call a doctor for you," said Stephie.

"I've seen a doctor, and I've been discharged."

"You were in hospital?" Tycho asked. He was holding a tray of food and a large glass of water.

"Long story," Wilder replied.

"We have plenty of time," said Stephie.

"I'm sorry, I will tell you. Only I'm too tired."

"That's fine," said Stephie. "We don't need to know. You're welcome to stay with us for as long as you like."

"I just need somewhere until I'm better," Wilder said. And then what? When she was better Cherry would have no reason to hound her. She would be able to return to her tree home, find Piddle and Puddle, and resume normal life, though her relationship with General Cherry would be shattered forever. Wilder would never help out that woman by giving the pulse emitters additional maintenance ever again.

Stephie was holding sheets, a pillow, and a bed cover. She began to make up a bed on the other sofa. Meanwhile, Tycho put down the tray and handed Wilder the glass of water. She popped one of the pain medication tablets into her mouth and swallowed it with a sip of water.

Tycho lifted the tray of food onto her lap. "We're not leaving until you've eaten every scrap. And we both know how you love your alone time, so that's a real threat."

Wilder smiled and began to eat. Some of the food was from the ocean, which wasn't surprising considering the proximity of Tycho and Stephie's home to the sea. Before they retired, they'd both worked on ocean harvesters, which skimmed shallow water for sea plants, algae, and tiny marine creatures.

According to the tales they'd told Wilder of the years of colonization that had passed while she'd been on her mission, Concordians had balked at first at the idea of eating animal life, no matter how small and unintelligent. The colonists who had grown up aboard the *Nova* eating crickets and other animal protein had nearly all died out, and even after the Woken had okayed the consumption of certain Concordian life forms, later generations were unused to the idea of eating non-plant life. They took a supplement instead, in order to protect themselves against the risk of nutritional deficiencies. But after tasting patties made of hundreds of the ocean creatures compressed and fried in oil, many had changed their minds.

Wilder had only tasted the patties once, on a visit to her friends' home, and she had to admit that the slightly salty, slightly crunchy patties were tasty. Though the idea of eating animals still turned her stomach a little, she didn't want to be rude, and she was so famished she would have eaten a sluglimpet if offered.

As well as the still-warm patties, Tycho had made her a plate of sea weed ribbons, roasted hypogeal fungi, and baked sweet potatoes with peanut butter. Ordinarily, she would never be able to eat so much in one sitting. In fact, the food Tycho had piled on her plate seemed more than she would eat in an entire day. But her instinct to consume calories overcame her usual indifference to eating. She picked up a fork, dug it into a chunk of fungi, and lifted it to her mouth.

"Great," said Stephie. "It's good to see you eat."

Wilder barely noted the grandmotherly tones in her hyper focus on her meal.

"I forgot to say," Stephie continued, "you can talk to the Fila while you're here."

This remarkable sentence broke through Wilder's distraction. "What?"

"I'll show you," Tycho said. He uttered a voice command, and half of the circular wall turned transparent. Water lay beyond them, illuminated by gentle lights set into the wall's exterior.

"The grand kids begged for a Fila playroom," said Stephie. "Their parents couldn't afford it. How could we say no?"

Wilder forced down a half-chewed lump of fungi. "Your grand kids play with the Fila?"

"I don't know if they exactly play with them," Tycho said. "But they talk to them, and sometimes the Fila put on an entertaining light display. The kids love it. Keeps them occupied for hours."

"I bet," said Wilder. She used the edge of her fork to cut a patty into quarters before stabbing one section and popping it into her mouth.

"I think they were originally the Fila's idea, weren't they, honey?" Tycho asked.

"I believe so," Stephie replied. "All we had to do was create the basement and send our house's coordinates to the Fila. They do the rest at their end."

"Are you sure it's safe?" asked Wilder, imagining a maze of tunnels among the foundations of the houses.

"The Fila say it is," said Stephie. "I guess they would know. They always try to help us. I don't think they would do anything risky."

Wilder hadn't had much to do with the aquatic aliens since her mission, when she had spent long hours chatting with Quinn, one of the Fila ship's operators. She'd been working with Kes on researching the creatures. Wilder had to agree with Stephie. The Fila wouldn't ever knowingly do anything that might harm a human.

They also exerted a not inconsiderable influence in the colony. The Leader was known to regularly consult with them about colony affairs, even taking advice on subjects that didn't relate directly to the Fila's relationship with humans.

Wilder had an idea. "How do your grand kids talk to them?"

"They open the room comm and chat," said Tycho. "But they have to wait until one happens to come by. There's no way to summon them, but somehow they usually know when the wall is set to transparent and one turns up within a few minutes."

"All this talking must be tiring you out," Stephie said. "We'll leave you alone to finish your meal. Then you'll probably want to rest. I'll come down again later with some night clothes. If you want anything, contact us through the house comm. You can use the interface in the armrest."

"Thanks," Wilder replied. "I am tired and I would love to rest for a while. Thanks for the food too."

"It's our pleasure," said Tycho.

The couple climbed the stairs. Wilder continued to eat. After a few moments, she saw movement from the corner of her eye. She opened the interface and the room comm that would allow her to talk to the tentacled creature. "Hi."

"Hello," the Fila replied, its voice broadcast over a speaker.

"Hello," Wilder replied. "Could you help me with

something? I would like to speak to Quinn."

CHAPTER TWENTY-TWO

Blissful, pain-free ease and comfort blanketed Wilder. Feeling like she was floating on soft, warm clouds, she came slowly to consciousness, not knowing where she was or what had happened to her but also not caring. All she remembered was that she was safe.

Finally, somewhat reluctantly, she opened her eyes. A low ceiling hung over her, and she was lying next to a transparent wall. Tentacles writhed slowly in the water beyond it.

Wilder sat up, causing her stomach muscles to ache dully. How long had she slept? The pain medication was beginning to wear off again, so it had to be around ten to twelve hours. Tycho or Stephie had returned while she'd been asleep and left her more food and water.

A single, very large Fila was floating a couple of meters away from her. She recognized its patterning immediately.

"Quinn?"

"Wilder," the Fila replied. "I didn't notice you had ceased sleeping."

"I only just woke up. How long have you been waiting

there?"

Silence followed Wilder's question, and she realized Quinn was trying to translate Fila time measurement into human terms and failing.

"Never mind," she said. "Thank you for coming to see me. I hope you weren't doing anything important."

"Nothing that couldn't be done by others. It is pleasant to meet with you again."

"It's good to see you too." Wilder hadn't realized it until that moment, but she'd missed Quinn. She'd spent months sitting in the operations room aboard the *Opportunity*, just talking to him and watching him and his fellow crew members, trying to learn all she could about the Fila.

In the years that had passed since returning to Concordia, she hadn't met up with him again. Living in a tree far from the ocean hadn't made it easy, and, as always, she'd been concentrating on her work.

Wilder turned to face the Fila and crossed her legs.

"Is this place your new home?" Quinn asked. "I could come here to visit you. I enjoyed the time we spent together on the journeys to and from the Galactic Assembly."

"I did too!" Wilder exclaimed. She reached out to touch the transparent wall, but the movement hurt her ribs. She winced. "Wait a minute." Wilder found her medication and took a pill with a swallow of water.

"Please, eat more if you're hungry," said Quinn. "I can wait."

"I'm not eating," Wilder replied. "It's medication."

"Medication." Quinn paused as he pondered the word's meaning. Or perhaps he was consulting with other Fila. It had never been clearly established if the Fila had true telepathic ability or their ultra-sensitive tentacles were picking up subtle movements in the water carried across long distances.

"Medication," the Fila repeated. "So you're suffering

from a sickness?"

"Not exactly. I got hurt in an accident. The medication is to take away the pain until I'm better."

"I hope it isn't rude of me to say that your bodies are not very efficient. If I suffer an accident or my body is invaded by pathological microorganisms, I only have to sever the affected part and regrow it."

"I have to admit, your method is way more efficient. But what happens if you're injured or infected all over? You can't sever all of you."

"It is very rare for that to happen, but when it does we simply die. We don't have medication. Humans have the advantage in that area."

"Quinn," said Wilder, sparked by the conversation to ask a question that hadn't occurred to her during the entire trip to the Assembly, "how long do Fila live?"

"That's difficult to answer."

Realizing she'd hit upon the time measurement translation problem again, Wilder re-framed the question. "When do you die? Is it after you have children, or do you live on for a long time after that?" Wilder was more interested in physics and engineering than biology, but she recalled Kes telling her that humans were unusual in Earth species in that they were one of the few whose females lived on for decades after they could no longer bear children.

Though Quinn was male, Wilder hoped her question would provide relevant information.

"Aside from the circumstances of disease or accident, Fila do not die," Quinn replied.

"What, never?" asked Wilder, flabbergasted. "Don't you grow old?"

"We do not. This is another big difference between our species, and between humans and other intelligent galactic species. Humans are very short-lived. I was surprised and saddened when I returned to Concordia and discovered that Ethan had died not long after our arrival."

"Wow, yes. That must have been a shock."

"It was a shock. If I had known that taking you all to the Assembly space station would separate you from the people you knew when you left, I would have warned you."

"It's okay," Wilder said. "You didn't know, and we've gotten used to it, I guess."

"Is your medication working?" asked Quinn. "Is your pain reducing?"

"Hmm." When Wilder thought about it, she realized the pain that had threatened to return had been beaten back again. "Yes, it is."

"What was your accident?"

"Oh..." Wilder was about to give the same response as she had to Tycho and Stephie—that it was a long story—but she hesitated. Quinn might not understand the underlying meaning that she didn't want to talk about it, but not only that. She *did* want to talk about it and unburden herself of her traumatic experience and Cherry's later outrageous behavior toward her.

Wilder had never had a family to confide in. The closest thing to that had been Ben, and he'd died years ago. For some reason, she felt close to Quinn too, despite him being not only not family, but another species.

She told him everything that had happened, leaving nothing out. It took her so long that she paused for a moment to pick up her tray and begin eating breakfast while she talked. Quinn listened without responding, only slowly swirling his tentacles in the water.

As Wilder finished explaining how she had walked from Annwn to Oceanside over the course of a day in order to hide at her friends' home, she heard the basement door open. Footsteps sounded on the upper stairs, and Tycho came into view.

"I heard you talking," he said. "I'm glad to see you

were speaking to someone and not chattering to yourself. I would wonder if everything you told me had been words of madness." He reached the bottom of the stairs and held out his hand, palm upward. "Brought you a little something." He was holding an ear comm. "It's new. Fresh from the factory."

"Thanks," Wilder said. "But I don't think I can use it. The minute I access the network, anyone looking for me will know exactly where I am."

"Are you really in that much trouble?" asked Tycho. "I know you like to do your own thing, regardless of what the authorities might say, but I'm sure you didn't do anything harmful."

"I didn't do anything harmful," Wilder replied. "All I want is for people to leave me alone so I can do my work. Apparently that's too much to ask." In response to Tycho's continued apparent puzzlement, she added, "I got on the wrong side of someone high up. Someone who I thought was a friend."

"May I suggest something?" Quinn asked. "After listening to your story, I believe this is one of those situations where both sides would benefit from spending some time apart."

"You got that right," Wilder said.

"As you know, I am familiar with the person you fear wants to confine you against your will. Admittedly I'm not as familiar with human behavior as I would like, but among my kind I am considered an expert. You feel forced to hide away in order to escape this person's efforts to find you."

"I *am* forced to hide."

"For how much longer?" Quinn asked. "And is this person in danger of retribution if he's discovered to be hiding you?"

"Honestly, I don't know. She seemed pretty mad and she has the power to do whatever she wants, as she pointed out to me. I don't know what's gone wrong with her. Sorry for dragging you and Stephie into this, Tycho."

"Don't worry about it. I guess I know who you mean now. I'm not frightened of what she might do to us. Me and Stephie are only a pair of old folks. We aren't worth throwing in prison."

"Nevertheless," Quinn said, "I have a solution that would allow Wilder to remain safe while she heals and the only person who would be in danger of suffering from repercussions as her accomplice would be myself."

"If you're about to suggest what I'm thinking," Wilder said, "I'm sorry, but I really don't fancy spending a couple of weeks in one of those underwater tanks you guys kept the old Leader in."

"I wasn't about to suggest that. Confining Ethan and the other man and his daughter was a great mistake that we deeply regret, and for which we have been trying to atone."

"Wait," said Wilder, "is that why the Fila have done so much to help us over all these years?"

"One of the reasons, yes. But we would help you anyway. We would prefer the galaxy to be a peaceful home to intelligent life. We try to support non-aggressive intelligent species."

Quinn had clearly never seen Cherry in a temper. Wilder asked, "So if you don't want to put me in an underwater tank, where are you suggesting I go?"

"To the *Opportunity*. I could arrange a shuttle to take you up to it."

"The *Opportunity*?!" The starship the Fila had built for the colony had been in orbit around Concordia for years. Wilder hadn't ever hankered to return to the ship, not after spending several months living within its cramped quarters with nothing to eat except the Guardians' ration bars. Though she hated her current predicament, hiding aboard the *Opportunity* to evade Cherry seemed like overkill.

"You could continue your work with anti-gravity while aboard the ship, too," Quinn added, "in relative safety." Wilder had complained at considerable length that Cherry and Kes had allowed her a-grav machine to escape.

She gasped. "You're right!" In its orbital position, the *Opportunity* only experienced micro gravity. If she managed to hit upon the right formulation again, the effects on the machine would be noticeable but minor. She would have plenty of time to turn it off, and even if she was slow to deactivate it, the machine wouldn't exert enough force to damage the ship.

The more Wilder thought about Quinn's suggestion, the more she liked it. Aboard the *Opportunity* she would be in absolutely no danger of anyone disturbing her. She could work for as long as she wanted in peace and quiet. It sounded like bliss.

There was only one impediment to the plan. "Quinn, I accept your proposal, with one caveat. I want to try to go home and collect a few clothes and other things I'll need, and I have a couple of very small companions I'd like to take along with me."

CHAPTER TWENTY-THREE

It was all decided. Tycho would go with Wilder by autovan to a friend's house where she could pick up spare parts to build another experimental prototype a-grav machine. Then they would go on to Wilder's tree house, which Tycho would check wasn't being watched before she went in to collect Piddle and Puddle. Quinn would arrange two shuttles to land nearby—one to transport Wilder and her pets, and the other to carry the a-grav machine parts and other supplies.

Tycho estimated it would take them most of a day to accomplish everything Wilder needed to do before leaving to board the *Opportunity*. Quinn said he could have the shuttles in place by late afternoon. Stephie objected to the entire plan.

"I'm sure you'll be perfectly safe here," she said when she came down into the basement to see what was taking Tycho so long. "No one knows you're here."

"Except for the kids and the grand kids," Tycho said.

"Yes, but they wouldn't say anything to anyone."

"Are you sure?" asked Tycho. "Little Bobby's only five. Do you think it's safe to trust a five-year-old to never mention someone collapsing at the front door to his grandparents' house?"

"Well, what if he does? Who pays any attention a five-year-old's prattling?"

"Stephie," Wilder said, "I know you're worried about me, but I do think this is the best option. Besides, I'm dying to get back to work on the a-grav machine. The fact that I think I'm millimeters away from a solution is driving me nuts. If I have to wait until I'm better and Cherry has no more excuses for locking me up, I think I might go crazy."

Stephie's expression of doubt and concern remained.

Suddenly, Wilder chuckled.

"I don't see what's so funny," said Stephie in an offended tone. "I care about you, Wilder. I don't want you to come to any harm. When you're up in that starship, you'll be all alone. What if you take a turn for the worse and no one's there to look after you?"

"Wilder won't be alone," said Quinn. "A minimal crew remains aboard the *Opportunity* at all times. I've decided that I will board the ship, too, as a crew member."

"You're going to be with me?" Wilder asked. "Fantastic!"

"But a Fila can't help you if you have a medical emergency," Stephie said.

"My medical emergency is over. All I need is time to rest and recuperate. A couple of weeks aboard the Opportunity will give me that and more besides. I understand your concerns, Stephie, and I'm sorry for laughing just now. It was only that I was reminded of when you were twelve and begging to be allowed to come and live in my tree village. Now our roles are reversed."

Wilder was actually being kind in consideration of Stephie's feelings. She was adamant she would take up Quinn's offer, whether Stephie agreed to it or not.

Stephie looked downward. "Gosh, you're right. I was forgetting. I changed my mind. You didn't stand in my way then and I won't stand in your way now. I'm sorry. It's only that I'm nearly fifty years older than you and I feel like I should mother you."

"Don't worry about it," Wilder said. "I made it this far without a mother. I reckon I can make it a little farther."

"Let's prepare some food supplies for Wilder to take with her," Tycho said, and the older couple climbed the stairs out of the basement.

"That was an interesting interaction, if you don't mind me saying," Quinn said.

"It was? Why's that?" asked Wilder.

"I rarely visit the homes of humans in these underground rooms as other Fila do, but on the few occasions I've witnessed your behavior and listened to your conversations, I find it remarkable how deeply emotionally connected you are to those who are genetically related to you. When I say 'you' I don't mean you in particular, but humans in general."

"That's a correct observation," Wilder said. "Human families are emotionally close. The bonds between parents and children are strong. Isn't it like that with the Fila?" Wilder realized she'd never asked Quinn about his family in all the time she'd spent talking to him aboard the *Opportunity*, probably because families didn't mean a lot to her.

"It is not at all like that with the Fila. I have thousands of offspring and I don't know who they are or where they are. I spawned aboard the seeding ship while it was on its way to Concordia. Perhaps some of my children were deposited on this planet or perhaps they journeyed onward to a new world."

"Huh," Wilder said. "I was 'spawned' aboard the *Nova*, and I have no idea who my mother and father were or if I have any brothers and sisters. I guess I'm a little bit like a Fila."

"I guess you are," said Quinn.

***

Tycho checked that the street was empty before giving Wilder the signal that it was safe to leave. She walked quickly down the path to the sidewalk and then climbed into the seat of the autovan. Tycho and Stephie had already packed plenty of food and other supplies in the back.

As Tycho started the engine and input the destination, the autovan pulled away from the curb. Wilder gave Stephie a wave. The older woman waved back before smiling and giving a thumbs up. Wilder was glad they hadn't parted on bad terms. She'd already lost the friendship of one person who she'd thought cared about her, she didn't want to lose another.

Wilder wondered if she should be wearing a low-brimmed hat to conceal her identity while she and Tycho were driving around. She didn't know what lengths Cherry might go to in order to capture her. She gave a slight shake of her head. The entire situation was ridiculous. Over the years she'd done a few borderline illegal things that she probably could have been arrested for, but wanting her liberty while she was recuperating from an accident wasn't one of them.

It was late morning in Oceanside. The rush hour was over and the streets were reasonably quiet. It had only been a year or two since Wilder had been there, but in that time the place had noticeably changed. The town had grown in more areas than the one Wilder had encountered when she'd walked into the place the previous day. New developments were going up everywhere—not only residencies, but shops, offices, services, and small manufacturing plants too. The colony was expanding at a rapid rate.

"How many grandchildren do you have now?" Wilder asked Tycho.

"If you count the one on the way, seventeen."

"Seventeen!" Wilder exclaimed.

"Five children, and they've all had two or three kids of their own. It happens faster than you realize."

"And I suppose all your children could go on to have more kids."

"I'm sure they will. And my family isn't unusual by any means. I have friends who are younger than me and have more grandchildren."

Wilder gave a low whistle. Then she noticed they were drawing near their first stop. She sat upright and peered through the van's window. She was very curious to meet the person they were going to see.

The network of people working on a-grav rarely met and when they did it was only in twos or threes, just in case they were arrested. Wilder had never met the person who had offered to give her the spare machine parts. She only knew him by his code name of Jamie Bond. When she'd heard the name she'd thought it was his real name, but he'd once explained that it was the name of a famous spy in Earth history.

Wilder had thought the name was very boring and it was no wonder that Jamie Bond's story had been lost to obscurity.

But what did the real person look like? During their comms on the secret network, Wilder had been impressed with his insightful comments and quirky sense of humor. She'd formed a mental image of a man in his late twenties, highly intelligent and probably quite handsome too. In her most candid moments, she admitted to herself she'd developed a bit of a crush on him.

The autovan had reached its destination. It parked itself outside a one-story home that looked as though it had only just been built.

"It's so small," said Wilder.

"Not necessarily," Tycho replied. "This is one of the

new designs. We're only seeing the upper story. The rest of the structure is below ground."

"To talk to the Fila?" Wilder asked.

"To talk to the Fila. I haven't been inside one yet but I've seen the plans. These places contain two or more floors where the Fila have access to come and visit."

"Two or more floors just to speak to them? That seems excessive."

"At our place it's only really our grandchildren who interact with the Fila, but many adults are getting into the habit too."

"Wow," Wilder said. "We'll be hearing about the first human and Fila marriage next."

"I wouldn't be surprised."

"I wonder what their kids will look like."

The front door of the dwelling opened and a boy who looked about twelve years old came out. He trotted up to the van's window, which Tycho lowered.

"Are you Deadly After Midnight?" the boy asked him.

Wilder's stomach sank in disappointment. "No, that's me. I take it you're Jamie Bond?"

The boy's eyes widened. "I thought you were a man."

"I thought you were different too. Do you have the stuff?"

"I do. But I'll need a hand bringing it all out."

"I can do that," said Tycho. "You wait here, W—I mean, Deadly After Midnight." He seemed to be stifling a smile as he opened the door and climbed out of the van.

"Shouldn't you be in school?" Wilder asked Jamie Bond.

He grinned. "Probably. I'll be back in a minute."

It took Jamie Bond and Tycho three trips to carry all of the parts Wilder needed from the house to the van. When everything was safely stowed, Tycho climbed into his seat.

"Thanks a lot," Wilder said to Jamie Bond, sincerely.

She'd quickly gotten over her letdown over the boy's true identity and her feelings had altered to admiration. She assumed his parents didn't know he was working on a-grav. Hiding the truth from them would take plenty of smart thinking.

"It's no problem," Jamie Bond replied. "Good luck with whatever it is you're doing."

The temptation to tell him about her breakthrough was huge. The only thing Wilder liked more than working on interesting stuff was talking about what she was working on, and she was very proud to be the first person in the underground group to have achieved success. But she couldn't afford the delay. She had to collect Piddle and Puddle and meet the shuttles Quinn was arranging.

"Thanks," Wilder said. "You too. I'm going to be off network for a couple of weeks. Could you tell the others? Then I hope to have something very important to announce."

"Not if I get there first," said Jamie Bond.

The autovan drove away from the low home. The first part of Wilder's preparations for leaving Concordia for a while was over. Now all she needed was her two small friends.

***

After leaving the highway outside Annwn, it was a twenty-minute drive to the remaining patch of forest that had once covered Sidhe and kilometers around. The road to Cerberus was well paved, but the offshoot that ran to the forest was falling into disrepair. No one except Wilder had lived out that way for years.

Autocars, and the autovan Wilder and Tycho were using to take her home, had no function for avoiding potholes, perhaps because they were rare in the rest of Concordia. The vehicle hit the holes at full speed, jerking Wilder in her seat and making her teeth judder.

She was studying the view closely, looking for signs

of Marines or military transports Cherry might have sent out to pick her up, but the surrounding landscape was empty of human life. Low scrub land was growing taller and rougher, and in the distance the darker green of the forest was growing larger.

"You know, there's still time to change your mind," said Tycho. "We can turn around and go back to Oceanside. Stephie and I would be happy for you to stay with us for as long as you like."

"I know, and I appreciate it," Wilder replied. "But now that I've had time to think about it, I'm really looking forward to this vacation on the *Opportunity*. I know it must seem weird, but the idea of spending days and weeks utterly alone is blissful to me."

"No, you don't sound weird. I understand, and don't forget I've known you a long time. And I have to say, you haven't changed."

After they'd driven another couple of minutes, Tycho said, "How are we going to play this? I don't see anyone lurking around to catch you. Where do you want to park?"

Wilder had already given some thought to the question. "If someone's already watching us from the cover of the forest, there isn't a lot we can do about it. I'm going to have to go in alone, keeping my ears and eyes open. I know that place like the back of my hand. I should be able to spot anything suspicious right away. If I spot an ambush in the making, I'll skedaddle and come running back to you. Hopefully, I'll make it before they catch me."

"No way," said Tycho. "I'm coming in there with you. I'm not going to let you take the risk alone. You're just a girl."

Wilder cocked an eyebrow at him. "I might be *just a girl*, but you're an old man, my friend. I'd beat you in a race any day."

"Hmpf." Tycho folded his arms. "Not in your current

state, you wouldn't."

"Let's not argue about it, okay?" said Wilder. "I know the forest much better than you. The part I live in, at least."

"I have to admit you're right on that score," Tycho said. "It was a sad day when we left the tree village. The trees were all dying by then, so there was no point in staying. In another few weeks we would have had nowhere to live. But it was sad all the same. That was where Stephie and I grew up, fell in love, and got married. It was while we were working on Cerberus. It was a hard time in some ways, especially after we realized you might not be coming back for a very long time, if ever. But we built many happy memories there. And now it's all gone."

"Thanks to the Scythians," said Wilder.

"Thanks to the Scythians. If it weren't for them there would have been no Sidhe. There would have been no Cerberus nor any of the other *secret* military bases. The trees wouldn't have died. Concordia would have been a different place."

"There's no point in mourning over might have beens," Wilder said. "Look, we're nearly there. Tell the car to stop near that tree that overhangs the road. After I get out, turn it around so it's ready to drive the way we came. The track pretty much peters out in another couple of hundred meters."

The autocar stopped in the shade of the tree Wilder had indicated. It was around the spot where Quinn would be landing the shuttles, but they hadn't arrived yet. It was mid afternoon. Wilder estimated she had another hour or so before the shuttles were due to arrive. It was plenty of time to pick up Piddle and Puddle, providing she didn't meet any obstacles.

A few moments later, she was stepping carefully and quietly through the undergrowth, heading toward her home. She was taking a circuitous route, approaching her tree from a different direction than her usual one, hoping this might give her an advantage if Cherry had stationed anyone there.

Though she'd only been away four nights, it felt like much longer. The forest felt fresh, new, and foreign, as if she were visiting it for the first time. The sensations she experienced were acute: the cool, moist air on her skin and in her lungs, the scent of damp, rotting organic matter, and the dappled, shifting sunlight slanting through the canopy.

Yet she also knew exactly where she was and where she was going. Nothing looked unfamiliar, out of place, or disturbed. Perhaps Cherry had decided to leave her alone after all. But Wilder wasn't going to take any chances.

She crept closer to her tree.

CHAPTER TWENTY-FOUR

"I'm sorry for threatening to call the CED," said Cherry as her autocar neared her home. "I'm sorry I overreacted. And I would never have you forcibly sedated." She gave a shudder and put her hand over her eyes. What the hell had she been thinking?

When she'd heard the Guardians had sedated Aubriot, she'd been outraged. Even though the man was an asshole, even though if she'd been forced to choose someone to be sedated, it would have been him, she'd been incensed. She couldn't believe the gall of the creatures, their arrogance in deciding to deprive someone of their consciousness.

And then she'd gone and threatened to do the same thing to Wilder. Would the girl ever forgive her? Probably not, and she wouldn't blame her. In Wilder's shoes, she certainly would never forgive anyone who threatened to do that to *her*.

It was easy enough to tell herself she'd done it out of concern for her young friend, who was hurt and vulnerable. But depriving someone who was entirely sane of their freedom *for their own good* made no sense at all.

Were her constant worries and fears over the safety of the colony getting to her? Ever since Aubriot had resigned she'd felt her responsibilities weighing even more heavily on her shoulders. He'd been the only one who had taken the threat to the colony seriously, but even he had lost interest and commitment. Even Meredith was putting politics before planetary security.

Cherry's car stopped. She was home already. Her rehearsed speech entirely disappeared from her mind. It didn't matter. She would just tell Wilder exactly what she thought, offer her a deep apology, and express the wish that Wilder would remain living with her until she was better. But if she wanted to leave she could and no one would stop her.

Cherry got out of her car and paused a moment before going into her house. The street was dark, like the rest of Annwn that time of night. Solar-powered lights in the sidewalk would turn on to guide approaching pedestrians, but they were the only source of light. The windows in the houses in the little dead-end road gave out no rays. Either their occupants were not home or they had made the windows opaque.

It was something, Cherry admitted to herself. In all the settlements in Concordia everyone followed the same rule: no visible lights at night. The autocars did not carry headlights as the ones on Earth had done. They did not need them in order to navigate. The cars only carried small side lights to warn pedestrians of their presence and avoid accidents. The cars could stop or swerve to avoid people in the road except at very short distances.

Cherry walked up the path to her small home. It was quite late. Finishing up at the hospital and visiting Meredith had taken more time than she would have liked. She hoped Wilder had made herself plenty to eat. Maybe she was asleep already. If she was, Cherry wouldn't wake her. She could apologize to her in the morning.

She opened the security panel and touched it. The door unlocked and opened.

As soon as Cherry stepped into her home, she felt something was wrong. She felt air move over her. That was it. She always kept her windows closed whenever she was out.

Had Wilder opened a window?

Unease settling over her, Cherry tried to guess the source of the breeze. It seemed to be coming from the door to her kitchen.

"Wilder?" Cherry called softly, not wanting to wake the girl if she was asleep.

The kitchen door was half open. Cherry opened it the rest of the way and stepped into the dark room. The motion-responsive light turned on. The window above the sanitizer was open. Immediately, night creatures began flying in, drawn by the light. Cherry reached over the sanitizer and pulled the window closed.

Her stomach sank. A scenario was building in her head. In her mind, she saw Wilder come downstairs and try to open the door. The door locks only responded to Cherry's touch. The security devices were an experimental design that read the unique mixtures of chemicals on the surface of her skin. She'd been trying them out on an informal basis for the military technology division. The doors would not have opened for Wilder.

Not to be foiled in her escape attempt, Cherry's young friend had gone through the kitchen window instead. Cherry looked through the closed window into her yard. It was impossible to see anything in the blackness and the window's reflection of the indoor light, but Cherry knew it was empty anyway.

Her heart heavy, she checked the kitchen for Wilder's pain medication. It was gone. Some food seemed to have been taken too. Cherry didn't mind in the slightest. She wished her friend had taken more.

By the time she climbed the stairs and went into the spare bedroom, she had no expectation of finding Wilder sleeping peacefully in her bed. There was no sign of the girl, of course. Dolefully, Cherry sat down on the empty bed. Where had Wilder gone? Was she okay? She was still far from well, and she had no comm. Cherry had requested a new one for her but it hadn't arrived yet.

Had she returned to her tree house? Cherry called the CED and introduced herself to the operating sergeant.

"Good evening, ma'am. How can I help you?"

"I'd like you to send someone to..."

After a pause the sergeant said, "Yes, ma'am?"

"No, it's okay. Never mind."

"Are you sure, ma'am?"

"Yes. Sorry to bother you." Cherry closed the comm. Wilder's home had no address and even if it had, sending over a CED officer to find her tree house and check on her would only add fuel to the fire. Cherry also couldn't go over there herself. She would be the last person in all of Concordia Wilder would want to see.

Cherry had another idea. She comm'd Kes. Wilder might also be angry at him for allowing the a-grav machine to escape, but he hadn't entirely betrayed her trust. Wilder might be prepared to talk to him.

But Kes didn't answer the comm.

Cherry wondered what to do. She hated the thought of Wilder, injured and angry, trying to get home, perhaps fearing that the CED or even the military were looking for her.

A comm arrived.

"What?" Cherry barked.

"Uh, something's happened at the Chimera excavation site, ma'am."

"Something's happened? What kind of statement is

that? Who am I speaking to?" In her preoccupation with Wilder, Cherry had missed the caller's ID.

"Colonel Fletcher, ma'am."

It was the officer she'd met at Cerberus. "Please be more exact in your language, Colonel, or we could be here all night."

"There's been an accident at the Chimera excavation site."

"Right. Was anyone seriously hurt? Is the project delayed?"

"No, and...I don't think so. Or—"

"So why are you comming me?" Cherry was fighting to keep her anger from spilling over into her tone. She wasn't having much success.

"Ma'am, if you would give me a moment to explain..."

Cherry rubbed her temples. "Go ahead, Fletcher. You have my undivided attention."

"I only just received the news, but apparently the incident happened about an hour and a half ago. One of the excavators was working at the edge of the site, removing bedrock, when he broke through into a massive underground chamber. His machine nearly fell into it, but the other workers managed to get a few lines fixed to the excavator and they pulled it back from the brink. He's okay."

Cherry bit her tongue as she waited for the non-story to come to an end. Caves might be interesting to some people, but she had more important things on her mind.

"Ma'am, the cavern he broke in to, from the recording the supervisor has sent, it looks like an underground city."

"Huh?" Now Fletcher had Cherry's full attention. "A city? Are you sure?"

"I'm positive, ma'am. I have no idea what it means, but I thought you should know about it. Should I send you the vid?"

"Yes, please do," said Cherry. She had an idea what

the discovery was, but she didn't want to jump to any conclusions. On the other hand, if there really was a city beneath the desert in Suddene, there was no doubt in her mind about who had built it. "Colonel, about the man who broke through into the chamber, are you sure he's okay? He didn't suffer any breathing difficulties?"

"I'm not sure about that, to be honest. All I know is his supervisor told me they got him out and he seemed fine."

"Tell them to take him to a medical facility immediately for a full checkup, especially his lungs, okay? I don't think there's a hospital on Suddene yet, but there must be some kind of health center there. And tell the supervisor to evacuate the entire excavation site and seal the entrances." Cherry didn't know anything about the atmosphere the Scythians breathed before screwing up their planet's ecosystem. She didn't know if the gases that might remain in the city could be poisonous to humans, but it wouldn't hurt to be cautious. "Oh, and tell the supervisor to remind his workers about the secrecy clause in their contracts. I don't want a single word of this to get out."

"Yes, ma'am. Can I ask...Do you have an idea what this place might be?"

"Anything you have the clearance to know about, you'll find out in due course."

"Yes, ma'am. I'll pass on the message. I've sent the vid."

"Good. Thank you for passing on this information so promptly, Fletcher. It could turn out to be extremely important."

"Just doing my job, ma'am."

Cherry closed the comm. She needed to speak to Meredith, but she would watch the vid first and check that Fletcher wasn't seeing things that weren't there. But she doubted it. He seemed to be an intelligent, rational man.

After informing Meredith, she would travel to Suddene and see this 'city' for herself. If it really was what she thought it was, the place might yield a huge amount of information about the Scythians, potentially useful information that would help Concordia repel them if they attacked.

She also had to address the problem of the Guardian, Faina, if that was what it was. She hadn't given up on getting the thing destroyed. At least for the moment it was safely secured in the Oceanside prison.

Cherry stood up in order to go to the tabletop interface in the room. As she rose to her feet, she remembered Wilder. She'd temporarily forgotten about the girl and the plight she'd forced her into. She sat down again. *Shit!* What a time for this to happen.

But could she help Wilder now anyway? What was done was done, and Cherry couldn't take her words back. She decided to comm Kes and tell him everything that had happened. Perhaps he could help Wilder. It would be an imposition when he was already busy with his work, but he really cared about the girl and he would want to help her.

Cherry comm'd him again. Again, Kes didn't answer. She left him a message as she went to her interface, then opened the vid Fletcher had sent. All she could do now was to hope Wilder didn't come to any harm.

CHAPTER TWENTY-FIVE

Cherry had to wake up a pilot to fly her to Suddene. She waited for him impatiently on the roof of a government building. It was past one in the morning, and a cold wind had risen. Cherry waited in the dark silence, hugging herself with her one arm to try to keep warm. She hadn't even thought to put on a jacket before leaving home.

While she waited for the pilot to arrive, she pulled out her interface from her bag to watch the recording of the underground city again. The clarity of the vid wasn't great. Low light conditions and the basic interface recorder the supervisor had used meant that the images were often fuzzy and too dark to make out clearly. But even on her very first viewing, Cherry had been forced to agree with Fletcher's assessment: the excavator had broken through into a vast subterranean metropolis. No geological formations could resemble the curved, towering edifices and detailed, regular constructions.

The city hadn't been built by humans. It looked nothing like the streets and houses of Oceanside. But it had been built. And the shapes Cherry saw struck a pang of fear in her guts. They were reminiscent of the curved, pointed Scythian ships.

Cherry's comm received a request from the pilot, whose name was Zapata. "Yes?" Cherry said. "Where are you? I've been waiting fifteen minutes."

"I'm here, ma'am," Zapata replied. "I'm downstairs. I can't get in."

"Yes, you can. Go to the panel. I've input your profile to the system." The building was locked up with only autonomous security protecting it from unauthorized entry. It was a situation that had surprised her, and one that she intended to rectify at the earliest opportunity. She would explain to Meredith that all government buildings required human security guards round the clock.

Cherry's clearance overrode all military and governmental security systems on Concordia. She could even walk right inside the Leader's Residence. So she had simply entered the building and gone up to the roof. But of course the pilot couldn't do the same.

Eventually, Zapata stood next to Cherry and the heli. He was a bulky man and not at all how Cherry had imagined a pilot who flew the small aircraft and even smaller helis would be.

"We're flying to Suddene?" he asked.

"Yes. Is that going to be a problem?"

The large, bearded man looked up into the starless sky and wet a finger to feel the breeze. "Feels like rain's coming, and I don't like the wind speed. But I'll give it a try."

"Good," said Cherry. "Let's go."

The heli was already straining against its docking clamps, the light blades lifting in the wind. Cherry had to hold on tight to the door frame in order to climb into the passenger seat. Zapata's weight soon settled the craft, however, as he entered on the other side. Cherry put on the ear mufflers and fastened her harness.

"What are the coordinates?" Zapata asked through the comm as he started up the engine.

"I'll input them," said Cherry. "Just get us into the air."

There was no need for the pilot to know Chimera's location. As soon as the trip was over Cherry would wipe the trip from the heli's log and tell Zapata to forget where they had gone. She tapped the numbers into the console.

The heli's rotor was already spinning. Zapata released the docking clamps, and immediately the machine swept upward at an angle, pushed sideways by the wind. Zapata gripped the controls, forcing the heli to turn. It banked sharply, caught by a sudden gust. Cherry reached out to brace herself against the window as the heli almost turned on its side.

"Windier than I thought," Zapata said.

"Are you sure you can make it?" asked Cherry. She wanted to go to Suddene, but she also wanted to arrive there.

"I'll try," said Zapata. "I'll have to fly on manual the whole way. The autopilot won't cope with this wind. We'll end up in the drink. If conditions seem like they're getting worse, I'll turn back. Is that a deal, General?"

"It's a deal."

Zapata was bringing the heli around in a circle as he rose higher, turning it to face the coast. The night was hellish black, and as the ground dropped beneath them, Cherry lost sight of any signs of civilization. The blackout rule seemed to be working, for all the good it might do when they came under attack.

When, not if. Others might not believe it, but there was no doubt in Cherry's mind that the Scythians would be back, and when they didn't receive their tribute, Concordia would be required to defend itself.

At least they now knew the secret of the Scythian spiders. Cherry had learned that, even before the building of Cerberus, Ethan had put defenses in place that would prevent the spiders from entering any constructed Concordian area unless dropped exactly onto it from above. If that happened, every Concordian knew how to defend himself or herself.

Or did they? Cherry made a mental note to check that the drill was still being taught in schools. The way things were going it wouldn't surprise her if it had been dropped from the curriculum.

The ETA was three hours away, according to the console display. Still worried about Wilder, Cherry tried to comm Kes again, but she didn't expect an answer and got none. He must have taken out his ear comm for the night.

Next, she sent the recordings of the Scythian city to Meredith. She'd held off on sending them until the Leader would most likely be asleep and wouldn't see them until she awoke. Cherry didn't mark the file as a priority. It was a sneaky, underhand move, but the more Cherry had thought about the situation, the more reluctant she'd been to allow Meredith to dictate what should happen in the situation.

Since their discussion about the Guardian, Cherry had lost faith in the Leader's ability to do the right thing. What if Meredith ordered the site to be closed off due to safety concerns? There might be a crucial clue to the Scythians lying somewhere in the abandoned city that would never be found.

Cherry couldn't allow that to happen. She wouldn't allow that to happen. And so she'd taken it upon herself to try to prevent it from happening by accessing the site before Meredith even woke up. It was a risky move. Meredith might demand her resignation, but Cherry had to do whatever she could to protect Concordia.

***

The sun was tinting the horizon of Suddene's desert as the heli neared Chimera's construction site. All there was to identify the place was a handful of monster trucks and a large hole in the ground.

"Taking her down," Zapata said.

He'd flown the heli well in bad conditions. A head wind had wrestled them all the way across the ocean, adding another half an hour to their flight duration. Buffeted by unpredictable gusts, Zapata had managed the light craft with skill. He hadn't spoken much, but Cherry had seen his lips thinning with tense concentration several times.

She guessed she was lucky they hadn't ended up 'in the drink'.

Just as she was finally relaxing and thanking the stars the journey was over, the wind gave them one last parting blow, whipping the heli upward when they weren't far from the ground.

For the first time, Zapata cursed. Cherry admired his restraint.

He brought the craft downward again.

"No restraints," he said, nodding toward the ground. "She'll blow away as soon as I get out, maybe even before. You'll have to jump. I'll take off and try to land her near the coast. I heard there's a heli pad at the port."

"Okay," said Cherry. "Tell me when." She prepared to slide open the door.

The heli was fifteen or so meters above the ground and dropping fast. Zapata did something to slow their descent.

"Five, four, three," Zapata said. The wind-blown, gray desert sand was rushing up at Cherry at a dizzying pace, despite Zapata's efforts. "Two...one. Go!"

Cherry tore open the door and leapt out. She hit the sand, which felt surprisingly hard for sand. She managed to roll to lessen the impact, but the breath was knocked out of her all the same. As she came to a stop she craned her neck to look upward and saw the heli rising, though its flight was erratic. The strong wind blew into the cabin through the door she'd opened, creating even more problems for Zapata as he tried to control the craft.

Panting, she rose to her feet, watching the heli. It flew higher, catching the rays of as-yet invisible sun. Its flight evened out. Cherry guessed Zapata had managed to close the door. The craft banked, and Zapata flew away in the direction of the coast.

"Have fun," came Zapata's voice over her comm.

Releasing a held breath, Cherry brushed the sand from her pants. A man was walking toward her from the trucks parked fifty meters away. It had to be the site supervisor.

Now was Cherry's chance to see this secret city. If she was unlucky, she probably only had a couple of hours before Meredith found out what she was doing and possibly put a stop to it. Realistically, Cherry knew she couldn't hope to explore the Scythian metropolis in that time, but perhaps she might discover something that would prevent the Leader from giving a stupid order.

CHAPTER TWENTY-SIX

Cherry was annoyed to discover no gas masks were available for entering the Chimera construction site. She'd assumed they would either be on site or easy to acquire quickly.

"Don't the workers wear them routinely?" she asked the supervisor, whose name was Alun, glaring up at the tall, scrawny man. She was forced to raise her voice over the noise of the wind. "What about the risk of poisonous gases leaking from underground vents?" Cherry was no geologist, but even she knew of the dangers of entering unexplored subterranean regions. There had been a couple of incidents at the mountain mines where miners had been evacuated when methane had suddenly flooded an area.

"All our workers are protected in their cabs, ma'am," Alun replied. "And all the vehicles carry sampling devices that sound an alarm when they detect anything dangerous. We do very little on-the-ground work. That's the job of the finishing crew."

"Okay, I understand. Can you order some? How long would they take to arrive?"

"I can try. I don't know if any are available in

Suddene. Might have to order them from Oceanside. Then we're looking at this evening at the earliest, assuming the shippers can find a pilot willing to brave this wind."

Indeed, the wind showed no signs of dropping. If anything, it seemed to have increased in the short time it had taken Cherry to walk from the spot where Zapata had dropped her to the excavation workers' trucks.

Everyone was standing leeward of the vehicles, but the violent air whipped around them on both sides, carrying with it stinging sand that threatened Cherry's eyes. The rays of the rising sun were making no dent in the chilly atmosphere.

"Dammit," Cherry said, half to herself. The longer it took her to go into the Scythian city, the greater the chances were that Meredith would put a stop to her investigation.

"It's possible we could drive you in there, ma'am," said Alun. "You would be safe inside one of our survey vehicles."

"How would that work?" Cherry asked. According to what she'd seen on the recording Alun had sent, there was a deep drop from the point the excavator had broken through to the floor of the city.

"We could lower a vehicle on a few lines. It shouldn't be too hard to rig something up."

Exploring the city from within the confines of a vehicle wouldn't be ideal, but it was better than nothing. "Let's try it," said Cherry.

"I'll have to unseal the site, of course," said Alun.

"The excavator registered no toxic gases?" Cherry asked.

"None at all."

"I'm prepared to take the risk of going in there," said Cherry, "but I'm not going to command anyone else to do so. I only want volunteers to accompany me. I might need some people to help me move stuff." She didn't need to explain any further. Her lack of one arm was plain for all to see.

"You won't have any shortage of volunteers," Alun said. "I had a hard time forcing everyone out of the place. They're all dying to know what's in there."

"Let's hope it doesn't come to that."

***

The survey vehicle was small and boxy. It held four seats, but they were closely crammed together and the roof was low. The top of Alun's head brushed it as he climbed into the driver's seat. All the controls were manual. This was a car you had to actually drive. Alun passed Cherry a hard hat and a pair of thick gloves.

The tires were fat and there was plenty of clearance beneath the car to enable it to deal with rocky terrain. Two excavators had volunteered—begged, in fact—to come along. Both the volunteers had crowded into the back seat.

Cherry was in the front passenger seat. She turned to face the woman and man sitting behind her. "I know Alun has already told you this but I'm going to say it again: Nothing you see in there can be discussed with anyone else. Not ever. Not unless you receive clearance directly from me. Understood?"

The excavators nodded, appearing taken aback by Cherry's serious tone. They'd been excited to be allowed to come along.

"My name's Pearl, by the way," said one. She was blonde-haired, green-eyed, and pale-skinned, which was unusual among Concordians. The man's coloring was the same as Cherry's and the most common among the colonists: olive skin, brown-black eyes, and black hair. They both wore work overalls and hard hats. The man's eyes were almond-shaped. They reminded Cherry of Wilder's eyes.

Guilt arose in her as she recalled her most recent encounter with the young woman and the poor hospitality she'd received in Cherry's home.

"And I'm Laurie," said the black-haired man.

"Hi," Cherry replied.

"Ready?" Alun asked.

Cherry faced forward and nodded.

Alun pressed the accelerator and the car surged forward, pushing Cherry into the back of her seat. The survey car's engine was powerful for a small vehicle. In a few moments they were racing toward the site entrance, which was a tunnel that opened above ground but sloped quickly downward.

Alun drove the car under the tunnel roof and into darkness. The survey car's headlights beamed out. Alun issued a voice command into his comm. The sound of metallic gears grinding started up somewhere ahead. The tunnel continued to slope downward.

Cherry saw dark gray solid metal doors pulling apart and a line of lights running along the tunnel roof beyond. The constructed roof had disappeared and been replaced by roughly hewn stone. They were underground, heading along the access tunnel leading to the excavated chamber that would become Chimera: Concordia's fifth missile silo and pulse emitter site.

Cherry had never seen one of the military defense sites under construction. The other four had been built while she'd been offplanet. Each project was a major drain on resources. Cherry hadn't looked up the numbers, but she estimated that at least half of the colony's productive effort, from the mining operations to the munitions factories, was devoted to constructing and arming the missile and emitter silos.

It had become a source of contention in Concordian society. Cherry didn't follow current affairs as closely as she probably should but even she had heard the rumblings of discontent that so much effort and economic value was spent on the planet's defense. Still, it was no excuse for Meredith's decision to reduce the military budget.

They'd reached the end of the access tunnel. Cherry noticed, as they drove down it, the ceiling had risen higher and higher, marking where the tunnel had been dug deeper and deeper as the excavation progressed downward.

Alun drove directly into the excavation site. Powerful lights on stands were positioned roughly central though widely spaced apart, linked by wires to a generator. Though their beams were too strong for Cherry to look directly into, they failed to penetrate the darkness overhead. The gouged out, distant edges of the chamber were visible, however. The ground was roughly even but still bore the marks of excavation drilling. The rock was a uniform, sandy gray.

Several of the monster excavators stood abandoned. A flimsy portable building that seemed to hold two or three rooms and a row of portable latrines were the only constructions.

"We've dug to the lowest level," Alun explained. "We would have finished the job in four days, bang on schedule. Then this happened."

Ignoring the man's complaint about something entirely outside of her control, Cherry asked, "What's the atmosphere like out there?"

"The alarm will go off if the car's instruments detect anything dangerous," Alun replied.

"That's the spot over there, right?" asked Cherry, pointing at a hole at the edge of the site where the rear of one excavator was poking out. Two more of the machines were attached to the first by thick lines of twisted wire. "Let's check it out."

Alun drove them over to the spot. "If we want to take this into the city we'll have to move Bunny's machine out of the way," he said to the two backseat passengers.

"That won't take long," Pearl said.

"Yeah, no problem," added Laurie.

Alun stopped the car.

The excavators looked even bigger close up. They were bigger than many houses Cherry had seen. Pearl and Laurie jumped out of the car and trotted over to separate machines. They had to climb up the outsides on specially constructed steps to reach the cabs. When they started them up, their massive engines sent vibrations that Cherry could feel through the floor of the car.

In three or four minutes, Laurie and Pearl had backed up the excavators, taking up the slack on the lines that attached them to the third machine in the hole, and pulled it all of the way out, revealing the powerful drill. Laurie and Pearl hopped into the car, slammed the doors, and Alun spurred the car into the vacant space.

They soon lost the benefit of the brilliant site lights and relied once more on the vehicle's beams. They revealed more bare rock for a few seconds, and then... nothing.

"This is it," said Alun, slamming on the brakes.

He'd stopped just short of the brink of a hole. Beyond lay only blackness.

"I can't see anything," Cherry said.

"You wouldn't," said Alun. "I took that vid when Bunny's excavator lights were shining in. This car's lights are ten times weaker. We won't see much until we get down there. What we need to do now is fix the lines we brought along to this vehicle. Then Laurie or Pearl can lower us down."

"Pearl can do it," said Laurie.

"Forget it," she replied. "I'm going down there."

"No way," Laurie retorted. "I'm not sitting up here waiting while you three have all the fun."

"Quit fighting," said Alun. "Figure it out between yourselves. I'm going to start securing the lines."

Cherry was forced to wait impatiently. Pearl and

Laurie played a hand game to decide who would go into the city—Laurie lost, cursed, and scowled before getting out of the car. He stomped away into the dark tunnel. Then Pearl helped Alun with the lines.

The system they created didn't look particularly safe to Cherry. Laurie drove the vehicle to the brink of the hole that led into the city, then all three excavation crew members tied the flexible metal lines to certain parts of the survey vehicle and then wound them around the smooth end of the excavator's drill where it attached to the vehicle's body. The idea was that Laurie would gently nudge the survey car off the precipice and slowly turn the drill to lower the car.

"Do you know how deep we have to go to reach the bottom?" Cherry asked.

"Yeah, roughly," Alun replied. "Don't worry. I've been doing this kind of thing for a long time."

Cherry was pretty sure the supervisor hadn't been creating makeshift winches in order to lower vehicles into ancient Scythian cities for a long time, but she let it go. She didn't have time to wait for a better, safer option. Cherry was safe from interference for a short while, due to the fact she was in the excavation site and out of comm range, but if Meredith wanted her to stop badly enough she could send an order by human messenger.

Pearl sat between the two back seats to even out the balance of the survey vehicle. Alun released the brake so the car wouldn't resist when Laurie pushed it forward.

Faced by utter darkness broken only by two slim beams of light from the headlamps, Cherry couldn't resist gripping the side of her seat tightly. All three passengers were wearing seat belts, but they wouldn't provide much protection if the car plunged hundreds of meters to a rocky floor.

There was a bump as Laurie's excavator made

contact, and then a slow slide forward. The front of the car reached the edge and rolled off, dipping down. The lines attached to the front jerked as they took the weight of the vehicle. Cherry's heart was racing. The rear of the car also left the rocky ledge. The drop this time was lower and the jerk harder as the rear lines prevented the car from falling.

They began to move downward. Something about the way Alun and the others had wound the line made the car seesaw as it lowered. The front would dip and then the rear, in a rhythmic fashion. The movement didn't appear to surprise or worry Cherry's companions.

She concentrated on trying to catch her first sight of the Scythian city. The survey car's swinging beams revealed tantalizing glimpses: a sweeping curve here, a slender point there. But Cherry longed to see the whole place. It would be impossible, of course. She would be confined to viewing whatever was illuminated by the car and the powerful flashlights they'd brought along. The city hadn't seen the light of day for tens or perhaps hundreds of thousands of years.

A sudden puzzlement struck her.

"It's strange, don't you think?" Cherry said. "I don't know much about geology, but shouldn't this city have been filled in with sand from the desert? How come the space around the buildings is still hollow?"

"Yeah," said Pearl. "I was thinking that too."

"You're right," Alun said. "It's normal for man-made —or artificially made, I should say—structures to sink over time as the land around them changes and rises. A place this big and this deep in the ground should be a pile of sand and weather-worn remains by now. My best guess is that it's covered by a roof. A dome of some kind, probably. The land's risen up around it, covering it over, but the weight of the desert sand hasn't broken through the roof."

"Yet," Cherry said.

"Yet," Alun agreed.

"But when it does," said Pearl, "woo wee! That's going to be one helluva landslide!"

"A landslide we don't want to be under," Cherry said. Alun's explanation made even more sense, knowing what Cherry knew. Concordia's atmosphere had begun to become unbreathable for the Scythians, so they had enclosed their cities to protect their citizens from the dangerous gases.

Cherry hoped the city's dome would hold a little while longer.

CHAPTER TWENTY-SEVEN

Three flashlight beams swung over the facade of a construction. Now that Cherry was seeing one of the structures in real life and up close, there was no doubt in her mind that what she was looking at was not a geological phenomenon. The surface was too smooth and regular and three types of material in soft pink, green, and purple had been used to create it, each part slotting into the next to create a mosaic effect, but with no discernible pattern that Cherry could identify.

"Is it safe to touch, do you think?" Pearl asked softly.

"I don't know why you're whispering," said Alun, his voice booming and echoing in the vast, dark chamber. "Nothing's been alive in here for a long while. No one's going to hear you."

No one, and no thing, Cherry thought, wondering if they would be the first humans to discover what the Scythians looked like. Though the Galactic Assembly had furnished the colony with image files of all its members, it had been unable to supply them with any pictures of the Scythians. Did anyone in the galaxy know anything about the hostile aliens' appearance?

The Parvus had said they didn't breathe oxygen, but a different gas. Would that affect the form their bodies took? Cherry didn't know.

Pearl was creeping closer to the edifice.

"Don't touch it," said Cherry. "At least, not yet. We need to try to figure out if it's safe first." She wished Kes was with them. He would know the correct and safe procedure to follow in the circumstances. If only he'd answered his comm when she was trying to contact him about Wilder. But he'd been busy or asleep, and she hadn't had time to wait.

The air was chilly and musky, and the ground was so thick with dust Cherry was sinking into it ankle deep. It made walking difficult. It would also make running hard, if they had to get away from something, and winching the survey vehicle out of the chasm would be a slow process. If anything did attack, they didn't stand a chance.

As Alun had said, nothing could remain alive in that place after tens of thousands or perhaps hundreds of thousands of years, but that didn't mean the Scythians hadn't left behind something synthetic, designed to come to life if ever their ancient home was invaded.

They had all reached the construction. Pearl had waited at its outer face for the other two to catch up.

"What now?" Alun asked. "Do we go inside?"

"I can't see a way in," said Pearl, playing her flashlight's beam over the dusty surface.

Cherry pointed her flashlight upward, wondering if the Scythians had windows in their buildings, but all she could see was the same random arrangement of three or four differently colored and textured materials.

"I should tell you two something," she said, "before we go any further. I want you to know what you might be getting into. But, again, not a word of this is to go any further."

"I think I know what you're going to say," Alun said.

"You do? Tell me."

"You're going to say this place was built by the Scythians."

Pearl's eyes grew round. "Was it?!"

Cherry said, "I don't know for sure, but that is what I think. You probably heard about the delegation of Parvus who are currently visiting us? Well, one reason they came here was to tell us Concordia is the Scythians' origin planet. They evolved here and built a civilization. But then they did something to alter their world's ecological balance and over time the atmosphere became flooded with oxygen, which is poisonous to them."

"So they left," said Alun. "The roof over this place makes sense now."

"Whoa," Pearl breathed. Then, "Darn it!"

"What's wrong?" asked Cherry.

"I know one of the most significant facts in the history of Concordia and I can't tell a soul about it."

"I'm not sure it's going to be a secret for much longer," Cherry said. "But please control yourself for a while, until the news is out."

"So we've stolen their home," said Alun.

"So what?" Pearl said. "It isn't like they can live here. It's better for us to colonize Concordia than allow a habitable planet to go to waste."

"Let's save the philosophical argument for another day," said Cherry. "I'm going to try something." She gave Alun her flashlight to hold and gently wiped a green section of wall. She'd only been meaning to wipe off some of the dust to get a better look at the joint between two areas of different colors, hoping there might be a way to pull the sections apart, but what she discovered made her jump backward in surprise.

"What's wrong?" asked Pearl.

"It's soft!" Cherry exclaimed. She'd been expecting to encounter a hard, unyielding surface like the wall of every human building in Concordia, but the Scythian material had given way easily under the pressure of her hand. "Look, you can see an indent where I touched it."

A depression in the rough shape of four fingertips had appeared in the wall.

"It feels spongy, like a dessert I had once. I can't remember its name."

"Mousse?" Pearl asked.

"That's it."

Alun was already reaching out to also touch the wall. Before Cherry could tell him to stop, he'd made contact. His hand sank in. He continued to push. His wrist disappeared and then half of his forearm.

Cherry had a vision of Alun suddenly being yanked from his feet and pulled bodily into the wall. "Stop! Don't do that."

Alun's arm was buried up to his elbow.

"What can you feel?" asked Pearl.

"I'm through to the other side. I can't feel much, though. Just emptiness."

"Take your arm out," Cherry said.

Alun pulled. He grimaced. "I can't."

"Oh no!" said Pearl.

Alun pulled again, straining against the grip of the wall. "Shit. It's stuck hard."

"Dammit!" Cherry exclaimed. "I told you not to do that. Keep trying to pull it out. I'll try to think of something."

But what could they do? If she tied a line between Alun and the survey car and tried to use the vehicle to pull him out his arm could be torn from its socket.

"Do you have anything in the trunk of the car that might work as a solvent?" Cherry asked. "Maybe we could dissolve the area around your arm."

"There's a bottle of hydrochloric acid in there," replied Alun.

"Don't use that!" said Pearl. "That'll dissolve your

arm too."

Suddenly, Alun slipped his arm out from the wall. He burst into laughter, whooping and doubling up, his hands clutching his sides.

"Oh, Alun," said Pearl. "That wasn't funny. I was really worried about you."

The supervisor straightened up and wiped his eyes. "You should have seen your faces."

Cherry glared at him. "No more stunts like that, or you wait back at the vehicle."

"Sorry," Alun said. "Couldn't resist."

Cherry rolled her eyes. She turned her attention to the place where Alun had stuck his arm. A hole marked the surface, but it was closing. Material from all sides was oozing inward. As an experiment, Cherry touched a purple area of the wall. The material there was tougher and grainy. She pressed a pink section. This substance was the firmest of them all, but it still had some give to it.

"This purple part is wide enough for even me to fit through," Alun said. "What do you say? Should we all go inside?"

"No, not all of us," said Cherry. "Someone needs to stay out here to alert Laurie if we get into difficulties so he can go and get help."

"I'll stay behind if no one minds," Pearl said. "I was excited to come in here, but now this place is seriously giving me the creeps. I'd rather not go any farther."

Cherry knew exactly what she meant. There was something deeply disturbing about the Scythian city. The feeling it gave her was something akin to how she'd felt during her time at the Galactic Assembly space station, only it was much worse. This place made her skin crawl.

Alun was already pulling the green material apart to create an entrance. "Better check there's air in there." He put his nose at the gap and sniffed cautiously.

"Smells like shit. I'll bring the car over and run a pipe inside so we can use the car's instrumentation to test for dangerous gases."

While Alun returned to the survey vehicle, Cherry also leaned forward into the gap in the wall and gave a tentative sniff. This time, Alun hadn't been joking. The air inside the construction did, indeed, smell like human feces.

Alun drove up in the car. He leaned out of the window. "I had an idea. That patch of green stuff there looks big enough to fit the car through. I wanna try and drive her right inside."

"Good thinking," said Cherry. If there were pockets of dangerous gases within the Scythian structure, they would be much safer inside the car. They would be able to drive out as soon as the alarm sounded, breathing the air in the vehicle.

Cherry opened the car door and climbed into it. Pearl moved off to the side. Alun pressed the accelerator and drove the car directly at the wall. The surface gave some resistance at first. It seemed to be stronger when a wide area of its surface was impacted than when something smaller was pushed into it. The car's engine noise rose as it strained, but the material began to give way. The car inched forward and the green substance retracted, the wall stretching inward. A gap opened in front of them, and then all of a sudden, with an odd ripping noise, the surface broke and the car drove through the wall and into the inner darkness.

CHAPTER TWENTY-EIGHT

Kes was on his fourth beer and he was feeling light-headed. He wasn't used to drinking alcohol. He didn't like to drink in front of Isobel when she couldn't due to being pregnant, though she never objected. It seemed deeply inconsiderate to him to indulge in something while the person you loved could not—and you had contributed to the reason they could not. It was Isobel who was going through all the physical demands of carrying their baby and caring for a toddler at the same time. Giving up booze was the least he could do.

Had been, Kes corrected himself. Giving up booze *had been* the least he could do. Which wasn't to say he couldn't have done a lot more. He swallowed hard and put down his glass.

Coming out to a bar had been a bad decision. The place was heaving with people, all of them strangers as far as Kes had noticed. He wasn't sure if that was better or not. On the one hand, he wouldn't have minded seeing a friendly face right then; on the other, a word of comfort or commiseration from a friend could tip him over the edge. He was barely holding it together as it was.

He leaned both elbows on the bar and cupped his hands around the glass of beer, hunching over the alcohol—the purported memory and emotional pain obliterator. It didn't seem to be working for him.

The scent of beer, spirits, and cocktails hung in the air in the dimly lit space. Music was playing, louder than the chatter of voices. Kes didn't recognize the song, but then again he never did. He'd been out of touch with musical fashion for as long as he could remember. Even back on Earth, growing up, when all his classmates had raved about the latest hot band or singer, he'd had no idea what they were talking about.

Being unable to join in the discussions had left him somewhat isolated, but he hadn't minded much. All he needed was a few close friends and his work. Just a handful of people he felt close to and who liked him, or loved him, as Isobel had. He'd screwed up badly, and he didn't even know why.

Kes lifted his glass to his lips and gulped several mouthfuls of beer. He put down the half-empty glass. He debated whether he should make this one his last and head home. His visit to the bar wasn't achieving the desired effect. He didn't feel any lessening of the terrible, empty ache in the pit of his stomach or the overwhelming sense of regret and self-hatred.

Yet he also couldn't bear the thought of returning to his dark, silent house or his cold, empty bed. Just imagining it filled him with dread. Maybe he should find a place to stay for that night. If he managed to get a little sleep and take a shower in the morning, he might make it into work tomorrow. He hadn't comm'd them about his absence and everyone was probably wondering what had happened to him.

Earlier that day, he'd put in his ear comm and tried to contact Isobel, but, predictably, every attempt was refused. He hadn't blamed her in the slightest. He'd left messages, but even to him his words sounded hollow. Eventually, he'd given up. Next, he'd thought about contacting the office, planning on making up some excuse to take the day off work, but he'd felt his throat thicken and he'd known he wouldn't get through the conversation without his voice breaking. He'd received notifications that Cherry wanted to speak to him but he hadn't comm'd her either, knowing he was incapable of dealing with anything.

Kes drained his beer, still indecisive about whether or not to call it a night. He opened the interface set into the bar surface and scrolled through the lists of drinks, wondering if he should try something stronger. But nothing caught his eye. He didn't need alcohol. He needed his wife and child. His chest ached and something was forcing its way up his throat.

Closing the interface, Kes rose from his stool. But a heavy hand clamped onto his shoulder and pressed him down again. A large figure swung onto the stool next to Kes and released his grip on Kes' shoulder.

Aubriot.

"Don't tell me you're leaving already, Ginger," Aubriot said. "I only just got here."

"Yeah, sorry. I'm not feeling it." Kes moved sideways to remove Aubriot's hand and stood up.

"C'mon," said Aubriot. "Stay a minute. Have a drink. One drink. As mates. We never really bonded, did we, you and I? Now's our chance."

As far as Kes knew, Aubriot had never 'bonded' with anyone, except perhaps Cherry, though their relationship had seemed a matter of convenience for both of them. "Look, another time, okay? I'm not in a good—"

"For fuck's sake. One drink isn't going to hurt you, is it? Is one fucking drink too much to ask?"

Kes heaved a sigh and sat down. He didn't order anything. He decided he would stay five minutes to pacify the arrogant, bossy man and avoid an argument, then he would leave. He would go for a walk. He would walk all night if he needed to. Perhaps that would help.

Aubriot had pulled his sleeve down over his hand and was using the edge to wipe spilled beer from the interface screen in front of him. When the surface was reasonably clean, he opened the screen and swiped the drinks list from left to right.

Aubriot's lips moved but Kes couldn't hear what he was saying. The music and noise of the crowd was too loud. He finally made his selection and then straightened up and turned his attention to Kes.

"Funny seeing you here," he said. "I didn't think you came to places like this. You strike me as more of a family man."

"I *am* a family man," said Kes, leaving his response at that. He didn't owe Aubriot an explanation for his presence at the Annwn bar.

Aubriot gave him a long look. "But not tonight, eh? Been arguing with the missus? She kicked you out?"

Kes didn't answer. He didn't know where to look as he stoically bore Aubriot's scrutiny.

"Nah, it's worse than that, isn't it?" Aubriot said. "If you'd had a fight, a bloke like you wouldn't make things worse by pissing off down the pub. You'd be banging on the door, begging forgiveness, or on your way to buy flowers."

Kes' lips thinned to a line. Normally, Aubriot's rudeness didn't get to him. In fact, he barely took any notice of what the man said unless he had to, but tonight his skin was not so tough. He glared at Aubriot, warning him with his eyes that if he continued pressing buttons, there would be consequences. Not that Kes stood the remotest chance of beating Aubriot in a fight. He would have his ass handed to him. But he wasn't in a state to care, and getting in just a few blows would feel damned good.

Aubriot's eyebrows rose. "Don't tell me she left you."

Kes' fist slammed into Aubriot's jaw with such a force he was thrown from his stool. He hit the floor. Kes stood over him, pain radiating from his knuckles, poised to hit Aubriot again.

A hush had fallen over the bar as the patrons took in what had happened. Only the music played on.

"Someone comm the CED," said a woman's voice.

Aubriot raised a hand. "It's all right," he called out, beginning to rise to his feet. "No harm done. Just a misunderstanding."

Kes took a step backward, his fist remaining raised. He guessed Aubriot's reaction was a trick, designed to make him let down his guard so that Aubriot could retaliate.

"Sit down," said Aubriot. "I don't wanna hurt you. Let's forget about it."

A drink was traveling along the narrow conveyor belt on the inner edge of the bar. The cocktail stopped in front of Aubriot. He picked up the yellow-green concoction, pulled out the curled lime peel garnish, and poured the entire contents of the glass down his throat.

Kes realized that Aubriot was very drunk. He wondered why. Though Aubriot had many faults, Kes had heard no rumors he was an alcoholic. Curiosity about what was going on with the man, and a weird sense of camaraderie, drove Kes to stay for a while. He remembered Cherry telling him Aubriot had left the military.

"What are you having?" Aubriot asked. "Don't make me drink alone. It's not polite."

His speech was slightly slurred. How much had Aubriot drunk? Kes was certain that resistance to the effects of alcohol was built into the man's genetic code, along with every other physical and mental advantage that was available at the time. Aubriot must have already downed a considerable amount of booze.

Kes was clearly not the only one with sorrows to drown that night.

"You should have one of these," said Aubriot, raising his empty glass. "Bloody good. Gets you drunk fast. That's what we want, right?"

"What was it?" asked Kes.

"Dunno." Aubriot chuckled. "I forgot. Wait a minute. I'll find it again. Order one for both of us." He opened the order screen, swiped it, and jabbed it a couple of times. When he'd finished ordering he said, without looking at Kes, "I was married once. Bitch left me too."

"My wife isn't a bitch," Kes said between his teeth.

"All right, wind your neck in. I was talking about my ex, not yours."

"She's *not* my ex!"

"Christ on a bike!" Aubriot exclaimed. "Ah, here's our drinks. In the nick of time." He grabbed the two cocktails from the conveyor belt and passed one to Kes. "Get that down your throat while I think of something to say that won't offend you."

Kes sipped the cocktail. It was as strong as Aubriot had promised, the citrus flavors failing to disguise the powerful taste of mixed liquors. He swallowed and took another drink.

"She only wanted me for my money," Aubriot said. "Thought she could get it too, despite the pre-nup. What an idiot she was, suing the richest man on Earth. But then, I didn't marry her for her brains. Maybe that was my mistake."

Kes vaguely remembered the story of Aubriot's divorce in the news. The woman lost her claim for alimony and was required to pay Aubriot's court costs, which bankrupted her.

He felt the effect of his cocktail spreading through his body. "What do you care?" he asked Aubriot. "With looks like yours, you could have any woman in this place. In Concordia, even."

"Could I?" Aubriot looked at Kes sidelong. "And if I could, would *you* want that? If you could swap places with me, would you?"

Kes considered for only a moment before shaking his head. He had no interest in having every woman in the room. He knew himself too well. He would find no satisfaction or happiness in that.

"See?" Aubriot said. "It's not so great when you think about it."

"Not so great for *me*," Kes said. "We aren't the same."

"Aren't we? I'm not sure about that."

Kes gave a short laugh. "I am." He took another sip of his cocktail.

"No, you're wrong," said Aubriot. "In some ways we're very similar."

Kes turned to face him. The man was physically flawless. He was also cocky, overbearing, boorish, and often deeply offensive. Kes realized he'd been wrong to say Aubriot could have any woman in the bar. He could have the ones who only wanted a good time and those who weren't discerning, but in fact Aubriot would struggle to attract someone like Isobel. Cariad had never liked him either. "Sorry, but you're the one who's wrong. I can't think of a single thing we have in common."

Aubriot leaned in so close to Kes he could smell the alcohol on the other man's breath.

"We're fucked," he said.

"What?" Kes craned his neck backward to avoid Aubriot's exhalation.

"Fucked," Aubriot repeated. "We all are. Me, you, Cherry, Wilder. But especially me and you. In here." He poked Kes in the head.

Kes grabbed his hand and pushed it down onto the bar. "Don't touch me."

"You can't expect to travel fifty years into the future

and be normal," said Aubriot, picking up his drink. He saw the glass was empty and opened the interface. "Want another one?"

"No, thanks."

Aubriot ordered his third drink in that bar. "We're men out of our time," he said, half to himself. He spoke so quietly Kes could only just make out the words. "The last Earth-born. We're out of place. It's different for Cherry and Wilder. They grew up on the *Nova*. Concordia's the only planet they know. It's their home." After a pause, he said, "Tell me, Ginger..."

Kes gave him a look.

"Tell me, Kes, is this what you imagined? Is this how you thought our lives would be?"

"No, it isn't."

"Not at all, right? Never imagined I would be sitting in bar getting smashed on cocktails. Never in a million years. It's strange, don't you think, how ordinary everything turned out? How similar to how things were on Earth. I mean, I expected some things to be the same. The Manual was supposed to create a fledgling Earth-like civilization because that was all we knew. But it's funny how, decades after the Manual became redundant, everything's continued along the same lines. Families, cars, residential estates, offices, factories. If there weren't four fucking massive missile silos hidden underground, Concordia would be like something off a soap opera."

"It isn't that odd," Kes said. "This is what we do, as a species. People have experimented with different systems: communes, monasteries and nunneries, anchorites living in caves. They're all anomalies. Those ways of life never become popular. For hundreds of thousands of years, we've lived in small or large family units and within tribes of about a hundred people we know. It hasn't changed and it isn't going to. It's encoded in us."

"Huh," Aubriot said skeptically. "Speak for yourself." His cocktail had arrived but he didn't remove it from the belt.

"So family life isn't for you?" asked Kes, smiling. "You're different. You're a *loner*."

"Fuck off," Aubriot said, though without conviction.

"I have to admit," Kes said, "when I went into cryo, I didn't expect my life to end up as it has. I expected a bigger struggle. I expected things to be harder."

"They were, for a time," said Aubriot. "We missed out on most of that."

"I almost wish..."

"What?" Aubriot asked.

"Nothing." For some reason, the unanticipated encounter with Aubriot and their somewhat bizarre conversation had made Kes' mind feel clearer. He was wasting his time at the bar with his dysfunctional drinking buddy. He should be trying to speak to Isobel, to apologize, and to ask for another chance. She might listen to him now she'd had time to calm down. She did still love him. He was sure of that, or last night wouldn't have happened. He could make things better.

"I'm leaving," he said, standing up and pushing his empty glasses onto the belt. It carried them away, Aubriot's untouched drink with them.

Aubriot watched the cocktail disappear into the hole in the wall at the end of the bar, his expression listless. Kes wondered if the alcohol he'd drunk had finally caught up with him and he was about to slump onto the bar.

"Call you an autocar?" Kes asked.

Aubriot shook his head.

"Are you sure you'll be okay?"

Aubriot nodded.

"Well, if you're sure..." Kes hesitated. He didn't want to leave the man alone in the state he was in. Something was definitely going on with him. "Is there anything you want to talk about?"

The question broke through Aubriot's drunken haze. He looked at Kes and the corner of his mouth lifted. It was an attempt at a ironic smile, but the effect was ghastly.

Just as Kes was about to suggest Aubriot go home and sleep it off, a young woman appeared from nowhere and draped an arm over Aubriot's shoulders. Her eyes were half closed and her movements languid.

"Are you all alone, honey?" she asked, "now your friend's leaving?"

Aubriot's arm snaked around the woman's waist, pulling her in. "Not now you're here, darlin'."

The woman laughed and allowed herself to be pulled closer. Aubriot tilted his head back and she leaned in for a kiss, her hair falling in a curtain to obscure their faces.

Kes left Aubriot to his latest encounter. As he was on his way out of the door, however, exclamations of surprise and consternation made him turn back. The bar's patrons were holding their hands to their ears and staring at each other as they all listened to what had to be an emergency message.

He wasn't wearing his comm. He'd put it in his pocket to stop himself from constantly trying to comm Isobel, knowing he was hounding her. He reached for his pocket, but before he retrieved his comm, the emergency message played from the bar's speakers.

CHAPTER TWENTY-NINE

Alun pressed gently on the accelerator, and the survey vehicle moved slowly forward. Cherry leaned closer to the windscreen, trying to make out what lay ahead. The headlight beams revealed a black floor, free from the dust that covered everything outside the building. The floor appeared to be hard, solid, and made from a different substance than the walls.

"The air's breathable," said Alun, peering at the display on the dashboard. "Want to get out?"

"No, not yet." If anything happened to them, they would be safer in the car. Would the Scythians have booby trapped their abandoned city? Cherry didn't think so. She doubted they would have thought that far ahead. When the time came they were forced to flee their planet, they would have been filled with fear for the future of their species, she guessed.

But then she remembered the words of Vasquez, Kes' fellow xenobiologist who had passed on long ago: *We mustn't imagine we can predict how they think.* Who really knew what the Scythians' thought processes had been when they departed their home? Perhaps they *had* been fearful that another galactic civilization would take over their home planet and make it their own. Perhaps they had put plans in place to prevent that from happening.

Yet there had been no sign of any plans so far. The colonists hadn't even suspected the Scythians had once lived there until the Parvus informed them of the fact. There had been no 'Private Property, Keep Out' signs in any noticeable form. Concordia had appeared to be a pristine world, untouched, and its life in the early stages of evolution. And it hadn't been until the Scythians detected the *Mistral's* trace and followed it they had discovered humans living on their origin world. They hadn't been keeping watch as far as anyone knew.

Another fact indicated to Cherry that the Scythians weren't excessively protective of Concordia: where were they? It had been decades since they had accepted the 'tribute' of the Guardians' sacrifice. With the acceptance came the implication that they would return to collect further tributes, but no sign had been seen of them for so long that the colony was becoming slack in its preparations for defense. Cherry wouldn't have been surprised to learn that some colonists even doubted the Scythians' existence.

Well, one thing was certain—the revelation that a Scythian city lay beneath the sands of Suddene would convince the most stubborn doubter.

The survey car had continued to crawl ahead, its lights illuminating nothing except the dark floor and empty darkness in front.

"This is less interesting than I thought it would be," said Alun.

"Try turning to the right," said Cherry. "Maybe we're on some kind of indoor road system."

Alun turned the steering wheel and the car curved smoothly to the right.

"Whoa!" he exclaimed, and slammed his foot down.

Cherry was thrown forward against her seat belt. "What is it?"

"Nothing," said Alun. "There's nothing there."

The headlights were no longer shining onto a smooth black surface, they were shining into a void. It was only Alun's fast reflexes that had prevented them from tumbling into the pit. Cherry's heart thudded as she realized what had almost happened.

"You'd think they would have a guard rail or something," Alun said. "Or a sign at least."

Cherry mentally agreed, but then she realized they were approaching the situation all wrong.

"Were you alive when the Scythians attacked for the second time?" she asked. "When the colony was living in Sidhe?"

"No. Before my time, thank the stars."

"But you've heard about the spiders, right? The ones the Scythians sent down to kill us?"

"Of course. My ma used to threaten me with them to make me behave. She used to tell me not all of them had been destroyed, that there were a few that had never been found, and that they were living out in the woods, waiting to catch naughty boys and girls."

Cherry stared at him. "I'm guessing your ma wasn't alive when the Scythians attacked either."

"She was. She was about two or three years old though and she doesn't remember it."

"I thought so," Cherry said. No one who had witnessed what the spiders did would ever have turned them into bogeymen to frighten little boys and girls. The memory of seeing Garwin cut to ribbons before her very eyes was seared into her mind like it had happened yesterday. Just the thought of them made her stump ache.

"Anyway," she continued, "we knew the Scythians would be back to try to finish us off, and we knew we didn't really stand a chance against them. All we had was the *Mistral* and a pulse emitter the Guardians had built on the wreckage of the *Nova*. So we tried to hide everyone as well as we could. We built Sidhe and we hid all signs of its presence. We erased all tracks leading to it, and we camouflaged the entrances so they couldn't be seen.

"We made a huge mistake. We were thinking the Scythians were like us. We put ourselves in their position and imagined what *we* would do to find something that was hidden. We imagined they would look for us. But the spiders didn't look, they smelled. They followed our scent from the place where they landed right to the doors of Sidhe within minutes. To them, our scent trails must have been like great illuminated lines traced on the ground and in the air. So..."

"I get it," Alun said. "The Scythians might not have a guard rail on a road, but they might have a guard scent."

"Exactly. You probably don't know it, but all the highways and military and metropolitan areas of Concordia are regularly sprayed with chemicals that break down human odors, precisely because of what happened with the Scythian spiders." At least, Cherry hoped the de-scenting program had remained active and Meredith hadn't cut it without telling her due to 'budgetary constraints'.

"That isn't a lot of help," said Alun. "This car doesn't detect scents."

"And neither do we."

They both sat and pondered the problem.

"For all we know," Cherry said, "there could be alarm scents going off all around us, or scents giving evacuation information still hanging in the air. We just don't know."

She was crestfallen. She'd been hoping to discover something within the remains of the city that would reveal a weakness in the Scythians the colony could exploit, or some other clue that would help in the defense of Concordia. Now she realized that, if such a thing existed, the information could be held in a form that was impossible for humans to access or understand: the language of scents.

"What's that?" Alun blurted. He was looking at the rear view screen on the dashboard. Immediately, he turned and stared out of the rear window.

Cherry turned around too. A light was flashing in the darkness. The white beam swayed and swerved. Cherry's mind was thrown into confusion. Had everything she'd been thinking about the Scythians been wrong? Did they have a visual sense after all?

Had her and Alun's presence triggered something?

But there was something familiar about the light.

"It's Pearl," Cherry said. "She's come inside and she's waving her flashlight at us."

"Of course!" Alun exclaimed. "She must want us to go back." He put the car into gear and began to reverse in a curve away from the edge.

For a moment Cherry wondered what could have made Pearl force her way through the wall and into the building when she'd said how uncomfortable the place made her, but then the understanding hit: Meredith had listened to Cherry's message. She'd sent someone to Suddene to tell Cherry to halt her exploration of the Scythian city. Or if she didn't want to stop her, she probably wanted to interfere.

Cherry gave a mental groan. Meredith had no appreciation of how serious and urgent the situation was. It might take years to explore the city and find out useful facts about the Scythians. The work had to be started right away without the intervention and intrusion of politicians.

"Damn," Alun said.

He'd steered the car to the left, apparently planning

on turning it around to go back the way they had come, but a second void opened on that side too. They'd been extremely lucky that they'd happened to drive through the wall at a spot where the road—if that was what it was—stood.

"Road's too narrow," he said. "Gonna have to reverse it all the way back."

The car did carry rear lights but they weren't as powerful as the ones on the front.

"Are you sure you can do it?" asked Cherry.

"Yeah, no problem." Despite his words, the space between Alun's eyebrows was creased with concern. He righted the steering wheel and put the car into reverse again. He hooked his arm over his seat back and looked out of the rear of the car. Cherry gazed in the same direction, but she could barely see anything. The mark between the black roadway and the drop of unknown depth on each side of it was nothing more than a faint line.

The car moved backward, and Pearl stopped waving her flashlight. She'd seen they were coming.

Cherry's concern about the risk of tumbling into an abyss was mildly offset by her frustration with Meredith. Concordia needed a new Leader. It had gone on re-electing Meredith too long, imagining she was as wise and competent as Ethan, but she was not. She even knew it herself, Cherry was sure, and she was only continuing in the role through a sense of duty and perhaps to honor the memory of her father.

The only answer was a new Leader for Concordia: someone who would take the Scythian threat seriously and who would act decisively to protect the colony. Not someone who pandered to public opinion because she lacked the strength of her own convictions.

"Whoa," said Alun, slowing down the car. It had veered toward the edge of the road. "Must be a slight curve I didn't notice." He corrected the car's direction and returned them to the center of the road.

Cherry heard a voice outside the vehicle. Pearl was shouting something, but Cherry couldn't make it out.

"Are you sure it's safe to open the window?" Cherry asked Alun.

"That's what the panel says," he replied.

If there was anything poisonous in the atmosphere inside the building, it didn't seem to be affecting Pearl. Cherry lowered the window and called out, "What did you say?"

"You have to come back!" Pearl yelled.

Cherry noticed that the woman's voice fell dead. There was no echo, in spite of the size of the building's interior.

"I realize that," called Cherry. "The Leader's sent an order telling us to stop exploring, right?"

"No!" shouted Pearl. "The Scythians are coming!"

CHAPTER THIRTY

When Cherry emerged from the tunnel that led to the surface, she had to screw her eyes up against the light. But when she saw the sun's position in the sky, she realized it was late afternoon, or evening in Oceanside. Nearly a day had passed while she'd been below ground investigating the Scythian city. The wind hadn't dropped, and the car was immediately hit by a scouring blast of sand.

As soon as she entered into comm range, she contacted Meredith. Predictably, she heard a 'busy' tone, but the Leader quickly ended her conversation and opened contact with Cherry.

"Cherry, thank the stars! What the hell are you doing in Suddene? It took me ages to find you. I had to ask an engineer to trace the last comm you received."

"You didn't get my message?"

"What message? I've been busy with government business all day. I didn't see anything urgent. Look, never mind. It doesn't matter now. How soon can you get back to Lyonesse? I haven't made any announcements yet. I don't want to create a panic."

Meredith sounded as if she were trying to prevent herself from panicking too, and only just succeeding.

"Well, now you've told the excavation team here it'll be all over Concordia within the next two minutes. You'd better make that announcement after we finish speaking. Our plan is in place, and we only have to put it into action. Do we have an ETA on the Scythian fleet, and how many ships are coming?"

"Yes. The Fila told me they would be here in three hours and seventeen minutes, but that was over half an hour ago."

"Right. What's been happening while you were trying to comm me?"

"Nothing. I've been trying to find you."

Cherry was stunned. More than half an hour had passed since Meredith had received the notification that an enemy fleet was on its way, and in that time all she'd done was try to contact her general. What if she'd died in the Scythian city? Would Meredith have done nothing at all, only waited for the Scythians to turn up and annihilate them all when they didn't receive their tribute? Or would she have turned over some sacrificial victims to appease them?

Cherry swallowed her shock and anger. "Okay, we have time to implement our defense strategy. Make the announcement. Now that I have comm I can give the order to roll out the defense plan. Refresh your memory on your part in case you've forgotten any of it. I'll be back in Lyonesse as soon as I can. I need to comm my pilot now. Wait. What about the Parvus? Are they still in orbit?"

"No, they left as soon as the news arrived. In fact, I think it may have been them who told the Fila that Scythian ships were coming."

"They left?" Cherry echoed. "Wait, don't tell me. They said they *intended* to help us."

"That's right! How did you know?"

"Just a guess."

"They left right after they sent the message."

"Okay, I get it," Cherry said. "We're on our own. I'll be in touch." She closed the connection. The temptation to unleash her frustration on Meredith was great but it could wait for later, after the crisis was over, assuming both of them remained alive.

The Fila seeding ship that had helped them last time was probably on the other side of the galaxy. It had taken months to arrive before. They couldn't hope for any help from the Fila this time. If anything, it was up to the humans to protect the Fila, who would no doubt feel the weight of the Scythians' wrath when the colony didn't comply with the hostile aliens' demands.

The only ship they had was the *Opportunity*, but it was too small to be an effective defense against the Scythian fleet. It would be better to leave it out of the battle plan.

Cherry needed her pilot.

"Zapata?"

"Yes, ma'am?"

"I need you back here. Now."

"Er..."

"Don't tell me you have a problem with that." Looking out at the gusts of wind filled with stinging sand, Cherry didn't doubt he had a problem but she needed a heli regardless.

Zapata said, "I'll be there in fifteen."

"I'll be waiting." Cherry opened the survey car door. Immediately, the wind slammed it closed again, spattering the glass with sand. She had snatched her leg out of the way just in time.

"It's probably a good idea to wait in here," Alun remarked. He'd been following Cherry's side of her conversations without comment.

"I guess you're right," she replied. All the excavation crews had retreated to their trucks. The ground around the entrance to the Chimera site was empty except for swirling sand, which was growing so thick it was cutting out the light. Cherry hoped Zapata would be able to land in the gale.

"Tell your people to go to the nearest shelter," she said to Alun. "You go too."

Alun gave the order to his crew. The trucks started up and began to move out.

Cherry calculated how long it would take her to return to the main continent. It would take fifteen minutes for the heli to arrive. How long had it taken to fly to the Chimera excavation site? Three hours in total from Annwn, but that had been with a following, if turbulent, wind. On the return flight they would be battling a head wind.

Before Cherry reached Lyonesse, the Scythians would be on Concordia's doorstep.

She would have to deal with them from the seat of the heli, but that couldn't be helped. First, she needed to alert all the senior officers. Cherry went to comm Aubriot to tell him it was time to put his plan into action, but then she paused. *Shit.* She'd momentarily forgotten about the man's resignation.

Shit. Shit. Shit.

Aubriot was the best military strategist they had. The only reason Ethan hadn't put him in charge of the defense force was due to his terrible personality. No one would want to serve under such an obnoxious and self-centered man.

In the months following their return from the Galactic Assembly, she had worked with him on developing and honing the plan Ethan had created that detailed the colony's defense tactics when the Scythians returned. In subsequent years—before he went astray—Aubriot had tweaked the plan, especially after Hydra came on-line.

Cherry could give the orders to set everything in

motion, but Aubriot should be at her side. It was his duty and responsibility. These were not things he should be able to step aside from. The colony needed him. She opened a comm to her ex-lover.

"Cherry," he answered. "I thought you'd never call." His words were slurred. He was clearly drunk.

"Who's that?" said a woman's voice. "Is it your girlfriend?"

"Shuttup," Aubriot said. "I'm trying to talk."

"Well!" the woman exclaimed. "That's pretty rude."

"Aubriot," said Cherry. "Did you hear the news?" It was possible that Meredith still hadn't made the announcement about the imminent arrival of the Scythians, or that the gossip emanating from the workers at the Chimera site hadn't reached him yet.

"You mean the news that our unfriendly neighborhood aliens are on their way? Yeah, I heard it."

"So, what are you doing?"

"Making the most of my final moments."

"*Seriously*?!"

"I'm kidding. Well, not really."

"C'mon, honey," the woman's voice whined. "Let's get back to business."

"In a minute," Aubriot replied.

"Aubriot, you have to sober up and get to work," Cherry said.

"No, I don't. I resigned, remember?"

"I never accepted your resignation." It was true. Cherry hadn't formally responded to the carefully worded message that had arrived from Aubriot after their conversation at his house. He'd simply stopped turning up for duty and she hadn't done anything about it except to assign another officer to take his place.

"What difference does it make?" Aubriot asked. "I have to go now."

"No," said Cherry. "You need to get back on duty. The colony needs you."

There was a long pause.

"I gotta go," Aubriot said.

"Wait! If you aren't going to help, at least go to a shelter."

"I will. We've got a couple of hours yet. I'm gonna make the most of them." He closed the comm.

Cherry cursed under her breath. Aubriot was being as self-centered as ever. She wouldn't have been surprised if he'd suggested offering up a few colonists to the Scythians in order to save his own skin.

"Problems?" Alun asked.

Cherry started. She'd forgotten the supervisor was sitting next to her. "Shouldn't you be on your way to a shelter?"

The surrounding desert was empty. The rest of the crew had departed.

"Do you need this car to get there?" Cherry asked.

"No, I don't," Alun replied. "There are a couple more vehicles in the tunnel. Or I could wait out the battle in the excavation site. It'll probably be the safest place on Concordia. But I thought I would keep you company until your heli arrives."

"That's kind of you, but there's no..." A buzzing noise coming from above distracted her. She peered upward into the hazy sky. Darkness was falling that had nothing to do with the sandstorm. Night was approaching. She saw the heli's lights in the dusk. Zapata had made it, faster than he'd predicted. The following wind had to have been very strong. Would they be able to make it back to Lyonesse?

CHAPTER THIRTY-ONE

The first thing Kes thought of when he heard the announcement was Isobel and Miki. He didn't know where they were. Were they near a shelter? Would they be safe?

A dreadful pall fell on him. Was anywhere on Concordia safe? What would the Scythians do when Meredith refused to give up anyone as tribute? If past experiences were anything to go by, the aliens would attempt to annihilate the colony.

Well, if they were all to die, Kes wanted to be with his wife and child when it happened.

The atmosphere in the bar had flipped from drunken congeniality to fear and confusion. After shock at the announcement of the imminent arrival of the Scythians had frozen everyone, chaos descended on the place. Some people roughly pushed past Kes as they ran for the door, others had sunk to the floor and were hunched over, weeping. Still more were standing motionless, trapped in indecision.

Aubriot detached himself from his prospective one-night stand and stood up, taking her hand and leading her toward the exit.

Kes beat him to it. Like the others crowded there, he pushed forward, eager to leave. Then he remembered an important fact: as Chief Xenobiologist, he had a role to play in the planned response to the return of the Scythians. He was supposed to head to the control center in the bunker at the Leader's Residence. He was supposed to support the Leader in her dialogue with the Scythians.

But what about Isobel? He couldn't just leave her to endure the attack alone, solely responsible for their little girl. He and Isobel had never discussed what they would do if Concordia was attacked. Isobel knew Kes would have a key role to play, and he guessed she must have accepted they would have to be apart during the attack. But that had been before she'd left him.

He tried comming her, but there was no answer. Sorrow was a knife in his heart. Even with the threat of death hanging over them she wouldn't answer him? Had he hurt her that badly? He guessed he must have. He couldn't allow everything to end with her thinking he didn't love her. He wouldn't allow it.

Kes burst through the crowd into the cold night air. A strong wind was blowing that immediately sucked all the warmth from his clothes. The street outside the Annwn bar was pitch dark. The only the light came from the open door of the bar. More people surged into the street from it, and Kes moved out of their way.

He began to trot along the street, the chill night clearing the final dregs of alcoholic muddle from his mind. He opened a comm and ordered an autocar, directing it to zero in on him rather than telling it to go to a particular location.

He had to get to the bunker, but he also had to find Isobel. The announcement had said the predicted arrival time was two and a half hours hence. That was time enough to find Isobel and then get to Oceanside, assuming she hadn't gone too far. Where could she be? Her parents had retired to a little place out in the mountains. If she'd gone there she was in one of the safer places on Concordia but he would never reach her.

"Kes?"

It was Meredith.

"Just checking in. You're on your way, right?" Meredith sounded tense and fearful.

"I am, but I…"

"What?"

"I have to find my family."

"You don't know where they are?"

"No. It's complicated."

"Concordia can't wait on you finding your family. You're needed here."

"I know, and I'm coming," Kes said with a sinking heart. He had to do the right thing. "I'm in Annwn now. I'll take a government autocar to get there."

"Good. I would suggest taking a heli but none of the pilots will fly. The wind's too strong today. They say the helis are too light and it's too dangerous."

"I can see that," said Kes. The wind was incredibly strong. He was leaning into it as he ran, forcing his body against the chilly stream of air.

"I know I said in the announcement that we have a couple of hours yet, but I need you here as soon as possible. The Scythians may open a dialogue before they arrive. The Fila are already hailing them but haven't received a response."

"If they do respond, just patch me in," said Kes. "I can work with you while I'm on the road. It won't be a problem." Exactly how he or Meredith were going to persuade the Scythians to leave Concordia alone when they didn't receive their tribute, he didn't know. He'd discussed all potential avenues of the conversation many times, but an effective argument was impossible to find. So little was known about the Scythians, it wasn't possible to know what might dissuade them from attacking.

An autocar appeared out of the darkness. Kes didn't see it until the last minute. The car swerved around him and then stopped. He climbed inside. He hesitated, but eventually he gave the vehicle the Leader's Residence coordinates. It nearly killed him to do it.

The car set off, navigating its way through the darkness. Kes tried Isobel's comm again, and again he received no answer. He held his head in his hands. He couldn't bear the thought of not seeing his wife and child one more time before devastation rained down on Concordia. He had to speak to Isobel and make things right with her.

CHAPTER THIRTY-TWO

The heli couldn't touch down. Whenever the landing skids neared the ground, a gust of wind would lift the heli into the air, or another would force it downward, causing the skids to touch the sand but then zoom upward as Zapata fought the downdraft.

The pilot had opened the vehicle's passenger door for Cherry too, so the wind was affecting the machine even more.

"Can you make it?" Cherry asked Zapata over her comm.

"Doing my best, ma'am."

"I understand. I just don't want you to kill yourself."

"Me neither."

"Or land on me."

Zapata chuckled.

The heli hung about fifteen meters up in the air, buffeted by the gale. Cherry had her eyes closed to slits to try to keep out the sand, and until the heli drew near all she could see of it was its lights. Her hair whipped around her head.

"I think we need to face the fact that I'm not going to

be able to land," said Zapata. "But I'll get as close as I can, and then you'll have to jump aboard."

"Okay," Cherry said. "Let's try." Her voice sounded braver than she felt. If she'd ever missed her left arm and hand, it was now.

The heli's lights approached, and then the bulbous belly of the machine above its skids came into view. Its main rotor was a dark, whirring blur. Cherry stepped backward as the heli veered toward her. She couldn't imagine what it had to be like to try to control the light air vehicle in the fierce wind.

Suddenly, the heli dipped downward. Another gust had caught it. The open passenger door zoomed close. Cherry leapt. One of her feet landed on the edge of the cockpit. She caught the edge of the open door with one hand. Mustering all the strength she had, she pulled herself forward. She saw Zapata, his head turned half toward her while he still tried to keep an eye on his controls.

She felt the heli rise abruptly. She'd been leaning into the cockpit, but the sudden movement forced her backward. The whine of the heli's rotor combined with the roar of the wind was deafening her. The night was a maelstrom of sand and empty air.

Her grip on the door was torn away. Her foot slipped. She was falling.

But then a large, strong hand fastened on her shirt and yanked her forward. Cherry landed on the heli's passenger seat, knees first. She grabbed the seat back. Zapata released her. The door closed, cutting down on the racket from the rotor and the howling wind.

"Thanks," Cherry said, fastening her safety harness.

"No problem," said Zapata.

The heli veered sharply left and down. For a second Cherry had an alarming view of Suddene's desert rising up toward her, but then Zapata swept them upward again and drove the heli forward into the battering wind.

How long had the pick-up taken? It had seemed an awfully long time between the moment Cherry had said goodbye and good luck to Alun, left the survey car, and waited while Zapata had made his many attempts to land. But when she checked the interface on the pilot controls, she saw it had only taken ten or eleven minutes.

Still, each minute could count.

Anxious to begin preparations for the impending Scythian attack, Cherry had comm'd her senior officers with the code word. All over the inhabited regions of Concordia, men and women were running to their stations, readying their weapons, and putting their equipment through checks. Finally, they would be watching the skies, wondering if they would outlive the night.

As Zapata fought the wind, flying her toward Lyonesse and the bunker beneath the Leader's Residence, Cherry wondered the same.

She checked in with her officers on how everything was rolling out. To her slight surprise, there hadn't been any hitches so far. Perhaps she'd underestimated the commitment and training of the defense force personnel. After the series of brief conversations, she was left with nothing to do other than wait as the heli battled its way into the headwind. The minutes to their ETA at the Leader's Residence were not reducing as fast as the minutes on the clock passed. It was as if time was expanding inside the heli and speeding up for the rest of Concordia as the Scythians drew nearer.

Ahead of them lay utter darkness, the night sky a thick, black shroud. Zapata was flying on instruments only. Below them lay the ocean. When Cherry had first set eyes on the expanse of precious water, the sight had amazed and delighted her. Now, she feared tumbling into its watery depths, leaving Concordia to endure the

Scythian attack without her.

"Do you have family to contact, ma'am?" Zapata suddenly asked.

"No need to call me ma'am, Zapata," Cherry replied. "Not now. I always hated that. Just call me Cherry. And, no, no family to con..."

Wilder! Cherry had entirely forgotten about her. Where was she? Was she safe? Did she even know the Scythians were coming? If she didn't have an ear comm yet she might not have heard Meredith's announcement, not if she'd gone back to her tree house, far from the nearest community speaker.

Cherry tried to comm the young woman, on the off chance she'd acquired an ear comm. When there was no answer she tried twice more, just to be sure Wilder either had no comm or was refusing to answer—the latter would be understandable.

It was time to try someone else.

"Kes?"

"Cherry," he replied. "Are you at the bunker already?"

"No, I'm flying back from Suddene."

"In this wind?"

"Do I have a choice? Look, Kes, I'm worried about Wilder. When I returned home after that day we were at the hospital, she was gone."

"You mean yesterday?"

Was it only the previous day? "Yes, yesterday. She'd left, not surprisingly, I guess."

"I'm not surprised either. You know how strong-willed she is."

"I know, and if I ever get to see her again I'll apologize. But I don't know if she's heard the Scythians are on their way. I have no idea where she is."

"And you want to know if I do? I don't, sorry. She hasn't been in touch."

"I was worried you would say that. Could you go to

her house in the forest and check she's okay? Maybe you can persuade her to go to a shelter."

"I would love to," Kes replied. "I'm worried about her too, but I can't."

Cherry realized that Kes' voice sounded strained, as if he was under extreme pressure. She guessed they all were.

When Cherry didn't respond immediately, Kes continued. "I have to get to the Leader's bunker. I'm on my way there now. The Scythians might comm us at any time."

"But what if she's all alone?" Cherry asked. "Someone has to help her."

"I know, but it can't be me. I'm sorry." Kes closed the comm.

Cherry blinked in surprise. It was very unlike Kes to be so abrupt. She guessed the tension of the situation was getting to him. She was reminded of those terrible hours and minutes before the second Scythian attack when everyone was waiting in fear in Sidhe, but Ethan had been there to keep everyone calm then.

What could she do about Wilder? All the military personnel had jobs to do, and civilians would be making their way to shelters.

There was only one person Cherry could think of who could help. She comm'd him, and after several moments he accepted.

"Aubriot, I need—"

"This is getting annoying."

"I need you to find Wilder. She's all alone and—"

"I'm busy."

"This is important."

"Nothing's important anymore. This is the end, so if you don't mind..."

"Don't say that!"

"Face up to it, Cherry. It's over. It was nice knowing you."

"Damn it!" Cherry exclaimed. "Don't you dare close this comm!"

The connection remained open. Cherry heard a sigh. She wasn't sure if it came from Aubriot or the woman he was with. He sounded as though he'd sobered up a bit.

"It is *not* over," said Cherry. "No one knows for sure what will happen."

"I think it's pretty clear."

"No, it isn't. Everyone thought it was clear when the Scythians attacked last time, remember? When the spiders landed and found us despite everything we'd done to hide ourselves. I thought it was over then too. I gave up, and I ran outside so it would be over for me quickly. But I was wrong."

Aubriot was silent.

"I was wrong," Cherry continued. "And you could be wrong now, too. No one knows what the future holds. And even if we think we do, even if we're sure, we still shouldn't give up. Don't hand your life to the Scythians on a plate, Aubriot. It's worth more than that. All of our lives are worth more than that."

After a pause, Aubriot said, "What do you want me to do?"

"Wilder was in an accident and she was recuperating at my house, but we got into a fight and she ran off. I don't know where she is and she isn't answering her comm. She might not know about the attack. She has to get to a shelter. She lives in the forest, near Cerberus. I want you to find her and take her somewhere she'll be safe."

"She still lives up a fucking tree? What's wrong with that kid?"

"That doesn't matter now. What matters is that someone tells her what's happening and takes her to a shelter. As soon as the Scythians realize Cerberus exists they're going to try to blow it out of the ground. There isn't anything going to be left of that forest but smoking ashes."

Aubriot said, "So you want me to go into a forest in the middle of the night, find a tree house, and tell an idiot kid she's about to die if she doesn't get out of there?"

"She isn't a kid. She's seventeen."

"Still an idiot, though."

"Just do it."

"I dunno. I'm in Annwn. By the time I get to the forest, find the stupid girl, and bring her back here, the Scythians will—"

"Aubriot, for once in your life, think about someone other than yourself!"

Silence.

Cherry held her breath. Had she pushed him too far? He generally hated any kind of personal criticism. Nothing could make him shut down faster. But he was the only person she knew who might succeed at finding Wilder and getting her to safety.

"There's no need to be rude," Aubriot said.

Coming from one of the rudest people she knew, Aubriot's comment almost made Cherry laugh. But the situation was too dire for that. "I'm sorry. Please do this for me. Find Wilder."

"I suppose I might as well die on a pointless quest in a forest as opposed to doing anything else."

"Thank you. Let me know what happens, okay?"

"All right. Where are you?"

"About halfway between Suddene and Lyonesse."

"Huh?"

"It doesn't matter. I'll explain later, after the Scythians go home, or we destroy them."

Aubriot snorted. "Keep dreaming." He closed the comm.

250

CHAPTER THIRTY-THREE

Kes' autocar was speeding along the main highway into Oceanside, but due to the blackout, the roads and streets leading off it were shadowy and vague. The road was empty of other vehicles except for a solitary pheromone-neutralizing truck making its final rounds, spraying the street with the liquid that removed all traces of human scent. No one walked the streets as far as Kes could see. Everyone was in a home bunker or had gone to one of the municipal shelters.

He was reminded of the second Scythian attack, when all two thousand colonists had crowded into Sidhe. After months of preparation and tension, the nightmare had come true. The enemy had returned, and all that stood between them and the last outpost of human civilization had been a few meters of earth and some reinforced doors.

Kes gave a mental shiver. Now they were better prepared, but if it came to a fight, could Concordia really defend itself against the might of the Scythians? They had only sent a handful of ships to enact their previous attack and the colony hadn't stood a chance against them. How many ships had they sent this time? Meredith hadn't mentioned a number. Kes decided not to ask her. He would find out the facts soon enough.

Light from above was brightening the dark road, turning iron gray to somber silver. Kes looked up. The clouds were tearing apart and starlight was glimmering through the raggedy gaps. He wondered if any of the stars were Scythian ships.

When he returned his attention to the road, his eyes widened. He suddenly knew where he was. One of Isobel's sisters lived in the neighborhood. A detour to her house would only take a few minutes out of his journey. It would be a long shot. Isobel had several siblings she could have gone to stay with, or she might not have gone to any of them at all.

"Car," he said. "I have a new destination." He quickly looked it up on the console and input the coordinates. The car passed two exits then at the third it turned left. After passing five houses it stopped. Kes jumped out of the car, telling it to wait, and ran to the front door. Rather than taking extra time to find Isobel's sister, Nancy, on the comm system, he banged on the door.

Realizing he'd probably just alarmed everyone inside on this already terrifying night, he took a step backward and tried to locate Nancy via comm.

The door opened.

Nancy and Isobel looked alike except for the fact that Nancy was taller and somehow overall 'harder'. Her nose was sharper, her eyes narrower—giving her a resting suspicious look—and her mouth thinner. As she saw who was waiting outside her door, Nancy's mouth thinned even further to a barely perceptible line.

"She isn't here."

Kes' shoulders slumped. "Do you know where she is? Is she in Oceanside?" If Isobel was somewhere nearby, he might still have time to see her before going to the bunker.

"No, I don't know where she is, and if I did, I wouldn't tell you."

Kes wasn't sure if Nancy was telling the truth. "I just want to see her. It might be for the last time, after tonight. So if you—"

"Kes!"

It was Isobel. She pushed past her sister but then halted, hesitating. She was the most beautiful sight Kes had ever seen. Kes couldn't help himself from grabbing her and holding her, though he took care not to crush her swollen belly.

Nancy tutted. She turned on her heel and strode away down the hall.

"I'm so, so sorry," Kes said.

"It doesn't matter," said Isobel. "Not now. I was so angry and hurt, but none of that is important now. I wanted to see you, thinking it might be for the last time. But Nancy had hidden my comm and wouldn't let me use hers."

What a bitch, Kes thought. "That wasn't very nice of her."

"It's only because she cares about me."

She has a funny way of showing it. "I wish I'd spent more time with you and Miki. I wanted to but...I don't know what was going on with me. I think I've been struggling with some things, though I didn't really know it."

"No, I was wrong to be so demanding. You have an important job. I should have been more understanding."

"No, you're wrong, Isobel. I..." Kes sighed in frustration. He didn't have time to have this conversation. There never seemed to be enough time. Then he had an idea. "I want you and Miki to come with me. I'll take you with me to the Leader's bunker. You'll both be safer there."

"We can't go there, Kes. It's only for officials, not

their families."

"I don't care. If I bring you both with me, what are they going to do? Turn away the Chief Xenobiologist? Tell the person they're relying on to communicate with the Scythians that he can't come in?"

Isobel touched his cheek. "You're being crazy. We can't go with you. I bet every other person in that bunker would love to have their family with them, but they can't. It's just the way it is. It wouldn't be fair if Miki and I went down there with you."

Kes' arms fell to his sides and his head bowed. His wife was right, but he couldn't bear the thought that this might be the last time he would see her and his daughter.

"Where's Miki?" he asked. "Can I see her?"

"Of course." Isobel called their daughter's name, and a moment later the two-year-old appeared at the top of the stairs that led from the basement into the hall.

"Daddy!" The toddler ran toward Kes as fast as her little legs would carry her. The hall light caught the red sheen in her black hair. Kes swept her up in his arms and she cuddled into his neck. He thought his heart would break.

"I can't leave you both," he said to Isobel.

"You have to," said Isobel. "I know what you're thinking. If this is the end I'd rather I was with you too, but you can't think like that. Go to the bunker and talk to the Scythians. I know we don't have much of a chance, but I know you'll do your best. If anyone can communicate with them, it's you."

Time was ticking away. Kes knew he had to go. He'd already taken too long on the detour.

"At least we had a chance to see each other again, didn't we?" said Isobel. Though she smiled, she was weeping. "At least we had the chance to put things right."

Kes couldn't speak. He nodded and held her and Miki

close. He huskily told his wife and child that he loved them before handing Miki to Isobel and striding down the pathway to the autocar. After he climbed inside and closed the door, he took a final look at them as the car drew away.

Isobel and Miki were silhouetted in the doorway by the light from the hall. He couldn't see their faces, only their outlines against the brightness, but he deliberately fixed the image in his mind, knowing it might be the last one he had of them.

When the autocar reached the end of the street he turned and looked at Nancy's house but the door had closed and the street was in darkness.

256

CHAPTER THIRTY-FOUR

There was a problem at Cerberus. Fletcher's tone was professional but Cherry could hear an edge of fear and panic in his voice. It was hardly surprising. Concordia's military had been preparing for decades for this moment, but it had never encountered a real enemy. Drills and exercises could not prepare you for the real thing. Cherry remembered too well the cold sweat and the painful tingle of nerve endings when faced with your mortality.

"Send people to visually inspect each system," she said. "Tell them to try percussive maintenance, then run the checks again."

"Percussive maintenance?"

"Hit the mechanisms with hammers. Not too hard, but enough to dislodge any rust or grit."

"Oh, okay. They're pretty large."

"I understand that, Fletcher, but unless you have any better ideas it's worth a try. Cerberus is our oldest silo. We'll be lucky if everything works as it's meant to after all this time." Cherry wished she'd asked Wilder to service the massive mechanisms that opened Cerberus' roof. But the focus had always been on the armaments. When the time came, they would be vital in the effort to protect the planet. But if the roof didn't open they would be useless. "Just do whatever you can, and keep me updated." She closed the comm.

The flight from Suddene to Lyonesse had passed quickly as Cherry dealt with the flurry of progress updates from Concordia's military arms. The three other silos were reporting all their checks were clear and they were ready for action. Companies of ground troops at all major metropolises were at their stations. The anti-spider devices had been activated. The community shelters were full and locked.

Concordia was ready and waiting.

"ETA has been revised," said Zapata suddenly.

"It has?" Cherry asked. She looked at the display. Even as she watched, the minutes until the heli was due to arrive at the Leader's Residence rapidly reduced.

"The wind's dropped," Zapata explained. "Didn't you notice?"

She hadn't. She'd been concentrating on the military's preparations. But as Cherry looked out into the night, she saw the clouds were opening and starlight shone through. She could see the water beneath them and in the distance was a line of blackness: the coast of Lyonesse. She checked the arrival time again.

"We'll make it to the Residence before the Scythians arrive," she said.

"Yes," said Zapata. "Just."

For the first time in the last hour, no comms were waiting for Cherry. No one had anything to report or anything to check with her. Zapata said nothing else. His features were tense with concentration as he extracted the maximum power from the heli.

Did he have a family he might never see again? Cherry realized she didn't know anything about him, except for the fact he was a damned good pilot.

A comm arrived, this time from a non-military source. Or perhaps ex-military. "Aubriot? What's happening? Did you find her?"

"After a lot of tramping through wet undergrowth in the dark, I found the tree. Then I had to climb up into it, getting covered in scratches and—"

"But did you find her?"

"Nope. Not here. Total waste of time. And now I have to get back to Annwn."

"Damn," Cherry said. "Did you see anything to indicate where she might be?"

"No. Place is a mess and it's too dark to see anything. No one would spend any longer here than they had to, though. There's a hole in the roof and the rain's got in."

"I wonder where she went," Cherry said. "I hope she's safe."

"Yeah, so...I'm going to try to get to the nearest shelter now."

Shit. Aubriot was kilometers from a shelter. He'd spent all the time since Cherry had last spoken to him searching for Wilder and now he was alone in the dark in one of the most dangerous places on the planet.

"Thanks for looking for her for me," Cherry said. "I appreciate it."

"No problem. You know, I have to admit she's a smart kid, even if she does live up a tree. She will have gone somewhere safe. And I have to go now too."

"I know where you can go!" Cherry exclaimed. "Cerberus. I'll tell Colonel Fletcher you're coming and he'll let you in."

"Cerberus? Why the hell would I want to go there?"

"Where else can you go? You'll never make it back to Annwn. There's no time."

"I suppose you have a point."

"And you can help them. They're having a problem with the roof opening mechanisms. Some of them are reporting faults but the maintenance team can't figure out what the problem is."

"And? I'm no engineer. I used to pay people to do that kind of thing."

"Just go there," said Cherry. "It won't hurt, and you'll be underground." And not alone. Aubriot had many faults, but there was something about the thought of him dying alone that tore at her.

"All right," he said. "I'll give it a try."

"Good." Cherry swallowed. Aubriot was sounding more 'human' than ever. And he'd tried to find Wilder, wandering around a forest at night while the imminent threat of a Scythian attack hung over him. It was probably the most selfless thing the man had ever done. "Good luck."

"Yeah, you too."

CHAPTER THIRTY-FIVE

Piddle and Puddle could not get used to micro-gravity. Wilder regretted bringing them aboard the *Opportunity*. The two small creatures vomited up whatever they ate not long after eating it, and the vomit was not easy to deal with when it was floating in mid air. Her pets' toilet habits—or lack of them—were even more inconvenient.

Wilder gently launched herself by pushing her feet against the side of the living quarters. As she floated past the small lump of Puddle's partially digested dinner, she swept it up into a tissue and folded the tissue over it. When she reached the other side of the living quarters, she pulled herself along the wall until she reached the trash disposal and deposited the tissue inside it. She returned to her work on her a-grav machine.

Piddle and Puddle had even puked and peed during the long hours it had taken for the shuttle to rendezvous with the *Opportunity*. Not that such small animals generated a lot of waste, but it was unpleasant nonetheless.

After several such accidents aboard ship, Wilder had made a bag out of a sweater by tying the bottom in a knot and the sleeves to two cupboard handles and installed her two little friends inside it. They would nap in there, cuddled together, and sometimes they would come out and run around the ship, clinging to the walls. They had quickly learned the dangers of letting go. Wilder had only had to rescue them two or three times as they floated helplessly, unable to return to a solid surface.

Technically, in micro-g, everywhere was a wall, and there was no a floor or ceiling. As soon as the shuttle had moved beyond most of the influence of Concordia's gravity well Wilder had been vividly reminded of her own poor coping skills with micro-g on the journey to the Galactic Assembly. She'd wondered if she'd made the right decision when agreeing to Quinn's suggestion to recuperate on the *Opportunity*. But by then it had been too late. She had borrowed the a-grav machine parts from Jamie Bond and Tycho and Stephie had loaded her up with supplies. After her friends had gone to so much trouble to help her it seemed wrong to back out at the last minute, especially over something as trivial as her discomfort in micro-g.

She'd told herself she would get used to it, though she hadn't noticed any signs of that yet. At least she was doing marginally better than Piddle and Puddle. She could use a toilet, for instance.

An unforeseen difficulty of working on a-grav while, ironically, in a micro-g environment, was that nothing remained where it was unless you fixed it there. Before, she'd been able to rely on Concordia's gravity to hold the a-grav machine on the ground. Aboard the *Opportunity*, she'd been forced to tether it to the 'floor'. She'd kept all the parts in boxes to avoid a room full of floating pieces of metal, but the boxes themselves had been dangerous floating objects too, of course. In the end, Wilder had put all the parts into a cupboard and then taken them out one piece at a time when she'd needed them.

The ship had been cool and smelled of dust and mold when she'd first come aboard. As far she knew, no human had set foot, or hand, on the *Opportunity* in all the years after she had disembarked with Cherry, Kes, and Aubriot. She personally had certainly felt no desire to revisit the place where she had spent so many months in close quarters with her three shipmates.

Quinn had already arrived and was waiting for her. Wilder had been pleased and relieved to recognize the distinctive patterning on his skin as he floated within the crew's section of the ship. The first thing she'd done was to ask him to turn up the heating. Things had become a little more comfortable after that.

Wilder pushed the final part into place. Her first stage of effort was now over. After many hours of work the new machine was built. Holding onto a chair that was fixed to the floor, she floated next to the a-grav machine, her hands on her hips, appreciating the satisfaction of completing this first essential task.

"Have you finished?" Quinn asked over the ship's comm.

"I've built it," Wilder replied. "Now I have to get it working. I can't remember exactly what I did before but I'm sure I'll figure it out through trial and error."

"Maybe have something to eat and take a nap. You're here to recover from your injuries, don't forget."

Wilder was tempted to ignore the Fila's advice and push on, but then she thought better of it. She hadn't yet forgotten the sight of her skinny, bruised body in Cherry's mirror. "Yeah, I'll do that." Once the words were out of her mouth she realized she felt hungry and fatigued. Her pain medication was wearing off, too. She could feel the discomfort beginning to build in her ribs and abdomen. It was weird how her mind managed to ignore the signals from her body when she was concentrating on something.

Wilder pushed off from the chair in the direction of the cupboard where she'd stored her food. After retrieving a container of pasta in lentil sauce, she opened the lid a little bit and scooped out noodles with a fork.

"Do you want to check your comm messages while you're eating?" Quinn asked.

"You make a strange kinda mom, Quinn," said Wilder. "You know that?"

"Are you implying that I'm trying to mother you?"

Smother me, Wilder thought, but she didn't say it. Quinn was only being kind. "I guess that is what I meant, but I know it's only because you care."

"I'm pleased I interpreted your underlying meaning correctly."

"You did, didn't you? You're getting good at understanding us."

"So, are you going to check your messages?"

"Wow, you're *really* good at understanding us," said Wilder, marveling that the Fila hadn't been deterred by her effort to change the subject. "Okay. In a minute. I'll eat this first."

Wilder had found her ear comm on the floor of her tree home and popped it into her pocket while calling Piddle and Puddle. Her two little friends had been hiding at first, but they'd poked out their heads when they recognized her voice.

Wilder ate the rest of the pasta and then sucked water from a bottle. She pulled out her medication packet and swallowed a tablet, followed by more water. Finally, she took out her comm and pushed it into her ear.

There was a message from Jamie Bond. "It was great to see you yesterday, Deadly After Midnight. I hope you make some progress with the sandwich—" 'Sandwich' was the code name for the a-grav machines. "I have a feeling you'll be the one to find the perfect mix of ingredients. I was wondering, do you want to meet up sometime and talk about recipes face to face? Just us, I mean."

Wilder smiled. Jamie Bond sounded sappy, but sweet. And he had to have guts to ask for a date with a girl who was at least five years older and a head taller than him. Maybe she would comm him back when she returned to the surface, but by then she hoped she would have made the 'sandwich' work and their shared project would be over.

Next in her list of comms were some attempts from Cherry to contact her. Wilder was glad she hadn't been bothered by those. In all of Concordia, Cherry was the last person she wanted to talk to. All that remained to listen to was a short message from Tycho and Stephie, wishing her good luck and telling her to visit when she was better.

That was it. No one else had tried to contact her. Ordinarily, this would be a good thing. She hated wasting time on boring small talk and gossip. But this time Wilder felt a tiny bit sad and, for the first time in her life, a little lonely.

Perhaps it was because she was many kilometers above the planet surface and the only human aboard the ship.

"Quinn, can I comm the surface from here?"

"Yes, that won't be a problem. However, if you wish to speak to someone you should do it now. It is evening at Oceanside and Annwn and most humans will be going to sleep soon."

"Okay, maybe I'll do it in the morning." Wilder put the empty meal container in the trash and pulled herself along the wall to go to the bathroom, change into pajamas, and brush her teeth.

When she was ready for bed, Wilder climbed into the sleeping bag on the floor of the living quarters. It was the same one she'd used for all those months on the trip to the Assembly. Plans for what she would do the next day circulated through her mind, gradually slowing down and transmogrifying into strange shapes and figures. The a-grav machine melted into a pulse emitter. Then it took flight and sped into the distance toward a setting sun, becoming lost in the vivid red, pink, and orange of the evening sky. A figure was walking toward her from the distant horizon, taking impossibly gigantic leaps over the land. As the figure drew nearer, Wilder recognized Jamie Bond, though he was taller and older.

"Wilder!" Jamie said. "Wilder, wake up!"

She tried to answer him. "I'm already awake," she tried to say. But her mouth voiced silent words.

"Wake up, Wilder!"

She forced open her eyes. Her dream had been so vivid she was momentarily confused, but then she remembered where she was and realized that it had to be Quinn, not Jamie, who was speaking to her. "What's wrong?" she asked, pushing down the sleeping bag.

"I've just heard from our communication center that we have sighted the Scythians. They're returning to Concordia."

Wilder was so shocked, for a moment she couldn't speak. "The Scythians?" she asked, stupidly.

"You must return to the surface," said Quinn. "Please go to one of the shuttles. I will send it to Oceanside immediately."

"No, wait." Wilder sat up and floated half inside and half outside her sleeping bag. "When will they get here?"

"Not for a few hours. You have time to return to the surface and enter one of the shelters."

"What if I don't want to?"

"You have to. The *Opportunity* will be a target for attack."

"I *have* to?" Wilder asked. "Now you're really sounding like you're trying to mother me. I thought you invited me up here as a guest. Now you're kicking me out?"

"For your benefit. When the Scythians arrive and are refused their tribute, this ship will become one of the least safe places in the star system."

"I'm getting damned tired of people doing things for my benefit," said Wilder. "How about you let me make this decision for myself?"

A pause followed. Then Quinn said, "I cannot physically force you into a shuttle, but I strongly recommend it. However, we built this ship as a gift for your colony. Whether you remain or leave is entirely your decision."

"Thank you," said Wilder. "I'm not leaving. Let's think about what we can do when the Scythians arrive."

CHAPTER THIRTY-SIX

Zapata landed the heli on the roof of the Leader's Residence. This time round, the landing was easy. The wind had died away to a light breeze and the sky had cleared to brilliant starlight. Cherry leapt out the moment the landing skids made contact, keeping low to avoid the still-spinning rotor. She ran out from under the blades before straightening up and jogging across the roof to the exit door.

By the time she opened the door Zapata was already high in the sky, making his way to the nearest shelter. Cherry ran down the steps two at a time. Before landing, she'd confirmed with Meredith that the Scythians still hadn't answered the hail the Fila had been sending them ever since they'd been spotted. Now, the enemy ships were minutes from reaching Concordia's high orbit.

Ten ships were coming. Two of the largest type: the double crescent that carried a massive pulse emitter on a spike where the crescents crossed. The other ships were single crescents, less powerful but still deadly. And Cherry had no doubt the Scythians were also bringing tens or even hundreds of thousands of their relentless spiders with them too, ready to unleash on Concordia and strip it of human life.

She reached the first floor and ran across the lobby to the elevator doors.

"I'm here," she said to Meredith over her comm as she waited for the elevator to rise to her level.

"Thank the stars," Meredith replied. "You're the last to arrive."

The doors opened and Cherry stepped inside. The doors closed and the elevator began its journey down.

Suddenly, a hard shock hit and Cherry was thrown to one side. The elevator abruptly stopped. Her heart froze.

"Meredith, what just happened?"

No answer came. The lights inside the elevator flickered and died. Utter darkness surrounded Cherry.

"Meredith? Meredith?"

Cherry felt for the elevator doors. If it had stopped at one of the intervening floors between the first floor and the bunker, she might be able to prise open the doors and get out. Then she could take the stairs the rest of the way.

But the doors were firmly closed. With only one arm, Cherry didn't have a hope of opening them.

The elevator light returned. The emergency backup power had kicked in.

"Meredith! Answer me!"

Cherry looked at the console. The lights for B3 and B4 were on, meaning she was between the two floors. The bunker was at B5.

Cherry was about to try to comm Meredith again, but she changed her mind. Something terrible had happened and the Leader was clearly distracted. Who else was in the bunker and could explain what had happened?

She comm'd Kes.

"Cherry?"

The voice that answered was strangled with emotion, the tone high, quiet, and distant.

"Kes? Is that you?" Cherry was honestly not sure. She'd gotten so used to her friend's voice—the Fila used something very similar as their standard for generating human speech—but this version of Kes' voice sounded like nothing she'd heard before. She wondered if whatever had caused the shock had disrupted the comm system, but he'd answered with her first name so it had to be him.

"I'm stuck in the elevator," she said. "What's happened?"

"They...They...Oh God! Oh my God."

Cherry heard a guttural sound, a horrible, heart-wrenching sound, as if the man's soul were being torn in two.

"Kes!" Cherry yelled. "Tell me what's happened!" She started thumping the elevator buttons with her fist. Desperately, she cast her gaze around the enclosed space, trying to find a way out. The only exit she could see was a hatch in the ceiling, but it was far out of her reach.

"They fired, Cherry," Kes whispered hoarsely. "They fired, before even asking us for tribute. They didn't say a word. All their ships fired at once. A simultaneous shot from ten ships." He choked, "Half of Oceanside is gone."

Cherry couldn't find the words to reply. Half of Oceanside? How many people was that? Thousands. Tens of thousands.

She kicked the elevator wall and then yelled as pain from her toes seared up her leg. "Kes, is there an engineer in there with you? Tell them to do whatever it takes to get me out of here. Now! Okay, Kes? Did you hear me? Find someone to get me out of here. Those fuckers are not going to get away with this."

She comm'd Aubriot, hoping to the stars that the damage the Scythians had inflicted hadn't taken down the network.

Aubriot took the comm.

"Have you heard what's happened?" Cherry asked.

"Yeah." His tone was leaden. "Wasn't expecting that."

"I need you to coordinate the response. We'll throw everything at them. Everything."

"What? Why me?"

"I'm stuck in an elevator. It was moving when we were hit and the shock's affected the system. I can't get out and I can't work inside a tiny box with no data and no vid feed. I need your help."

"You've got officers…"

"Just do it! It's mostly your plan, remember? You know it inside out. They've brought ten ships. We'll wipe them from the skies."

"Yeah. Okay."

He was gone.

Aubriot was no longer an officer—he wasn't even in the military—but Cherry didn't doubt his ability to make the senior staff listen to him and follow his orders. Despite his many faults if there was one thing he didn't lack it was the ability to take control.

She stared at the walls surrounding her, rigid with frustration. How many people had died? She'd been expecting an exchange of words at least. The Scythians should have demanded their tribute, then Meredith would have refused. And if the Scythians attacked or even threatened it, Cherry would have ordered the missile silos to be opened, the pulse emitters to be raised to ground level, and the surface armaments revealed. The Scythians would have discovered that they were not going to destroy the human colony or take the planet as easily as they might have thought.

But the Scythians had had a surprise of their own to deliver. What did it mean? Were they on the offensive because they anticipated a hostile reception and they were getting in the first blow? Or did they want to cow the colonists and make them agree to whatever terms the Scythians set?

Did it matter? No.

When she'd learned that Concordia was the Scythians' origin planet, their attacks had made more sense to Cherry. The fact didn't excuse them. There was no excuse for attempting to destroy another intelligent species, even if you did find them living on your former home. But to an extent Cherry had understood the Scythians' actions.

Now, things were different. The Scythians had allowed the humans to remain on Concordia. They'd been absent for decades, and the colony had thrived and built a civilization. To return now and launch a devastating attack with no warning, no parley, no attempt at a compromise...It was an evil act, and the Scythians deserved everything they had coming to them.

In her mind's eye she could see the gigantic roof covering Cerberus begin to pull back, shedding soil, rocks, and vegetation to the sides. Minotaur, along the coast from Oceanside, would growl into life, opening the cliff top, sending boulders crashing into the ocean below. Medusa, long-hidden below her high plateau, would shake free her icy cap and spill frozen shale down the mountainside. A rising waterfall would signal Hydra's arrival, rising from the ocean. The rumbling of the silos' mechanisms would shake the ground and echo through the air. The armaments would start to rise into the starlit night, their targeting systems locking onto the ten Scythian ships that threatened the planet.

A noise sounded above Cherry. Someone had landed

on the roof of the elevator. A moment later, the hatch in the ceiling opened. The head and shoulders of a middle-aged, bald man appeared.

"Thank the stars," said Cherry.

"You'll have to come out this way," said the man. "The elevator won't restart. Either the shaft has been damaged or something's screwed up the system."

"It doesn't matter," Cherry said. "Do you have a rope?"

"Yes, but that's all. I don't have a harness or anything like that. Maybe you can tie it around you."

"Just let it down. Hurry up."

The end of a hemp rope dropped into the elevator. Cherry grabbed it. "Pull me up!"

The man peered in. "Are you sure you can support your weight on one arm?"

"Yes. Stop wasting time. Pull me up."

The man disappeared and the tension on the rope tightened. Cherry's feet left the floor and she rose into the air, clinging tightly to the rope. When she reached the hatch, however, she hit a problem. The rope was scraping against the edge of the hatch. If she continued to hold it her hand would be scraped too and would block the rope from moving farther.

Just as she was debating whether to let go and fall back into the elevator, a hand reached in and grabbed the back of her shirt. She was unceremoniously hauled through the hatch and dumped onto the elevator's roof.

"Thanks," she gasped.

"The only way out is up the service ladder," said the man, "but it isn't far to the next floor."

Above them in the dark elevator shaft the doors to the nearest floor stood open. Cherry went up the ladder first, forced to go slowly so that she didn't fall when she released the grip of her only hand to move it higher.

She reached the open doors and crawled out of the shaft onto the tiled floor. Immediately, she rose to her feet and ran to the stairway that would take her down to the bunker. As she sped down the stairs she noticed cracks in the walls. The combined attack from all the Scythian ships must have had a devastating force to inflict damage so far underground.

In less than a minute she'd reached the bunker. She burst through the doors into the room, only to meet a scene of disarray.

Kes sat motionless at the table, his face ashen, his gaze a distant stare. Meredith was pacing in front of the transparent wall that separated the room from the Fila side, her hand on her forehead and her features riven with despair and confusion. Two officials were huddled together and muttering to each other, another two were staring at the screens embedded in the walls. The screens showed scenes of the open missile silos and other places in Concordia, as well as a visual on the Scythian ships.

"What's going on?" Cherry asked.

Meredith abruptly turned toward her as if only just noticing Cherry's appearance. She ran at Cherry and grabbed her shoulders. Before she could say anything, however, a comm from Aubriot arrived.

Cherry held up her hand to Meredith, palm outward. Then she touched her ear comm. "Yes?"

"Cerberus opened," Aubriot said. "And all the others. Everything's locked on target."

"Right, I'll give the order," said Cherry.

"No!" Meredith exclaimed. "Wait!"

Cherry gritted her teeth. "Standby, Aubriot." She asked Meredith, "What are we waiting for?"

"We received a message. Play it, Kes."

Woodenly, Kes swiped the interface set into the table he was sitting at and thumbed a key.

A screech pierced Cherry's ears. She covered one of them but had no way of protecting the other from the penetrating sound.

"Dammit, Kes," said Costello, Head of Civil Works, "can't you skip over that part?"

Kes betrayed no sign he'd heard the woman.

"Invaders of our planet," said a voice. The Scythians had somehow accessed the Fila's translation technology. The computer-generated voice was nearly the same as the one Cherry had heard a million times before when talking with the aquatic aliens. "We have tolerated your presence in our home and allowed you to benefit from its resources. You have multiplied your numbers and created a self-sustaining livelihood. We have been forgiving. We have been generous. But these things are...*Does not translate*...Now it is time for us to receive our recompense."

A pause followed by a second *Does not translate*.

"We are returning to our home," the Scythian message continued. "We have brought materials to construct habitations and settlers to live inside them. They will be the first of our kind to dwell on the sacred soil of our homeland in eons. But our people will not be able to survive outside of their habitations. They will require assistance. You will service them, supplying all their needs. In return, we will allow you to continue to live on our world. Refuse this offer, and we will destroy your colony and all life on our planet. No other species will ever besmirch our sacred land with its presence again. We await your answer."

CHAPTER THIRTY-SEVEN

Wilder endured the crushing pressure stoically, though she couldn't help harboring a wish that the Fila had the technology to entirely eradicate the effect of the *Opportunity's* fast acceleration on the human body, not only ameliorate it. She'd grown used to the feeling on her trip to the Assembly. But she worried about Piddle and Puddle. Would their little bodies and small bones cope?

Thankfully, the pressure eased after only a short time. That was all it took to travel the distance to the second planet out from Concordia in the star system. As soon as Wilder felt she could safely move, she asked Quinn to release the straps holding her to the padded, reclined seat. She climbed off the seat and walked to the living quarters, struggling against the forces pressing her down at first. By the time she reached her pets' separate pouches—she'd guessed they would be safer apart so their bodies would not crush against each other—the effects of the acceleration had decreased to roughly the same as Concordian gravity and she could move lightly.

Wilder opened the first pouch. Puddle's eyes glared up at her resentfully. She lifted him out carefully and gently ran her hands over his body. He didn't seem to have any broken bones. As to any internal damage, she simply didn't know. Time would tell if the little creature had suffered serious damage. She replaced Puddle in his pouch.

Next, Wilder opened Piddle's tied-up sweater. She sucked in a breath. Piddle's eyes were closed.

"No, no, no!"

Wilder reached into the pouch. Piddle was warm, but was she still alive? Even more gently than she'd handled Puddle, Wilder cradled Piddle as she lifted her out. She inspected the creature's face. Piddle's mouth hung open and her tiny tongue lolled out over her pointed teeth. As Wilder turned the small body, Piddle's head flopped to the side.

Puddle's head and front legs emerged from the hole at the top of the sweater. He was watching his little friend.

Wilder held Piddle's chest against her ear, the soft, warm fur tickling her, but she couldn't hear anything. Did Concordian animals even have hearts in the same way that Earth animals did? Wilder didn't know. When she'd been at school Concordian animals hadn't been a part of the curriculum. No one had thought complex life forms even existed on the planet they were journeying toward.

As Wilder carried out her checks on her pets, the *Opportunity* had been slowing further. Wilder grew lighter and lighter until her feet lifted off the floor and she was floating.

Piddle gave a little squirm. Wilder quickly moved the animal to where she could see her. Piddle's eyes slowly opened, her tongue retracted, and her mouth closed. Her legs moved feebly.

"Are you okay?" Wilder asked. "Please be okay!"

As if in response, Piddle wriggled some more. Her tail whipped from side to side. She also didn't seem to have any broken bones.

Feeling better but remaining concerned over the health of her pets, Wilder put Piddle in Puddle's pouch. He immediately began to groom her.

"We have entered low orbit on the far side of Camaret," said Quinn. "The Scythians may have observed our movements, but perhaps not. At their current distance the Scythians' instruments may not detect the *Opportunity's* trace against the background of solar radiation."

"But they know this ship exists, right?" said Wilder. "They won't have forgotten about it."

"No, indeed they won't."

Camaret was the next planet in from Concordia, closer to its star. Barren, rocky, and devoid of life, the place had not held much interest for the colony's scientists, who, after longer than fifty Earth years, had barely scraped the surface of investigating their own world.

But for Wilder, Quinn, and the other Fila in the crew, Camaret was somewhere to hide and wait while they tried to come up with a way to use the *Opportunity* to its greatest effect in the inevitable battle for Concordia.

As long as they remained shielded by the planet's mass, the Scythians might not want to weaken their forces by sending a ship to hunt them out. And though the *Opportunity* was not powerful enough to inflict serious damage on anything except the smaller ships in the Scythian fleet, it was nevertheless not without its sting.

CHAPTER THIRTY-EIGHT

All eyes were on Cherry. Even Meredith, the Leader, seemed to be looking at her for an answer. Only Kes' gaze was averted. He was in a world of his own, clearly deeply in shock.

"When did the message arrive?" Cherry asked. "Was it before or after we opened the silos?"

"We received it immediately after the assault," Meredith replied.

"And we've heard nothing since then?"

"No. They must have seen the silos opening but they haven't said anything about them yet. I guess they still think they can destroy us." Meredith slumped into a chair. "It was all a ploy, right from the beginning. The Scythians never wanted a tribute. During their second attack, when the colony was sheltering in Sidhe, they must have realized they could make use of our presence here. We could survive on their planet but they could not. If they used us as their slaves they could reestablish a civilization on the world they had been forced to abandon. They could come home. Telling us they accepted the sacrifice of the *Mistral* and its crew was only a convenient excuse for them to call off their attack and leave. Since then they've been waiting, biding their time until our population increased to sufficient numbers to serve their needs."

"You're right," Cherry said. "That's clear now."

"What isn't clear is, what do we do?" Meredith asked.

"What do you mean?" asked Cherry.

"What answer do we give them? Do we agree to their demands?"

"Why is that even a question?"

"Yes," Meredith said. "We don't have a choice, do we? We'll have to agree."

"What?!" Kes roared, slamming a fist on the table and rising to his feet so fast his chair clattered to the ground behind him. "No! They just killed thousands of people with no provocation. Thousands of Concordians are dead just so the Scythians could make a point!" He swiveled to face Cherry. "Give the order. Destroy them."

"I will," Cherry said. "We can't give in to them."

"No," said Meredith. "Do not give the order to fire. I'm Leader here and I forbid it. If we respond to the Scythians' attack we'll be committing suicide. Our families, our homes, everything we've worked for, gone. We'll all die, and we're the last outpost of human society. If Concordia falls it'll be the end of human civilization."

"Better dead than living as slaves," said Cherry.

Meredith seemed about to say something but then changed her mind. She turned to the other officials in the room. There were four heads of government departments. "I want to hear your opinions," she said.

While Meredith was listening to the department heads, Cherry comm'd Aubriot to explain the situation. She wanted to know what he thought about the

Scythians' demand. Would he prefer survival, no matter the cost?

"Fuck that," he said.

"That's what I thought you would say," said Cherry.

"What about our esteemed Leader?" Aubriot asked.

"She wants to agree to their terms, believe it or not. She's talking to the others, but I don't think she'll change her mind."

"Oh well," said Aubriot. "Who cares what she thinks?"

"Not me," said Cherry.

"Gotcha. Just let us know when."

"Keep those missiles and emitters targeted."

"Don't worry. They're all tracking the Scythian ships' movements perfectly."

A screech erupted from the room's comm. Cherry clapped a hand to one ear and pressed her shoulder to the other. A moment later the sound mercifully ceased.

"We must receive your answer. Withdraw your weapons. We must receive your answer. Withdraw your weapons." Silence.

"Elliot," said Meredith. "Open a return comm to the Scythian ship."

"Wait!" exclaimed Costello, the Head of Civil Works. "You can't answer on behalf of all of us. We have to put it to a vote."

"Who's Elliot?" Cherry asked Kes.

"The Fila representative," he replied. He was propping his elbows on the table and holding his head in his hands. His earlier fury seemed to have dissipated to extreme lassitude.

Cherry had almost forgotten the Fila on the other side of the transparent wall in the bunker. "What happened to Quinn?"

"He's aboard the *Opportunity*, with Wilder."

"Wilder went to the *Opportunity* with Quinn?! Stars, I'd forgotten all about that ship. I wonder where it is? I hope Quinn had the good sense to leave the area as soon as he knew the Scythians were coming."

Kes didn't reply.

Meanwhile, Meredith and the department heads had been arguing.

"I am the elected Leader!" Meredith exclaimed.

"So what?" Costello asked. "There's nothing in your mandate that gives you the right to consign the entire colony to slavery."

"It's my responsibility to protect you all," said Meredith. "Not sacrifice you to some noble-sounding ideal."

"Wanting to live free or not at all isn't an ideal," retorted Costello. "It's a right."

"Maybe it is, but that's an individual's decision. We can't go around all of Concordia and ask everyone what they would prefer. There isn't time. I have to decide for everyone. That's what I'm supposed to do. And I decide we should live. Who knows what the future may hold? If we agree to the Scythians' terms now, perhaps the Galactic Assembly will force them to release us later. If we resist now, that's it. Forever."

"You're forgetting a third alternative, Meredith," Cherry said. "What if we assert our right to live in peace on a planet that can sustain us, without hurting anyone? What if we fight back, and we win?Besides, I think you're optimistic to think the Scythians won't still kill most of us even if we agree. They didn't have to come here and slaughter thousands of our citizens in order to propose their plan. They could have approached us peacefully. But instead they attacked first so we would be intimidated into agreeing to their terms. They're murderers. Vicious, remorseless murderers. Living under them would be torture. Death would be better."

"I can't do it. I can't allow the destruction of all the men, women, and children under my care."

"You know what?" Cherry said. "Your father would

be ashamed of you."

Meredith gasped. "How can you say that? It isn't true! My father was all about protecting and nurturing every single person on Concordia."

"Yes, he was," said Cherry. "But not at any cost. No one seems to remember any longer—it's probably not even in the history books—but in the early days of this colony your father, me, and the rest of the Gens fought tooth and nail for the right to live our lives as we chose. We risked death for that cause because the idea of living without our independence was unbearable to us. Our actions were reckless, perhaps stupid even, when the colony was small, weak, and teetering on the edge of failure. But we did it anyway because we decided that our lives were not worth living any other way. Ethan *fought back*, Meredith. And that's something you aren't prepared to do.

"I've just realized I've been wrong about something. For months now, I've been worried this generation of Concordians wasn't up to scratch. I thought they were not prepared for the Scythians' return. They seemed lazy, undisciplined, and careless. To me, they weren't scared enough. But they've surprised me. After I gave the order, all the battle preparations went with hardly a single hitch. Our military knew what it was doing after all. I've realized it wasn't them I should have been worried about, it was you. I hate to say it, Meredith—I remember you as a baby in your mother's arms—but you're the wrongness I was sensing all along. *You're* the rot at the heart of Concordia."

Cherry opened a comm to all her senior officers and Aubriot. She spoke only two words: "Return fire."

CHAPTER THIRTY-NINE

Seconds later, fire erupted from Cerberus as the missiles launched. Minotaur followed next, then Medusa, and finally Hydra. Massive rockets rose into the air, pulling against Concordia's gravity, rising faster and faster, trailing brilliant white flames. They were locked onto their targets and wouldn't stop until they either reached their destinations and detonated or they were shot out of the sky.

Almost before the missiles left their launchers, pulse fire started up, its light turning night to day around the silos. Concordia was throwing everything it had at the Scythians. The colony had been a long time waiting for this moment and it had nothing to lose.

Cherry's gaze moved to the screen showing the Scythian ships. This scene was limited to a single viewpoint. The Concordians had decided against adding to the single satellite left over from the earliest days of colonization for fear of attracting the attention of the Scythians. The aging device had transmitted images of the first two battles with the Scythians. Now it was to transmit its third and last. Cherry was under no illusion that the Scythians would succeed in destroying the colony. If not that day, then eventually. They wouldn't rest until their origin planet was wiped clean of the interlopers. They had made that clear.

The bunker was silent as everyone watched the screens. None present except Kes and Cherry had ever experienced a Scythian attack. Meredith's features were frozen in horror. Others bore a look of fascinated dread. Kes' expression was intent but calm, as if already resigned to whatever happened in the battle.

The Scythian ships were firing. They weren't attempting to out-maneuver the missiles closing in on them, perhaps guessing correctly that their only chance at evading them was to destroy them. A shot from one of the largest Scythian ships hit the leading missile, bursting it into fragments that quickly disappeared into the ether of space.

A pulse from the surface arrived ahead of the next missile, successfully striking a small Scythian ship full on, bursting one half of its crescent away. More missiles were arriving, but the Scythians were hitting them all. The missiles' effect would be greater than a pulse strike but only if they managed to get through. And their supply was strictly limited, unlike the pulse emitters, which would continue to fire as long as they received sufficient energy.

On the surface of the planet, fire from the Scythian ships was arriving. The pulses they weren't aiming at the missiles were targeting the missile silos. Specifically, the pulse emitters that stood not far distant from the missile launch sites.

"Yes!" Kes shouted.

Cherry turned to see a Scythian ship dissolving in pale blue fire. Either a missile had gotten through the enemy's defense or a pulse had hit its mark.

One down. Nine to go.

The second tranche of missiles were moving into

position. Like the first swathe, these would be aimed at the two leading Scythian ships with their pulse emitter spikes. These two ships could cause the most damage, and it was possible their loss might cause the others to give up and retreat. Concordia might live a little while yet.

The two Scythian spikes flashed simultaneously. A pulse sped from both, they converged, doubled in size and brightness, and flew toward the planet. A second later, Minotaur exploded.

A collective gasp sounded in the bunker as the missile silo rose into the air in fragments, spurting flames hundreds of meters high. The Scythians' combined pulse must have hit the silo's fuel tanks. Less than a second later a tremor hit the bunker, the shock from the blast arriving from its clifftop site down the coast.

Meredith's frozen gaze of horror broke and she buried her head in her arms on the table.

Cherry felt strangely calm as she watched the battle. The path of its progress seemed inevitable. The colony would inflict damage on the Scythian ships, perhaps even destroying one or two, but slowly it would be beaten into the ground by their enemy's relentless fire. The ships could move. They could leave, repair themselves, and return to inflict more damage. Concordia had nowhere to go.

"What's that?" Costello asked, pointing at the screen that displayed Hydra. Black objects were raining down into the ocean. At first Cherry thought it was debris from the Minotaur explosion, but Hydra was too far away. The silo sat on a shallow area of ocean closer to Suddene than Lyonesse.

If the black falling objects were not debris, they had to be coming from the Scythians. The ships must have launched them while they were engaged in battle, but their dark color had prevented the human observers

CHAPTER FORTY

"Quinn, we have to see what's happening," said Wilder.

"Moving out of Camaret's shadow will expose us to the Scythians' scanners," Quinn replied. "At this distance they will spot us immediately, and then they will fire on us."

"Well, how about we fire on *them*?" Wilder was tired of hiding. She felt like she was skulking away like a coward when every other Concordian was suffering under the Scythian attack.

"I understand your motivation," said Quinn. "But firing on the Scythian fleet will most certainly attract their attention."

"That's the point!" Wilder exclaimed. "Maybe it will help the colony if we provide a distraction. The *Opportunity* is pretty fast. Maybe we can draw a ship or two away from the battle."

There was a pause as the Fila considered Wilder's suggestion. She was looking through the transparent wall at Quinn. She found it easier to talk to him that way, rather than chatting with his disembodied voice over the ship's comm.

"That may be an effective tactic," Quinn finally said. "I have spoken with the other crew members and they agree to take the risk."

"Woo hoo!" said Wilder. "Let's do it."

"You must go to your safety seat," Quinn said. "We will be piloting the *Opportunity* at high speeds."

Wilder suddenly remembered Piddle and Puddle. The poor creatures would have to endure another bout of high acceleration. She almost wished she hadn't brought them aboard, but then again the Scythians were probably attacking Cerberus and her pets' forest home would be razed.

"Give me one minute," said Wilder. After the previous period of acceleration, Wilder had remembered there was a soft, downy substance in one of the cabinets in the ship's head. She had no idea what the material was supposed to be used for, and neither had any other passengers on the trip to the Galactic Assembly, for it had remained untouched. But Wilder knew the perfect use for it now.

She pulled herself through the ship until she reached the head, took large handfuls of the fluffy substance out of the box in the cabinet, and went to the living quarters. Piddle and Puddle were floating in their pouches, looking ill with motion sickness.

"I hope I can take you home soon," said Wilder. "But until then, I have some lovely soft stuff for you to lie on when we get going. You should be more comfortable on this." She pushed the material into the tied-up sweaters, forcing it into the bottoms where her pets would end up when the ship began to accelerate.

When she was sure she'd made Piddle and Puddle as comfortable as possible, Wilder pushed off from the wall with her feet, sending herself zooming into the room that held the four reclined acceleration seats.

"Ready," she said to Quinn. "Oh, wait a minute. Can you give me a visual of what's happening outside the ship on the interface?"

In answer, the blank interface on the wall suddenly displayed a view of the exterior. A rocky, airless landscape filled the entire screen. They were so close to Camaret the ship's cameras were not picking up anything else. The landscape was bright with the reflected light of the system's star. Wilder wondered if it was day or night on Concordia. She'd lost track of time.

Then the scene switched, and Wilder saw the star itself, though it was smaller and dimmer than it appeared from Concordia's surface. Concordia itself was not visible. Wilder wasn't sure in which direction it lay.

"Starting to maneuver," said Quinn. "We will leave Camaret's cover in three minutes and eighteen seconds."

Pressure pinned Wilder down, but she ignored the uncomfortable feeling as she watched the interface. The scene switched again, back to Camaret's surface. It was moving. Distant rocks and dust flowed over the screen, followed by a curved horizon, and then open space. Even though millions of kilometers separated them, Wilder immediately saw the blue-green ball that was Concordia and the tiny flickerings of light that was the pulse fire of the battle.

"What's happening, Quinn?" Wilder asked. "Are you picking up any messages? Your people know you're here with me, don't they?"

Quinn didn't answer for several long moments. Wilder didn't press him for a response, knowing that he was probably busy listening to the messages she had asked about.

"Things are bad, Wilder," the Fila eventually said. "The Scythians are attempting to erase all life on the planet. They have dropped a biocide into the ocean that is killing my people."

Wilder almost sat up in shock but the safety straps prevented her. "They're monsters. Why would they do something like that? The Fila are no threat to them."

When Quinn said nothing Wilder was forced to come to the obvious conclusion by herself: the Fila were no threat to the Scythians by themselves but they'd helped the humans—the species who was competing for land to live on and planetary resources, and who had gone to the Galactic Assembly for military support in defense of their occupation of Concordia.

"We have to stop them," said Wilder.

"I fear it's already too late," Quinn said. "The message says the biocide is spreading faster than they can escape it. Eventually it will disperse throughout all of Concordia's oceans and that will be the end of us."

"Oh, Quinn," said Wilder. A lump formed in her throat. She didn't know what to say.

"The biocide has been deposited on the land too. Its dispersal out of water is slower, but within a few months all of Concordia will be a barren wasteland. The planet will not support life again for perhaps hundreds of thousands of years, if ever."

"Let's get them," said Wilder. "I know it's hopeless, but let's do all the damage we can."

"Yes," Quinn replied. "Let us do that."

Acceleration pressure hit Wilder like a hammer, driving the tears in her eyes down the sides of her face and into her hair. She was crying for the Fila, crying for the people of Concordia, and for Piddle and Puddle, whose home had been obliterated by the Scythians and would never grow again, thanks to their desecration of the planet.

On the interface on the wall, Concordia was growing visibly larger, such was the speed of their approach to the planet. Wilder still could not make out the Scythian ships, but the sparks of pulse fire were more noticeable.

The Scythians would not have a visual on the

Opportunity yet either, but they had to know she was coming.

"We will be within firing range soon," said Quinn.

"At this distance?" Wilder asked, fighting to speak due to the crushing pressure on her throat.

"Space battles are conducted at wider distances than you might imagine."

Concordia had grown from the size of a pea to a marble.

"You have been a good friend, Wilder."

"You too, Quinn. You too."

Wilder wished she had had another moment with Piddle and Puddle, to hug them one last time. She wished she could say goodbye to Tycho and Stephie and Jamie Bond and everyone else she knew. She wanted to tell Kes how much he'd helped her with his support and to thank him. She even wanted to make amends with Cherry.

But there was no time left. No time left for anything. She was only seventeen. She had barely begun to live her life. It wasn't fair.

A brilliant streak of light flew across the screen, heading from the *Opportunity* toward Concordia.

"That was from us, right?" said Wilder. "I hope it blows a Scythian ship to pieces."

"No," said Quinn. "It was not us. We haven't fired yet. We are only now within range."

Wilder blinked. "If it wasn't us, who was it?"

"I am trying to discover that."

The image on the interface screen switched. Wilder saw the system's star, brilliant white-yellow. "That's where the pulse came from? The sun?"

"Not quite. Please wait a moment."

As Wilder watched the system's star, another source of light appeared next to it, more brilliant than any star in the background. The spot of light grew gradually larger and brighter. It was moving toward the

Opportunity. Several minutes passed. The light became too bright for Wilder to look at. She narrowed her eyes to slits and saw the bolt narrowly pass the ship. She guessed it was heading onward to Concordia.

"Is it a Scythian weapon?" Wilder asked. Perhaps the aliens had a device that would destroy life on the planet even faster than their biocide.

A frustrating silence dragged out. The pressure on Wilder eased. The *Opportunity* was slowing down, and she had no idea why. "Is anyone going to tell me what's happening?!" Wilder asked, rather loudly.

"It is not a Scythian weapon," Quinn said. "It isHUMANITY'S FIGHT aimed at the Scythian ships, and it is destroying them."

"It is?" asked Wilder. "Let me see!"

The scene on the interface switched once more. Concordia was bigger than ever. Wilder saw the bolt that had passed them by. It was growing smaller as it sped away from them, drawing closer to its target.

"What is it, Quinn?" Wilder asked. "And who's firing? You must have some idea."

"We have sent out a hail, but the distances involved mean we may have to wait several minutes for a reply."

"You really don't know who it might be?"

"My best guess is that it is the Parvus."

The Parvus? At first the name made no sense to Wilder, but then she remembered the headline in the newsfeed the evening she'd had her accident with the a-grav machine. A delegation of Parvus was arriving, the headline had said, and she'd been reminded of Kes receiving the notification the day before. Wilder had asked Cherry about them but at the time she'd been too busy to talk.

"Who are the Parvus?" Wilder asked. "And what are they doing here?"

"The Parvus are members of the Galactic Assembly," Quinn replied, "and it looks as though they've saved your colony."

CHAPTER FORTY-ONE

Cherry thought she was dreaming. One of the largest Scythian ships was a ball of pale blue fire. What had happened? All the missiles had been launched, and even a direct hit from several pulse emitters should not have been able to take out one of the huge spiked ships.

"Did you see that?" Costello asked. "What was it?"

"I didn't," Cherry replied. "I was looking at another screen for a moment." Minotaur was rubble, and they had just lost Medusa too. Her mountaintop site was now a massive, smoking crater. The Scythians were continuing to try to pound the colony into dust despite the fact they had already ensured its eventual destruction with their biocide.

"The biggest pulse I ever saw arrived from out of nowhere and hit the Scythian ship."

"From out of nowhere?" Cherry was utterly confused. How could another pulse emitter be firing on the Scythians? It was impossible for anyone to have built another one in secret. Wilder working on an a-grav machine was one thing, but building something like an emitter, with all the specialized parts and materials needed, would require a miracle.

The Scythian firing was slowing down. They also seemed confused by this unexpected—and, to them, devastating—event.

Cherry comm'd Aubriot.

"What's going on?" he asked. "You didn't tell me you had another pulse emitter up your sleeve."

"I don't," Cherry replied. "I'm as much in the dark as everyone else. But while we have this advantage, don't let up. If you can squeeze any more fire out of your emitters do it. Let's kick them while they're down."

Long minutes dragged out. The Scythians continued to concentrate their attack on Cerberus and Hydra, the only remaining military sites. Cerberus and Hydra continued to fight back.

Then another mysterious pulse arrived, and this time Cherry saw it. The screen momentarily whited out, and when the image returned it showed the remaining spiked Scythian ship was no more.

"It is the Parvus," said a voice. Elliot was speaking. "We received a message from Quinn, aboard the *Opportunity*. The Parvus have been harvesting energy from this system's star. They have technology that allows them to do this, and then they can contain the energy within a field and direct it toward a distant object. They have passed on an apology that the process takes so long, but they hope their intention is well received."

"Oh, it's well received," said Cherry. "It's very well received."

The remaining Scythian ships were moving. They were turning around and leaving. They'd given up the battle.

Cherry said, "Please tell the Parvus..." But Kes touched her arm and pointed at the transparent wall. Elliot had ceased the Fila's customary swirling movement. His body hung motionless in the water. The biocide had reached him. He was dead.

304

CHAPTER FORTY-TWO

Kes wandered through the rubble that was all that remained of that part of Oceanside. The sun was rising, and the remains of the buildings still smoked with heat from the Scythian's initial, unexpected strike. Kes could feel it through the soles of his shoes. Cherry had wanted to make him wear a gas mask before going outside. No one knew exactly where the biocide containers had landed or how far or fast the poison would spread.

But Kes didn't care. What did it matter if he died now or later? They were all going to die eventually, along with the rest of life on Concordia. The Scythians had already done the job of killing everyone, it was only going to happen slower than they had anticipated.

All Kes wanted to do was find Isobel and Miki. He dared not imagine they might still be alive, but he longed to see their faces one more time. He wanted to touch them, to hold them, and to ask their forgiveness for abandoning them. If he could only do that, perhaps he could die in peace.

The problem was, the place was unrecognizable. Kes didn't know where he was. The Scythian strike had flattened all the houses and obliterated the roads. Fires had started that still burned. More than once, Kes had come across human remains in the debris. After ascertaining as quickly as he could that they did not belong to his wife or child he would skirt around them, trying to avoid looking at them any further. Other searchers were looking for loved ones too.

Kes stopped, put his hands on his hips, and tried to get his bearings. In the distance he could see a freeway running through an untouched portion of ground on the city's outskirts. From the appearance of the landscape that surrounded it Kes guessed that it was the road from Annwn. It would have been the route he traveled in when Meredith had ordered him to join her in the Leader's bunker.

He took a long moment to mentally reconstruct the street system as it had been, leading out from the arterial road. He pointed to where he guessed the rows of houses had been to help his mental process.

"One, two, three," he muttered. Three exits, and then the fourth had been the street where Isobel's sister, Nancy, had lived.

When he'd decided on a rough area in which to search, Kes strode toward it, stepping over the rubble-strewn ground. He was going so fast he almost didn't see a body until he was on top of it.

A man, lying face downward. His shoes lay some distance away and his back was burned.

Swallowing his horror and distress, Kes took a wide detour before re-orienting himself. He arrived at the approximate location of Nancy's street sweaty and shaking, either with exertion or anguish. Perhaps both.

"Isobel!" His voice was loud in the silent devastation. "Miki! Sweetheart, can you hear me? Isobel? Miki!"

A groan sounded in response. Kes' heart leapt and he raced toward the origin of the noise. But before he reached the person his heart sank again. It was a man, lying on his back, still alive.

"Help me."

The man's hair was gone. Singed away, and his skin bore the marks of burning. His clothes were burned too, but by some miracle the man hadn't caught entirely on fire.

"Can you stand?" Kes asked. "Try. I'll help you." He wasn't sure where to touch the man without hurting him.

The man slowly managed to sit up. He grabbed Kes' forearm. "Thank you. Thank you for stopping."

"Medics are coming out soon," said Kes. "They're trying to find gas masks for them first."

"Gas masks?" asked the man. "What do they need those for?"

He didn't know. Of course he didn't. Only the people in the Leader's bunker knew what had happened, what the Scythians had done, and what Concordia could expect.

"Someone will explain it to you later," said Kes. "Can you walk? I can help, but I don't know where to touch you. I don't want to hurt you."

"I can't feel anything. I don't think you can hurt me."

But when Kes tried to help the man to his feet, they found his legs were simply too injured to support his weight.

"The medics will be coming soon," said Kes, though he wondered what was the point. But he didn't want to tell the man the truth of the situation.

"Were you looking for someone?" asked the man. "I heard you shout a name."

"I was. I was looking for my wife and my little girl."

"You carry on. I'll be all right here. I feel better now I know help is coming."

When Kes hesitated the man urged him again.

"Okay," said Kes, "but I'll be back to check on you."

He resumed his search, calling Isobel's name and

Miki's over and over and wandering farther and farther until he had entirely left his original search area. A deep sorrow settled over him and obliterated his faint hope.

A comm arrived. Cherry wanted to speak to him.

"Any luck?" she asked.

"No. I found a survivor, but not Isobel or Miki. Are the medics on their way yet?"

"We're working on it. Kes, I'm sorry. Are you going to carry on searching?"

"Yes. I have to find them."

"I understand. I hope you do. I wanted to let you know something. You remember that strange arrival that claimed it was a Guardian?"

"The one that seemed to be Faina? Yes, I remember."

"It broke out of prison during the attack," said Cherry. "I found out a moment ago."

"Huh, really? That seems to be the least of our worries right now."

"Yes, but I thought it was worth mentioning to you. The prison isn't far from the area you're searching, though it escaped the worst of the blast. If the thing is a Guardian I find it odd that it would take advantage of the chaos to escape. The Guardians were programmed to help us."

"Perhaps Faina thought the best way she could help us was by escaping."

"Hmm. Maybe you're right," Cherry said. "Anyway, as you say, we have worse things to worry about. There must be plenty of people trapped in the rubble. We'll have to find them and get them out."

"And before the biocide arrives," said Kes. "The situation is hopeless, but I guess we have to keep going."

"We have to. What other choice is there?" Cherry was gone.

Kes sat down on a stone. "Isobel!" he called, more out of misery than in anticipation of an answer.

But then he heard a reply. Or had he imagined it?

"Isobel!"

There it was again. A faint cry. Kes couldn't make out what the speaker had said, but he knew the direction the response had come from. He got up and ran toward it, scrambling over hot rubble.

"Isobel!"

"Here! We're over here!"

He stopped. The voice replying to him was not his wife's. He did recognize it, however. It was Nancy.

Kes continued on. The sound of Nancy's voice had come from a demolished house, similar to all the other demolished houses. If it had been her house, Kes would never have been able to guess.

He reached the remains, a pile of smoldering building fragments.

He saw her immediately. A face in one of the gaps, close to the ground. He ran to her and knelt down. "Nancy?" He'd never been so pleased to see his sister-in-law in all his life. "Where are Isobel and Miki?" He held his breath, desperate and also terrified to hear her answer.

"They're okay, Kes." Nancy reached out through the gap. He gripped her hand tightly. "Or, Miki is. I think Isobel might have a broken leg. When the house came down—"

"Kes! Is that really him?" It was Isobel.

"Yes, it is," Nancy replied. "But don't move. You..." Nancy sighed in frustration. "You're going to hurt yourself."

Isobel appeared at the gap beside her sister. She looked in pain but her face was shining. "I knew you would come and find us. Miki! Miki! Come and see Daddy."

"Izzy, it's so good to see you," said Kes. "Is the baby okay?"

"She's fine. Kicking like crazy."

Soon, Nancy was holding up the little girl to the gap and Kes could touch his wife and child. They were alive. Miraculously, blissfully alive.

How much longer did they all have before the biocide reached them? Kes didn't know. He put the thought out of his mind. For now, they were together.

It was more than he had hoped.

The story of Space Colony One continues in:

Final Onslaught

Sign up to my reader group for a free ecopy of
Night of Flames, the prequel to *Space Colony One*,
more free books, discounts on new releases,
Review Crew invitations and other interesting
stuff:

https://jjgreenauthor.com/free-books/

ALSO BY J.J. GREEN

STAR MAGE SAGA

SHADOWS OF THE VOID SERIES

CARRIE HATCHETT, SPACE ADVENTURER SERIES

THERE COMES A TIME
A SCIENCE FICTION COLLECTION
LOST TO TOMORROW

DAWN FALCON
A FANTASY COLLECTION